Pennies From Heaven

PENNIES FROM HEAVEN

Dennis Potter

QUARTET BOOKS

LONDON   MELBOURNE   NEW YORK

Published by Quartet Books Inc, 1981
A member of the Namara Group
360 Park Avenue South (Suite 1300)
New York, N Y 10010

First publishd in Great Britain
by Quartet Books Ltd, London, 1981

ISBN 0 7043 3394 5

Manufactured in the USA
by Whitehall Company, Wheeling, Illinois

L. of Congress C.I.P. data

Potter, Dennis   Pennies from heaven.

    I.   Title. P.
PR6066. 077P4   1981.   823.'914   81-19187
ISBN   0 – 7043 – 3394 – 5   AACR2

To Nora Kaye
for seeing – and believing . . .

Pennies From Heaven

1

Arthur Parker was a sheet-music salesman, but the product he tried to peddle to the often reluctant storekeepers of Illinois meant far more to him than just his bread and butter.

Arthur dearly longed for life to be more like the songs. It wasn't only that he wished for blue skies by day and a silvery moon at night, nor simply for the right girl to smile at him in the right way at the right time across the crowded rooms of his travail. No, it was much more – too much more. He hoped against hope that somehow, someplace, *everything* was going to work out *all right*. Around the next corner, or the one after that, the cruel and misshapen old world was going to put on its dancing shoes.

But two seconds of waking thought behind clenched eyelids, to say nothing of a lifetime's experience making ends not quite meet, compelled him to realize that a dream worth a dreaming hardly ever did come true.

And so although Arthur usually had a song in his soft and squelchy heart, the same tune did not always successfully negotiate its tinkling way up into the rockier terrain of his head. Times were hard, and as far as he or anybody else could see, they weren't about to get any better come 1935. One of the happiest numbers he peddled to dumb storekeepers all through the corn belt insisted that life was just a bowl of cherries – but up until now, at least, Arthur kept breaking his teeth on the stones.

Aw, the hell. Come on, pal. A cherry is a cherry, and worth celebrating. Straighten your shoulders, good buddy, and crack your face into sunshine. Hadn't he always told himself, every morning of his adult life, that you could not sell anything without a smile?

And today his job was to sell himself.

Today was going to be different. It was going to open out into a bright new dawn, and, by Jiminy, he was going to keep his foot in the door, like he had done a thousand times before, out there on the road.

Today was going to be – *dee dum, dee dum, dee, dee.* Jee-sus, this bank is like a goddamn cathedral. It glistens with money. You can smell the stuff. The real incense. Surely to God they can spare some of that crisp lettuce for yours truly, the chirpy guy with the syncopated briefcase. Full to busting with the only hymns worth whistling this side of Paradise.

Arthur's grin had stretched itself into place. His neat white collar was properly starched. His necktie was as aggressively sober as Billy Sunday. And he had brushed and polished his shoes until you could near enough shave yourself in their shine.

He trusted that he was coming across in octaves as a really smart fellow. Brimming to the lid with what his disappointingly demure wife Joan would never in a million and one years call Piss and Vinegar.

Arthur hoped that the stuffy looking bank manager (was it?) on the far side of this intimidating expanse of walnut (is it?) desk would mistake the gleam in his eye for a pretty cute shrewdness or, better, an inspiring dynamism. Instead of what it really was: innocent avarice, and corrupted desperation.

Some hope. This, here and now, this was one of those times and one of those places which the people who run things always call 'the real world', and Arthur was a stranger in it. He didn't yet know it, but he had long since hung his harp in the trees and sat down to weep beside the waters for his own small Zion.

He had never been especially adept at seeing himself as others saw him. At this moment, for example, he genuinely had no idea that what he seriously imagined to be the confident grin of a real live go-getter (who anybody would trust with their life's savings) was being instantly translated by the bank official sitting opposite into yet another obsequious leer wasted on the mug of yet another worried and fawning supplicant.

Where do they all come from? thought the banker as Arthur

2

duly asked for his thousand dollars. Who do they think they are? More to the point, who do they think *I* am?

'A thousand dollars?' said the bank manager, allowing his eyebrows to make the politic arch. 'What on earth do *you* want with a thousand dollars, Mr – ah – Mr Parker?'

The apparently affronted incredulity in the question gave Arthur what he now felt would be the first of many nasty moments yet to come.

He could already feel the brazenly confident grin falling off the sides of his mouth. He dragged it bodily back on to his face and stuck it down again, a Band Aid on a cut that refused to heal.

'I want more capital for my business,' he made himself say. Irritatingly inappropriate, the words of a song lilted into the suddenly empty caverns of his skull. *Yes, Yes, My Baby Said Yes, Yes . . .*

But, oh God, the banker was looking back at him with the sort of coldly amused contempt which would shrivel a crocodile, let alone a salesman.

Arthur's heart wasn't sinking. It had already capsized. He had recognized one more po-faced spoilsport who refused to live in the land of the songs.

'Selling sheet music?' asked the banker.

'Yeah. Songs. On commission,' nodded Arthur, trying to ignore the snort or the snigger implicit in the question, and trying not to look down at the sad little details of his own sad little account laid in a sparse little file on the desk in front of the banker. 'I – well – I got a bad territory, see. East Central Illinois, God help me. I wanna muscle in on Indianapolis as well. You get me?'

The banker got him, all right.

He knew only too well, this banker, that whereas a poor workman only occasionally blamed his tools, a poor salesman almost always blamed 'his territory'. This silly fellow Parker needed a short, sharp shock of the kind best called Elementary Economics.

'With all such large sums, of course, the question of adequate collateral cannot, alas, be evaded,' the banker said, almost as an incantation. Elementary Economics had its own gratifying liturgy.

3

'Pardon?' blinked Arthur, not well versed in such priestly ritual.

'You see,' said the bank manager, spreading his hands in sacramental fashion, 'your wife has a deposit account with this branch, and if she or you could see your way to . . .'

'That's *hers*, that is!' Arthur interrupted, too quickly, too obviously agitated. 'That's something quite separate. Her Dad willed her that, so – '

'Yes. But if it could be put up as . . .'

'Don't you goddamn well understand?' Arthur flared, because he had had too many years of angry frustration about Joan's nest-egg. Too many lost arguments. Too much pleading. Too much humiliation.

The cold-hearted little bitch wouldn't let him touch a penny of it.

'Really, Mr Parker,' said the banker, unaccustomed to even the mildest expletives. 'That sort of language will not help one little bit.'

'What will help then? You tell me!'

'That is what I have been trying to do.'

'Without dragging in my wife's cash!'

'Which represents your best – indeed, your only' – and he was spreading out unctuous hands again, to Arthur's intense irritation – 'indeed, *only* chance of getting a loan of the size you are proposing.'

Arthur knew for sure now that his goose was cooked. There was not going to be any golden new dawn. Not for the bird nor for him. And now he was being made to eat the feathers.

He glared back at the intolerably smug face opposite. There never seemed to be a way to put one over on these people. They always said yes when you wanted no, and no when you needed yes.

'So it's no, then,' he said, more as an epitaph than a question.

The banker allowed himself to dole out the bromide of his business smile.

'It's nothing personal, needless to say,' he nevertheless said, 'but as far as the bank is concerned, you have very few tangible assets.'

Arthur tapped his head, hard. 'What about this?' he asked,

with all the vigour of his bitterness. '*This* is what you sell things with, brother. It's what's in here that matters. And I know what I'm talking about, see – '

'Mr Parker – '

But Arthur was not eager to be interrupted. Not now.

'I know the kind of songs that sell!' he insisted. 'I got an instinct for it. It's in my bones. And I get thirty per cent of every song sheet I push to the retailer. Nearly.'

The tacked-on 'nearly' bespoke hapless comedy rather than any sincere love of truth. It made the bank manager want to laugh, and he compromised by crinkling the used parchment on his face.

'Well, *nearly* thirty per cent of ten cents,' he allowed himself as a further indulgence, as one who knew there was no danger of his own zygomaticus getting out of control. He would as soon urinate on the sidewalk as be so unprofessional a banker as to laugh out loud at anything other than a very rich customer's joke.

But Arthur could see that the man wanted to laugh. And he resented it.

'Oh, what's the use!' Arthur said. 'What's the good of setting up your own business in America today!'

The dejection, and the resignation, in Arthur's voice was being echoed and amplified outside these gilded walls by millions of others. A great blight seemed to have fallen upon America, from shining sea to shining sea. Nobody seemed to know why, nor what to do about it. In the steelyards and the stockyards and the factories of Chicago all around them, the sickness had taken its grip.

'The times are hard,' conceded the banker, with the sepulchral resonance of one regretting a huge natural disaster, an Act of God. 'The Depression is still with us.'

'And why?' protested Arthur, angrily. 'Because of dry-rot, that's why! It was salesmanship that made this country great, and it'll be salesmanship that'll *keep* us great. Dry-rot! That's what's doing the damage. Dry-rot! The stuff you got between your ears, pal!'

The bank official lurched to his feet.

He was not going to be crudely insulted by some insolent ignoramus of a damned song-sheet salesman who didn't appear able to add up. Didn't the sap realize that two and two make five when you are lending, three when you are borrowing, and sweet nothing whatsoever when you have neither collateral nor good manners.

'Yes, well – ,' he sniffed, with a practised disdain. 'I think we've concluded the useful part of our business, Mr Parker.'

But Arthur did not get up. He was bruised inside, and he couldn't bear to walk out empty-handed into swanking Michigan Boulevard. Surely there must be *something* he could still say that would . . .

'I'll take my account somewhere else,' was all that came out. It sounded hollow even in his own ears.

'That is your privilege of course, sir. And now, if you will excuse me, I'm afraid I have another – '

'Course,' smirked Arthur, with one last throw. 'I'd settle for a hundred.'

Or five bucks. Or a new cotton shirt. Or a cigar. Anything, but anything, so that he didn't have to droop his shoulders out of this ornately sugared palace without some small victory, some minuscule justification for a face that ached with smiling and a heart that ached with hope.

'I'm sorry to have to say,' said the banker, not in the least sorry now, 'that the same difficulties would stand in the way of virtually *any* amount.'

Arthur found himself on his feet. Rage and humiliation swirled through his soul. He could feel his own blood thudding hard against his ear-drums.

'You mean you'd bring a man down just like that!' he raged. 'You bastard!'

'Good day, Parker,' said the banker. A man about to step hard down on a beetle.

Good day, Parker. This is the real world, Parker. O O O that old refrain. Let us put it another way, Parker. Sing it, swing it, dance it, it don't matter none, old buddy. This-is-the-Real-World, Parker. Got it? The REAL WORLD. Money doesn't grow on trees, and pennies don't fall from heaven. Understand, Parker? You have to be as sharp as a knife if you want to survive and prosper. You have to know how to add up. Most of all, you have to know how to *take away*.

'Good day, Parker,' said the banker. Show this bum out into the real world. The one which doesn't fool around. The one which sets aside a nice little space for your dreams: like, say, a square foot or two, rented out by the minute at the highest rate the market will bear.

Go on, Parker. Get out. You are on *this* side of the rainbow, mister. And you had better not forget it.

Trouble was, Arthur wanted to rewrite the script. The suffocating, so-called Real World was getting him down. The place could certainly do with a few better lyrics, and the horrible, dead materiality of things needed a bit more rhythm. Something to tap your toes and click your fingers to.

And even now, even here, in his angry disappointment, a movie musical unwound a few frames into his heart. A sweeter version of the bank and the bankers was lodging itself in some small corner of his mind or in some small space out of the corner of his roving eye.

A song. A song. Please cue in a song! A song and a dance and a few pretty girls with twinkling eyes and twinkling feet. Maybe even a few pretty girls with gleaming bodies bared in the right places. Girls who didn't feel like Joan felt about what she so regularly called 'all that stuff'. Love and kisses, as sweet and sticky as candy.

If money was to be the measure of a man, well – let it be *Yes, Yes, My Baby Said Yes, Yes*.

'Good day, Parker,' the banker had said, cold, and abrupt.

'O.K. King Kong,' Arthur snarled, bumping back into the real world as the real world's hard eyes and harder fangs snapped at him like a pack of goddamn bloodhounds. 'O.K.! I know my own way out!'

Arthur always knew the way out. His problem was, he so seldom knew the way in. And, look, the luscious cherries were still up there at the top of their protected tree, well out of his reach.

2

Good morning, Chicago.

This is the way the world begins. Not with a bang, but with a miaow, a bell, a hoot, a bark, a creak of bed springs, the click of a closing door, and a Wheaties commercial on a radio prattling into an empty room.

Good morning, Arthur.

This is the way the day begins. Not with a song, but a doubt, not with a radiant dawn but a grey ache deep in the ligaments of his being.

Good morning, Chicago. Rise and shine, folks. Today can't be any worse.

A creamy moon hangs slow and ripe over a city grimly hugging the polluted shore of the poisoned lake, but already the milkman is on his way.

Hesitant streaks of an emaciated blue are seeping into the sky with every semblance of shamefaced reluctance, furtively lifting velvet mantles off the buildings to stain pale blobs of shabby detail on the hunched silhouettes. The first train of the day is clanking and groaning around the bends of the Elevated, and on State Street (that great street) a patrolling cop whose grandfather burnt peat in a distant isle yawns in a shuttered store's doorway. A loaded barge hoots in plangent melancholy out on the sluggish river.

A few miles away, on South Campbell, occasional lighted oblongs leap out of the upper segments of the houses. Here and there on the street alarm clocks are jangling, people are waking, and prowling cats are returning home from their sordid assignations.

At Arthur's house, on the same street, the bedroom is still darkened, though a thin gruel of light is trickling around the drapes at the window. The couple in the double bed, Arthur and Joan, appear to be snugly asleep. Six o'clock in the morning, and all's well. But –

But, no. Arthur is as still as still can be. And he is awake. That is, his eyes are open, but it would not be easy to say what he is looking at.

Perhaps he was seeing the bank from the day before. Maybe it was the long, flat ribbon of road along which he would once again journey, later in the day. It was just as likely that he was staring deep and bleak into the ever-widening chasm between the silly little words of his silly little songs and what everybody else insisted upon calling (oh, again and again) the real world.

Time passed even as it stood still.

Arthur was now, clearly, staring at the heavily, drowsily ticking alarm clock on the bedside table. It was a minute or so before half past six in the morning.

He had an obscure sense that we make our lives, build our world, minute by minute, that each new moment was rich in newness and so in possibilities: but the thought was too vague for him to reach. What he certainly felt, and felt like a boulder rolling around in his mind, was that each new minute was only the tiniest possible extension of the great cumbersome weight of all that had gone on before. A weight which bore him down, and down, and . . .

The alarm jerked wildly into life. Arthur instantly reached out and slapped it into silence. Exactly as though it were a raucous little animal which needed to be punished.

In this new space after the jangle, Arthur considered that the day had now properly begun.

He consciously put down the swirl of dark thoughts, and tried to throw off the boulder pressing on his mind. He curled his toes under the sheets, and then listened to his wife's soft breathing in the bed alongside him. It took only a moment for the best thought of all, so far as he was concerned, to gush like a hot spring into his imagination.

As long as there was *that*, well, then things were still on the up and up.

He turned almost cautiously in the bed, and looked at her. She was asleep. Her hair was loose on the pillow, and she looked soft and pretty. The residue of the deadness went out of his eyes, to be replaced by a hopeful and speculative look. He stared down at her, and he began to feel hungry.

9

If something *real good* happened now, it would assuage him for the rest of the day. If, in waking, she were to turn into him in the same sleepy movement, and come alive under him, clenching her body and flaring her eyes and widening her lips and gasping so that the gasp was his own pleasure, his own . . .

'Joan?' he said softly, even as he hardened. 'Joanie, sugar . . .'

She did not stir, but he somehow sensed that she was now awake. He put his arm around her. He wanted her to nourish him.

'Mmwa – wha?' she murmured, reluctant.

'C'mon, Joanie. Sugar. Wake up, baby . . .'

His hand was already fondling at the swell of her breast, and she pushed it away.

'No – Arthur – don't – '

'Aw, sugar,' he began to plead, as one who knew the ritual. 'Come on, Joanie – '

''S too early – I'm not awake – ' she was complaining, pushing his eager hand away again, 'there isn't time – '

'There's always time for this – C'mon!'

But his hands were too urgent, his words too pantingly eager. She didn't want it, and she wasn't going to have it.

'Arthur! Stop it!' as he pulled her into himself. 'No, – Arthur, no, I said. No!'

Abruptly, she pulled the cord dangling above them, and the light came on. They blinked at each other, in one brief fraction of mutual astonishment. . .

'Why not?' he asked, anguished. 'Why not, Joan?'

'You said you wanted to get away early. That's what you said.'

She wasn't going to be nasty. She was smiling. She was going to be nice. It was just that she was *not* going to let him push *his thing* into her and – Definitely not.

'You never want to, do you?' he said, hope draining away through every pore. 'Never.'

Never was a silly word, she thought.

'Fix the coffee, will you, darling?' she smiled. Sweetly.

Arthur swung his feet to the floor, angry, and calamitously disappointed. 'Goddamn coffee!' he snarled. She was shocked, as she always was when he forgot his words like this. Expressions that had never been used in her father's house.

'Arthur!'

'Listen, Joan. I'm going to be away from home for the next four days and nights – '

'No need to swear, though. Is there?'

'It wasn't much of a cuss.'

Why the hell was *he* the one who was apologizing? What he ought to do, if he wasn't a bit scared of her, if he wasn't a bit scared of everything, was lay her frame down across the bed and –

'Well, I don't think it's very nice. Especially in your own home, Arthur?'

What wasn't? Oh, cussing wasn't. Saying goddamn wasn't. Christ Almighty.

He looked at her as she sat up in the bed, severe and bright, and pretty. The girl he had married. A slim, sweet creature waving to him from her father's veranda.

'You don't give me a chance,' he said. 'You gotta give me a chance.'

'I don't know what you mean, Arthur.' And she didn't.

She had scarcely any idea of the tunes he danced to. The depths of his yearning would have astonished her, as would their inchoate purposelessness, and his own inability to measure or grasp them. She knew he was careless of the literal truth, extravagant when he had the chance, a romancer, a day-dreamer – but she didn't know why, nor that these things, these failings, were but the surface ties pulsed through him by a much deeper ganglion. In truth, Arthur was one of those innately 'religious' who had never in his life given a thought to either God or morality.

Indeed, to him, 'ethics' were just another roll of barbed wire staked out around him by the omnipotently malevolent powers who controlled the very air in which he moved and breathed.

Joan, ignorant, smiled prettily back at him as he stared so desolately at her. Poor old Arthur, she thought. Showing off because he couldn't have his way.

He turned abruptly, lacking words, unable to tell her – what? Why, to tell her about His Life. Instead, he went to the window that looked down on to slow South Campbell, and opened the drapes.

And as he pulled them apart, letting the light flood in, he was momentarily transfigured by memory. Or by an invented memory. It didn't matter which, for it was all the same to him, the way he salted and flavoured the less than magnificent history of his own past.

He was seeing his courtship of pretty Joan, and as he looked out of the window, it was as though a silvered beam of light, moon-struck, had settled upon his yearning inner gaze. The shaft of thought glittered and became one of the songs that he so dearly loved, turning prosaic South Campbell into magical Sunnyside Lane.

Down there, as the song unfolded, Arthur and Joan were wandering hand in hand. Down there, the two of them were dancing in the street, and they were dancing because they were perfectly happy. And because each wanted what the other wanted, mouth to mouth, limb to limb. Like the song said: Together.

When he turned back from the window, he half expected her long bare arms to be opening out to pull him into her.

But she asked him, again, to fix the coffee.

Sipping his own, now lukewarm, coffee in the kitchen, deliberately morose, Arthur no longer had a song to express the pain in his loins. He looked so sorry for himself that he was funny. He had little enough sense of decorum, but his woebegone expression at that moment also showed that he had no sense of proportion either. And the latter virtue is certainly the most important, as the shopkeepers had never bothered to tell him.

He had gone so far as to refuse to eat breakfast. It was almost as though, in childlike fashion, he was trying to dramatize his contention that – because she had not given him the needed solace – he had been left with nothing inside himself.

'Well, I wouldn't go all that way without breakfast, Arthur,' Joan said, 'You must eat, sweetie.'

'I *like* feeling empty,' he announced.

'Now you know you don't. What funny things you say in one of your moods.'

'Empty,' he repeated in a hollow voice, full of self-pity. 'That's me. There's nothing inside me, Joan. Nothing at all.'

She smiled as she looked at him. He was just like a little boy, she thought.

'What? Not even a song, Arthur?' she said, to coax him out into his own ready sunshine. 'A teeny-weeny little tune?'

He was not to be quite so easily soothed. He reached down to the bulging briefcase, packed ready at his feet.

'I keep them in my bag. Not my heart,' he growled.

'And in your head,' she said, determined to soften him.

The implied flattery worked like a charm. Yes, it was true, he thought, too damned right. I'm a walking expert. Perhaps the greatest the world has ever known.

'That guy in the bank yesterday said he didn't reckon there's a fellow in all Chicago who knows more about the songs that sell than me,' he said, describing what should have happened. The way he would have written it.

'Did he say *that*?' The frown on her face did more than provide the question mark.

'Borrow what you like, he said,' Arthur nodded, shifting the scene around in his head, painting triumph over the humiliation. 'Fellow like you is no risk. No risk at all.'

She didn't believe him. He was talking nonsense again. This *must* be lies.

'Don't want it, I said,' Arthur swept on grandly, an effect only slightly spoilt by the furtive expression he didn't know had crept up alongside his expansive rewriting. 'No. Don't need it. My wife's got some cash, I said. She'll support me.'

She froze. Whatever else she had to do, she must keep control of Daddy's cash.

'We need that money, Arthur. For our old age.' Her voice, and her face, were as hard as she knew how. HE MUST NOT GET HIS HANDS ON THAT MONEY.

'No. We need it *now*, Joanie!' he blazed back at her. 'Honey – I'm a good salesman. I can pick the right songs! Jesus Christ Almighty!'

'Don't blaspheme, Arthur.' But this time it wasn't his language that was so important. She had thought the subject closed between them, but here he was prowling around it again like a hungry wolf.

A prowl which gave him a quick, unwanted picture of his hated.

enemies. Surely to God the money would in some way buy him release from these miserable creatures, and from that long flat road going south from the city?

'Corn to the left of you,' he growled. 'Corn to the right of you. And storekeepers as dumb and windy as my old granny's asshole.'

'Ar-thur!' She was genuinely shocked. It was unbearable, the way he talked. But he was taking no notice. He had opened his bag, and was thrusting a song sheet at her. It had a cowboy on the cover, silhouetted against a huge moon the colour of Philadelphia cream cheese.

'Now this one, see,' he was saying, with that pointless urgency of his. '*Prairie Moon*. Gonna be a hit. It's already on the radio two, three times a day!'

'Well, I haven't heard it,' she said, flatly, knowing that in this vein he would ignore any interruption which was even marginally less than enthusiastic.

'But how many orders will I take this trip?' he said, furious. 'These storekeepers – ach, they got corn syrup coming out of their ears! *Prairie Moon*? they'll say. *Prairie Moon*? We don't have no *cowboys* here in Illinois. Goddamn East Central Goddamn Illinois!'

'Arthur!'

'I'm a storekeeper now, ain't I? This is the *storekeeper* talking.'

'Is it?' she asked weakly. There was a cunning glint in his eye. He had given himself licence. God knows what else he was going to say. It was always dangerous when he started on about these poor storekeepers. No wonder they didn't seem to like Arthur . . .

'Ignorant as a two-day-old turkey,' he was saying. 'And some of 'em *cusses* a lot, oh, yes. Your hick storekeeper cusses a lot, believe you me.'

'*My* daddy didn't. Not ever.

'Ah, yes,' conceded Arthur grandly, but not entirely with magnanimity. 'But your father used to sing in the church choir. More a Christian than a storekeeper. He might overcharge you, but he said his prayers. He'd want to use that money he left you – '

'Money he'd worked hard for all his life,' she cut in, quickly. 'To save for a rainy day.' It was her own fault for bringing up Daddy again.

14

'It's raining, pouring!' he cried. And then crashed back into the swamp of his own depression. He knew he would get nowhere on this subject. The storekeepers, the road, the flat and endless fields got into the bog with him. He looked so crestfallen that Joan realized the dreadful topic of money had once more subsided. The victory put the warmth back into her voice.

'Oh, cheer up, Arthur. You won't sell anything without a smile.'

He turned his eyes upon her, and she knew at once what he wanted.

'Make me happy, then,' he said. 'It'd be really nice down here – huh? On the floor!'

'Ar-thur,' she protested.

Yes, he could see that the idea was as genuinely distasteful to her as it was *exciting* to him.

'It was only a thought,' he mumbled, and got up with his bag.

'A very peculiar thought, Arthur,' she said, following him into the hall.

His sloping shoulders did not show the rebellion in his mind. He was asking himself just *why* it was such a peculiar thought. It seemed a pretty damn good thought to him. You didn't always have to make love in a bed. There were plenty of other nice places. On the carpet. On the tiles. In a chair. Up against a wall. Frontways. Sideways. Every which way.

Out on the stoop, as new positions formed and re-formed in his mind, as flexible limbs in black silk stockings coiled and gripped at his own rampantly triumphant body, and rouge-red nipples thrust themselves erectly at his eager mouth, he turned to the slim and pretty wife who surely, surely ought to be all and more of this to him. His supposed sweetie-pie.

'Don't you ever listen to the words? In the songs? In these songs,' he asked her.

But instead of taking her clothes off, she was helping him on with his coat.

'Ah. But that's not real life,' she smiled.

There it was again! That insistent, brutal, invincible phrase! No good screaming at it, or beating your fists against it. Real Life. About the only thing left to do with it was to turn it into a downbeat joke, a verbal shrug.

'Real life?' he asked. 'You tell me what real life is, then. A bowl of dog biscuits.'

'Nothing wrong with that, Arthur. If you're a dog.'

She had meant it as a reassuring little joke, as sardonic as his, but it was a terrible mistake.

She realized it with a lurch inside herself as soon as she saw his reaction. Scarcely ever before had he looked at her with quite such naked hatred. The joke had tipped the balance, or broken some bond between them.

'That's what you want!' he hissed at her. 'A goddamn poodle. Not a man, a real man!'

'Don't be silly, Arthur,' she quavered with an uncertain smile, alarmed by the sudden venom in his face, and wanting to step backwards.

'Well, I tell you this! Here's one old dog that isn't coming back into the kennel!'

He had turned on his heel and was stalking away. There was such a dread, abrupt finality in the movement that a renewed fear jumped up into her throat.

'What do you mean?'

'Three guesses!' he snapped back at her, without breaking his stride.

As he opened the car door to get in, she raised her arm to wave him the usual good-bye. But this time – and it was for the first time – it seemed as though he was not going to look back to receive his benediction. She could feel the smile stiffening on her face.

And then he did turn back, at the last moment. He could see her raised hand, and he could see the smile fixed upon her face. But his glance was utterly cold, completely unresponding. He got into his old car, without softening, and started the motor.

Joan could hardly believe it. She stared after the departing automobile, and then remembered to lower her stranded arm. There was nothing left to wave at.

'Arthur?' she said, to no one in particular. Not even to herself. Along the road, a newsboy was throwing the papers on to the porches, and a mailman trudged along his rounds. Some kids were on their early way to school with their bookstraps and lunch boxes and cascades of laughter.

The world was going on as normal. But Joan had the bleakest premonition that things would never be the same again. Oh, dear God in heaven, what had she done?

3

The faithful old car had chugged and rocked its way under the girded shelter of the El, past its own momentarily polished reflection in plate-glass store fronts, beyond the glum brick skyscrapers, the run-down tenements, decayed villas and littered sidewalks of South Chicago. Arthur was now well clear of the city, and each mile was bringing him back in tune with himself and the world.

Anger, disappointment and humiliation had flattened out into the apparently endless and almost featureless Illinois country-side as it stretched away on either side of him. He began to hum and whistle the insistently simple rhythms of *Roll Along Prairie Moon*. There was a lot to be said, he thought, safe in his moving tin box, a lot to be said for being a cowboy. A singing cowboy. With guitar, spurs and a feed-bag.

A billboard loomed into his view. It advertised Carole Lombard in LOVE BEFORE BREAKFAST. Well, why not? Why not? thought Arthur, brooding anew about the events of the morning, and the disappointment in his loins.

LOVE BEFORE BREAKFAST slid out of view, quicker than his regret, and his reawakened sense of grievance. The road, too, was now sending back refractions of this heavier mood. He would see Joan's face interposing its refusal between a passing gas station and his own journey.

A blighted landscape closing around him. Greyer colours, more sombre glimpses of the world of other men's toil. Here, the Depression ceased to be a metaphor used by economists, and became actual depression, real dejection. Sluggish. Morose. He had reached the nowhere lands.

DEATH BEFORE DINNER. More likely than love before breakfast . . .

Arthur's eyes narrowed. Up in front, a strange figure was standing in its own shadow at the side of the road. A figure that could have come from – where? God knows where. Another planet. An open grave. A prison, or an asylum. He – or IT – had a battered old case, oddly shaped. He, or it, was tattered and tousled and altogether weird, something between an apparition and an accusation.

Roll Along Prairie Moon died on Arthur's mind.

The figure on the road in front of him was putting out his thumb and grinning cadaverously. And as Arthur's car got closer, the figure began to make more urgent, arm-flapping, jump-up-and-down gestures, comical, and yet disturbing.

A malicious glint came into Arthur's eyes. He slowed, deliberately, as though to stop. But then, with a cackle of glee, Arthur jammed his foot hard down upon the accelerator to zip past the waiting figure. Startled, the man screamed an incoherent obscenity.

Arthur braked hard, and stopped.

Behind him, on the road through the flat lands, the tattered figure looked hesitantly and anxiously at the car. In the driving mirror, Arthur watched him with puzzled amusement. He could see more clearly now that the figure was that of a Creole – not so much a black as an octaroon man.

The octaroon man scurried towards the car, carrying his case, moving with a funny, loping, half-limping sort of run. Neither his configuration nor his motion was that of anything like what Arthur considered a normal man.

Arthur set his own features into a pretended severity as the strange individual, the odd black man, arrived at his side-window.

'What did you yell?' he demanded, his eyes as hard as rock candy.

The black man's face shrivelled in real fear.

'Me - me?' he stuttered. 'I d - dud - didn't holler nothing, sir.'

The standard grammatical error was more than just a double negative for Arthur. It was one he had often committed himself,

18

and, at home, had as often been corrected by the punctilious Joan. And so Arthur, who was not at all adverse to being considered a superior sort of person, could not pass up the chance to put the syntax in order.

'*Anything*,' he said, with immense satisfaction. 'I didn't holler *anything.*'

'No. N - nor me, sir,' the man blinked back at him.

'Ignorant bum,' snorted Arthur, amused.

The man stiffened, and made to draw himself up. It was like an Ancient Senator pulling his cloak around himself, a gesture out of time but always meaning the same thing.

'Hey,' he spluttered, 'I got my d - dug - dignity, mister.'

Arthur examined him. True, there was an innate mystery about the black man which might, in certain circumstances, he called d - dug - dignity, or thereabouts.

'Yeah,' Arthur conceded. 'But you ain't got an automobile!'

'N - nu - not at the moment. No, sir.'

Amused, intrigued, Arthur played along. 'But you wanna ride,' he said. 'Is that right?'

The man at the side-window seemed to consider the question, as though it were an entirely new idea.

'W - well - um - ' he hesitated. 'Are you going - um - thataway?' and, ridiculously, pointed a wavering finger vaguely in the direction Arthur was so obviously already travelling.

'I'm a free man,' announced the driver, amused. 'I might. I might not. I'm unpredictable.'

The would-be passenger could not take this in all at once. He puckered his face in bewildered thought, looked at the road ahead, and then back at Arthur, waiting for a solution, but not finding one.

'Oh,' the man stumbled. 'Ah. I - um - ah -'

Arthur, with a grunt of amused disdain, swung open the car door.

'Get in, Einstein,' he said. 'And your case. No extra charge.'

The stranger was profuse in his gratitude, comically and excessively so. He clambered in with his battered case with the excited air of a child invited to ride on a fun-fair roundabout.

'Thank you,' he beamed. 'Oh, thank you – thanks a m - mum - million, sir!'

With occasional sidelong glances of amusement, irritation, curiosity and reluctant pity, Arthur tried to place his unusual passenger. The car was speeding along a good, straight road through the fields. Now and again a barn in the distance advertising Mail Pouch Chewing Tobacco, or a billboard screaming tattered delights, broke up the flat monotony. Arthur, an urban man, readily bored by what he always dismissed as 'scenery', kept his foot hard down on the accelerator.

But the faster Arthur went, the more his passenger hunched down into himself. He was now in the semblance of a foetal position, hugging his bony knees, staring straight ahead with fixed glittering eyes as the ribbon of road unwound towards him.

'N - nice - um - nice, this – ve - hic - le,' he said, suddenly, giving a little shudder on the longest word.

'Not bad,' said Arthur, less dismissively than he really felt.

'W - wish . . .' the passenger started to say, but then stopped, his eyes shining with a peculiar glint. As in a magical spell, whatever it was he wanted to say seemed to be too potent to utter.

Arthur didn't want 'a wish' to be so inconclusive. He had had enough of that sort of wish.

'Wish what?' he asked.

The passenger gulped in nervous awe, too afraid to take his eyes off the scudding road.

'Wish I had one,' he managed to say, in a surprised rush of speech.

'These ain't for the likes of you, old pal,' snorted Arthur. 'Try roller skates.'

'U - y - yeah,' agreed the passenger, taking the proposition seriously. 'W - w - well, anyway.'

But he had said nothing very much so wistfully, with such an oddly poignant yearning, that Arthur, who was himself no stranger to such hopes, looked across at him with an unexpectedly gentle smile.

Up ahead, a silhouetted water tower and a folded silo were encouraging the arrival of a little town. Each man fell silent, perhaps contemplating possible triumph in the streets that lay ahead.

A thought which triggered a question from Arthur.

'What you got in that case?' he asked, abruptly.

'P - pup - piano,' the other answered.

'Yeh. Right,' Arthur grimaced. 'Should have known.'

But the passenger had not finished. His words had got stuck in one of those catastrophic stutters that shuts the gate on all articulation.

'P - piano accordion,' he gasped, getting it out at last in another shudder.

'Yeh?' said Arthur, pleased. 'You can play it?'

'It's my living,' the accordion man said simply. And then he fell into a dark silence.

The car had arrived in the little town, and the streets were now pressing closer on either side. Arthur, even while looking for a place to park, found himself as much moved as amused by the accordion man's deep, brooding silence.

He felt that there was some as yet unspecified and inexplicable bond between them, and then as quickly disowned the thought for the nonsense it had to be.

A dozen and more miles away eastward across the flat lands great banks of cloud were rolling themselves together, and darkening at the meeting. The pale sky, which for the last few hours had been close to the insubstantial blue that can be glimpsed in a pail of fresh milk, was now growing sour.

By the time Arthur's car had come to a stop, and the accordion man had bundled himself out like one dropping from an aeroplane without a parachute, the air was distinctly heavier. A violent storm was on the way.

4

Nobody looking down upon the small town of Galena, Illinois, on that rain-threatened late afternoon would have expected it to be the kind of place where an old dream could come true.

Here, almost slap in the middle of the all but featureless Mid-West, and just as witlessly marooned in the middle of the dishonest 1930s, the town sprawled listlessly about its own centre like the paunch of a man too worn and too disillusioned to walk properly upright.

At the moment, under the heavy sky which grew upward in gradations of grey from the drab buildings, a visitor could have allowed himself a small and wry smile at the sounds of *The Old Rugged Cross* drifting somnolently along the otherwise unremarkable Main Street.

It was not so much that the old hymn spoke of blood, passion and hope in chords as dreary and muddy as a winter puddle, but that it was being played so badly, so lugubriously, on such a wheezing instrument. The inapt multiplied by the inept.

Did not Galena have troubles enough?

The accordion man – for it was, of course, he – stood backed up on the sidewalk, his instrument strapped about his unkempt frame, and his fingers digging at the ivories in a manner that might just have been a little more acceptable had it been a little less emphatic.

Worse, his face, already uncomfortably haunting when caught at the wrong angle, had slipped into the kind of trance which could have been called ecstatic did it not seem to be caused by the inadequacies of his own music. His eyes were half-shut, and his mouth was half-open, and his body swayed a little to the rhythmic dirge.

And when he stopped, for a brief spasm, he called out to whoever had the misfortune to be going about his business within earshot (or earshatter):

'Thank you very much folks,' he chanted, mechanically.

'Thank you. Thank you very much. Thank you very much.'

The words were bumping together, closing up all the spaces in between. The noise he made was so weird that the people passing in either direction were at such pains to ignore him they seemed, in the very pointedness of their alleged indifference, to be anything but passive listeners.

'Thank you, folks. Thank you very much. Thank you. Thank you very much.'

But no one dropped a coin in his hat. There was nothing to thank anyone for, let alone thank them so very much.

Further down the street, Arthur, too, was being refused satisfaction. The Music Shop, as it called itself, looked from the outside to be a haven for him. The window was an arcadia of sheet-music covers, where crescent moons silvered silhouetted lovers, full moons bathed upturned lips, roses decked and garlanded. A few musical instruments gleamed dully in the thickening light now rubbing itself against the plate glass. It should have been, for Arthur, better than a home from home.

'Oh, now,' the proprietor was saying, in tones suggesting both reproof and exasperation, 'I think I know what I can and can't sell in my own store, Mr Parker.'

Comment enough to meet Arthur's ingratiatingly open smile and ingratiatingly open order book. The Enemy was speaking to him yet again, in a voice that Arthur knew too well. But his salesman's smile scarcely wavered.

'Sure you do, Mr Barret,' he grinned. 'Sure! I'm not trying to . . .'

'And if there *is* a demand for *Desert Moon* – ' Barret interrupted.

'Prairie *Moon*. Prairie *Moon*,' said Arthur, for maybe the twentieth time that day. 'Great, *great* song, sir!'

'Well, *if* . . .' insisted Barret, not to be persuaded. 'I just call the wholesaler. Right?'

'And wait a week or more – whereas if you take a dozen *now* you'll be ready, sir, when they come in and out of that door asking for the sheet music. It's a seller, Mr Barret. It sure ain't no dog, sir –' Arthur was saying, stalking the moving storekeeper.

The little bell on the door into the store went TING! right in the middle of Arthur's pitch.

How nice it would have been for him if whoever were now walking in had come to ask for *Roll Along Prairie Moon*. But Arthur, eyes clamped importunately on Mr Barret, did not even look up. And the proprietor, irritated by the sales talk, shook his head in brisk refusal and went forward to attend to his customer.

'Can I help you, ma'am?'

A standard request, and certainly an inoffensive one. But it seemed to cast an aura of awkward shyness over the customer. She was a pretty young woman – potentially even a beautiful one – with hesitancy in the dart of her eyes and the very lilt of her walk.

'I wonder if . . .', she began, almost a whisper, 'you see, I'm looking for part-songs for a children's choir, and . . .'

Arthur, feeling glum, had at last turned without much curiosity to look at the customer whose entering TING! had so inopportunely interrupted what he incorrectly felt would have been a worthwhile sale, goddamn it.

And as he turned, he fell.

And as he turned, he ascended.

And as he turned, his insides imploded.

And as he turned, his heart exploded.

And as he turned – oh, come on, the list is endless, the moment instantaneous. Time stood still, and time sped to its longest horizon.

DID YOU EVER SEE A DREAM?

Arthur, before he turned, imagined that he knew all the songs and what they meant. But after he had turned, he realized at once that –

DID YOU EVER SEE A DREAM WALKING?

He realized at once that –

DID YOU? DID YOU?

He realized at once, or in the fraction of time it takes to widen an eye and narrow a throat, that his knowledge of THE SONGS had been all on the surface, the shell and not the depth, the skin and not the heart, the reflection and not the actuality, the shadow and not the –

DID YOU EVER SEE A DREAM WALKING?

Or hear Bing singing it?

Or even better still, even more wondrous, see the melancholy, rain-threatening light outside the window switch itself into bright pink shafts mixed with spiralling golden rays. Light specifically designed in the studios of the head to shame a dazzle of sunbeam?

Why, even the instruments around the store began to hurt the eyes with their new lustre. And much as the hesitant young woman might move around the store, awkwardly aware of the stricken intensity of Arthur's stare, the dazzling light followed her around as she pretended to examine the song-sheet covers which, in reality, were one of the primary causes of the lovelorn look which so puzzled and worried her.

Mr Barret had gone out to the small stock-room at the back. Arthur and the lady were alone in the music store.

So where was the serpent?

'It's not there, I'm afraid,' said Barret apologetically, returning to attend to his customer and responding to something the dumbfounded Arthur had not heard her say. 'But I'm sure we can get it for you, Mrs – uh – ?'

She leant forward to him, like a worried conspirator.

'Miss,' she all but whispered, excruciatingly shy, and indicating an embarrassed self-consciousness about her presumed virgin status that ought to have encouraged the now exceptionally alert Arthur. 'It's Miss Everson.'

Ah, Miss Everson! Adorable Miss Everson! Divine Miss Everson . . .

'I want it for the children in my class,' she added, still very quietly, still strangely apologetic.

'Can you give me an address, miss?' the storekeeper asked. And his store was as quiet as the moment before the first day broke.

The rain-carrying light at the window was once again all over the store. The instruments had crept back from their Aladdin lustre. Everything was Normal. Cunning was back in order. And Arthur, calculation restored to his salesman's eyeballs, was tilting his head like a sparrow, the better to hear her reply.

Miss Everson flashed a quick look at Arthur, conscious of the direction of his straining ears.

And could it be that, although still quietly phrased, her answer was pitched with *just* enough strength for Arthur to get it into his head?

'Miss Eileen Everson,' she said. 'Care of Lincoln Junior School.'

Here in Galena, wondered Arthur? Yes. Must be. Must be.

'Very good, Miss Everson,' Barret was saying, oblivious to the rhapsody. 'I'll see what I can do. Have a nice day.'

Smiling nervously, she turned to go. TING! of cheery valediction from the little bell over the door. ZING! of vibrant desire from Arthur, exactly in tune. He stared after her departing figure, hungrily. Barret noticed his glance, and, amused, misunderstanding, dropped into the secret male code for assessing the true wealth of the world.

'Know what *she* needs, don't you?' he smirked.

Arthur would not dream of deliberately offending a man who could give him an order for sheet music. Nor does he object to the normal exchange of ribaldry between men at their business about anything reasonably personable in skirts (except a stranded Scot a long way from home, that is). Many is the time that Arthur's lips have dampened in a much more lascivious comment. But . . . what is this? What is happening here?

Arthur, with a scowl, a genuine scowl, was imperiously thrusting his order book at Barret.

'O.K.,' he snapped. 'Just sign for what you *have* ordered – and don't talk about a *lady* like that!'

It was worthy of a peppery old maiden aunt. It was as good as anything Joan's father, the short-changing dry-goods Christian, could have managed.

Too startled to make any retort, and even a little intimidated, Barret signed for the few copies of *Whistling in the Dark* and the fewer of *Pennies From Heaven* which he had taken, while Arthur, in a desperate hurry, gathered up his stuff, jammed his hat upon his head, and made at speed for the TING! - TING! door.

Barret, slow to react, glared after him, extremely offended. He said something out loud as Arthur slammed the door shut. Arthur couldn't hear whatever derisive obscenity it might have been, but both men knew that he would never make another sale in that particular shop.

The commission on *Whistling in the Dark* was a small price to pay: but other invoices would soon be rendered. Arthur, without

really knowing it, was stepping out into the unknown ... hurriedly.
Have you ever seen a dream running?

5

Miss Eileen Everson, schoolteacher, had not emerged entirely empty-handed from the Main Street music store. She carried away with her a half-formed impression, more like a disturbance than anything else, of a man who had looked closely at her 'in that sort of way', as she thought. 'That sort of way' made her insides churn, not very pleasantly. But not unpleasantly, either.

She had her head down, and she was walking fast. Perhaps she was moving so quickly because heavy rain was obviously due. Maybe it was because she tended to be one of those who hate to dawdle anyway. But it was beginning to seem possible, from the way *that man's eyes* had lingered too long on the back of her own retina, that she was scurrying along the sidewalk in this fashion in order to escape from her own puzzling reactions. Trouble was, the reactions did not stay behind with the instruments and the sheet music, but were coming along with her.

And their most likely cause was coming along behind her.

Eileen was not aware of it, but Arthur, hurrying along with a determined but wary expression, was on the point of catching her up. He had no idea what he was going to do, and no sense of what he was going to say. He knew only that he had to stand toe-to-toe in front of her and stare into her face again.

From somewhere up ahead of both of them, the turgid but not entirely unmartial strains of *Onward Christian Soldiers* were drifting towards them. The sky was getting still darker, the air still heavier, and the accordion music swelled to marry evangelical theology with the meteorology.

Eileen could now see who was playing the old hymn.

The strange accordion man, his lineaments still those of a visitor from another time or another place, was playing much as he had before. His face, his whole body, was more than half-way into a trance. His eyelids were nearly shuttered. His fingers dug into the keys as though trying to excavate a rare ecstasy out of their wheezing intractability.

She hesitated, then stopped, staring at him.

This was Arthur's chance to stand in front of her. But he, too, stopped, in such a position that he could watch her, and what she was looking at. It was clear to him from what he could now see that Miss Eileen Everson was as moved or, at least, as intrigued, by the accordion player as he had been an hour or so earlier.

Eileen Everson, under a compulsion she was not able to resist, was suddenly stepping forward, the abruptness of her action only a little tempered by her evident shyness.

'It was very nice,' she said, awkwardly.

' - very, very much. Thank you very much,' the accordion man was continuing by rote, so unused to being approached, let alone congratulated, that he could not register what was happening.

Retreating a little, she dropped a coin in the hat at his feet. It did not chink against others.

'Pardon, lady?' he responded at last, utterly startled.

'It was nice - ' she retreated, embarrassed. 'A nice hymn - '

The accordion man could not believe it. He acted as though the heavens had opened and spiralled a luminous shaft right down into the centre of his puckering forehead. He went stiff with delight, then, letting the joy explode within him, he began to jerk and twitch. It was oddly threatening.

'Sh - shall I play you another one, lady?' he nearly screamed at her.

Properly alarmed, Eileen backed away faster, thinking she had tangled with a crazy man.

'I - sh - ' she mumbled.

'*The Old Rugged Cross*!' he yelled at her, unable to control his limbs. 'I'll play *The Old Rugged Cross*!'

'No - ' she gasped, scurrying now. 'It's all right - no - thank you.'

But he wasn't even looking at her hurriedly departing figure.

28

Ecstatic, incredulous, his fingers were probing their stiff way into the sonorous opening chords. Not so much clinging to the bloodied old wood of Calvary as digging holes into it.

Arthur, witnessing the bizarre exchange, made as though to follow Eileen once more. But she was running, and passers-by had enclosed her. He lacked the nerve, even if he could have caught her. Nothing would scare her off more quickly than the sound of a running man's footfalls.

He stared along the road where she had gone. His eyes were wistful and the old ache inside him had sunk deeper than it had ever done before. The first big drops of rain had started to patter down, but he was not aware of them. A building could have collapsed on the other side of the street, and he would have thought it less worthy of notice.

Gradually, however, the accordion music began to intrude into his yearning. The accordion, the rain, and the onset of disappointment and loss.

Arthur turned and glared irritably at his erstwhile passenger.

The accordion man, his violent enthusiasm dissipated by now, had lapsed back into the soporific, near-nigh imbecilic trance of before, eyes half closed, mouth half open.

'Shaddup, you fool!' shouted Arthur, unable to bear it any longer.

The accordion stopped, at once, with an injured wail. The accordion man looked at Arthur, blinking, bewildered, and defenceless. For a fraction of a second, the two men held the look, and they were mutually puzzled. In that small moment, an inexplicable emotion trembled on the edge of understanding. Certainly, something seemed to pass, or be about to pass, between them.

The rain was falling. Their eyes were locked.

And then, strangely, and without knowing why, the easily moved salesman was reaching out to touch the street musician.

The accordion man let out a strange sound. It was that of a man about to cry. Arthur broke away, quickly, more offended than embarrassed.

What the hell was he doing putting his hand out to a half-wit like this instead of – instead of Miss Eileen Everson, care of Lincoln Junior School, here in Galena.

Arthur looked at the inexplicably weeping accordion man, and felt his heart swell with a sense of wonder that had nothing to do with the broken-down busker in front of him.

A charitable impulse fell upon him, even as he turned up his coat collar to ward off the drenching rain.

'It's O.K.,' he wanted to say. 'Everything is all right.'

6

The rain was slanting down heavily now, spreading a hissing, swishing mantle over the dully gleaming streets of the dispirited town. Water gushed from the broken roof gutters and gurgled around half-blocked drains. It chased itself in racing drops along putter-pittering storefront awnings, smashed determinedly against steamed-up windows, puddled in violently angry reflections on the emptied sidewalks, and drummed like a troupe of demented tap-dancers on the tin roof of the cheap diner where Arthur, in the unbidden grace of fellow-feeling, had taken the no longer snivelling accordion man for a meal.

The diner could truthfully have marketed itself as a place where no-hopers might get a cheap meal and a later stomach-ache. It was occupied at the moment by a gaggle of morose or subdued individuals sheltering from more than the driving rain outside.

Their faces were mostly the colour of sawdust. Those who were eating tended, by their nature, to hunch down over bowl or dish with the furtive, hungry intensity of ill-used mongrels at feeding time who fear that their paltry scraps might suddenly be taken away from them.

The accordion man, especially, was shovelling and plunging food into his mouth in a way that both fascinated and repelled

Arthur. He watched him with a measure of distaste and then realized that the man was eating in this manner because such largesse did not come too often. Even so, it made Arthur feel less like his own meal than he already did.

'How long is it since you ate?' he asked, at last.

Loaded fork half-way up to his already pouching mouth, the accordion man stopped, guiltily, then chewed and swallowed in what must have been a painfully swift gulp, in order to find space on his tongue.

'I eat here and th - th - there,' he stuttered, evasively.

'Now and then's more like it,' Arthur snorted, and pushed his own soggy meat away, almost untouched.

He was still thinking about the shy girl who had come into the music store with a hesitant little lilt that had plucked at his heart: and if music be the food of love, this chopped steak (even decorated with oozing dollops of scarlet ketchup) was no part of the tune.

Arthur shifted and sighed and listened to the rain.

'Ain't you h - hungry, mister?'

The accordion man, mouth full again, words struggling, had stopped chewing. He was gazing in hopeful incredulity at Arthur's apparently abandoned food.

'Oh, I'm hungry all right,' Arthur answered, but meaning something else.

His companion was not equipped to pick up the wistful response, so he frowned in bewilderment at the uneaten meat.

'D - dud - don't you like it – ?' he asked, astonishment unabated.

Arthur was lighting a Lucky Strike from a crumpled pack. He blew out a long column of smoke, the colour of his thought.

'When you think about things,' he said, more to himself than to any possible listener, 'before you go to sleep at night, when your head is still, and – '

But the unwavering direction and unaltered intensity of the accordion man's gaze at the forsaken chopped steak broke back into Arthur's gentle melancholy.

'No, I don't want it,' he said, giving his plate another nudge away from himself. 'You can have it. And good luck to you, buddy.'

The delight, the entrancement, on the other's face was comically out of all proportion to the crumbling, congealing and lukewarm mess of minced-up old cow that was evidently its cause. He looked like a startled child for whom Christmas, Thanksgiving, his birthday, the Fourth of July and the last day of term at school had all been rolled up into one gloriously spangled rocket-burst of astonishment.

His day – or so his face said – had now brought reward enough. Neither the rain nor the misery outside mattered in the slightest. The drizzle inside his own head was no longer of consequence. And as for the sadness – was it? – on his benefactor's face – well, how stupid, how stupid – s - s - stupid . . .

My God, thought Arthur, wish *I* could be so easily pleased.

Part of Arthur had always wanted to bum along the highways of his native land. He saw even this in romantic terms, subsuming the degradation and poverty of it, and its enforced near-criminality, into such unlikely cameos as the picture he had of himself munching a sandwich in a buttercup field by the side of a five-barred gate. It would be a life where the unexpected visitations of good fortune – like the way he was treating this particular gentleman of the road, for instance – would place all the workaday troubles of the mean-minded world into a proper perspective.

Arthur, pleased by the radiant delight his uneaten chopped steak was provoking, pulled himself up through the thickening glades of drooping, blue-headed weeds.

And one released tendril of his imagination reached out to cast the hobo opposite in the role of the buxom and bespectacled Sunday School teacher from the lost land of his Chicago childhood. Back there in the scrubbed-faced, sexless days when he and his pals used to warble *Brighten Your Corner* to the faltering accompaniment of an asthmatic harmonium.

Except that Arthur did not care for that brand of music any more. It didn't swing properly, and never ever celebrated girls with, what was it?, *bee-kissed lips.*

But if the accordion man's busy fork were a band leader's baton, though, and the sawdust-coloured faces at the counter the members of the – No. The entranced gleam in the hungry man's eye was better made for one of those intimate solo numbers where the singer, up in front of the bow-tied band, cleaned his teeth with the microphone. Right? Two-three – And the lyric of 'Pennies From Heaven' issued from the other's hungry mouth. Right?

Words you could chew by, especially if you had not eaten for days on end.

The song was drumming in Arthur's ears now. He always loved the moment when the preamble hesitated on the very edge of the real lyric, like someone taking a deep breath before plunging from the diving board into a pool of aquamarine.

Arthur, blowing out more grey-blue smoke, leaned back in his chair to listen to a song that was not actually being sung. The rain outside, by the same token, had not turned itself into the copper-coloured sequins his mind was nevertheless conjuring up out of the unheard melody. Fantasizing, he let himself be drenched in a shower of small change. A small enough optimism, all said and done.

How about a soft shoe shuffle in the cascading coins? How about those sad-faced bums over there stooping down to pick up pennies ankle deep on the drab street outside? *How about pigs with wings?*

O.K. O.K. The mouth opposite is chewing and champing, not singing. So nobody is dancing in the rain, and few people outside the cuckoo house ever do. The bums in the cheap diner are not turning their umbrellas the wrong way up. They don't have umbrellas anyway. And the pitter-patter-splatter of heavy rain on pock-marked concrete is not at all the same as the chink of coins.

Whenever Arthur surfaced from his minuscule but techni-color dream-trips, the surroundings to which he returned had indeed transformed themselves: they had become darker, or more oppressive, or even further out of kilter from the tucked-away half acre which was the land of his songs.

Sure enough, the hobo opposite, the odd, half-witless coon plunging mucky food into his slack mouth – Come on. There are no lessons there!

'Where are you going to sleep tonight, buddy?' Arthur asked, with a trace of the compassion but a much larger slice of the incurious security of one who knows he has a bed in a rooming house to go to.

The jaws stopped grinding, and the lips stopped slurping, for a moment – but then resumed as the accordion man, furtive, bent his eyes back to the food he was so diligently demolishing.

'Hear what I said?'

Warned by the irritation in Arthur's voice, the troubled black man forced his glance upward.

'Alley,' he mumbled.

'What?'

'Wh - where I was playing,' the other gestured vaguely with his loaded fork, 'there was an alley – '

Arthur wanted to protest. Or to laugh. And in these circumstances the distinction is of no consequence. If the rain kept tumbling down, then sleeping in an exposed alley was – still. None of my business. There must be thousands and thousands in the same sodden plight on this and many another night without a moon and stars to silver the silhouette of young lovers out on the front porch.

Arthur smiled indulgently at the gobbling accordion man. 'Young lovers out on the front porch' had opened up a precious new fissure in the black rock. His expression changed. The wistfulness was still there, waiting.

'There was a girl, wasn't there,' he said, in a new voice, ' – who gave you some money just before we came in here . . .?'

The accordion man bolted a lump of fat and gristle, and beamed.

'Yes,' like an exultation.

Arthur looked into space. 'She was beautiful,' he said, softly. 'She was the sort to make a man feel – '

'She gave me a dime!'

'That's the one. Beautiful. Beautiful! The way she held her head. The way she walked. Funny how just one look can – '

Arthur broke off, on the brink of a rhapsody. The spreading, almost slavering grin on the black man's face seemed to be too knowing, perhaps even a simple-minded kind of mockery.

'What are you grinning at, you idiot?'

'She g - gave me a dime!'

An answer which radiated such genuinely innocent wonder

that Arthur was able to dismiss at once any fear of sniggering mockery. He warmed again to this shabby and simple stranger, his feelings of compassion once more shaped and pointed by the hauntingly brief image of the lady schoolteacher in the music store.

'Is that all you got?' he asked. 'Didn't nobody else drop anything in the hat?'

'No - o - o.' And the voice was touchingly hollow.

Arthur looked steadily at his strange companion, letting the husk of someone else's even more diminished or poisoned life intrude for a moment into his own usual, spectacularly self-absorbed pictures. Then, with a defensive snort, pushing the dangerous and alien configuration out of his imagination, he got up to pay the check.

'You can't live on a dime,' he said. 'You're doing even worse than me. Here's a quarter. Go on, Rockefeller. Take it. Feel rich!'

But instead of simply accepting the rather hesitantly proffered coin, the accordion man, shockingly moved, unbearably excited, clutched imploringly at Arthur's outstretched hand and began to kiss it with slobbering servility.

Arthur snatched his hand away, extremely offended.

'Hey! Cut it out!' he protested, for the accordion man would not easily let go and his lips were still trying to clamp themselves on Arthur's wrist. Arthur was forced to wrestle his hand free.

'What are you? A pansy?' he spluttered, in a fury of indignation and embarrassment. After all, people were looking . . .

'Sorry. S - sorry, mister! Mister?'

The scared and stuttered apologies were too late, because his enraged benefactor, who could imagine few things worse and nothing more un-American than being kissed by another man, had gathered up his briefcase and was storming towards the exit.

'Sleep on the goddamn sidewalk for all I care!' Arthur snarled over his shoulder before disappearing into the wet street of Galena.

The accordion man was left alone at the table. He looked oddly forlorn, like some bit player too old for the part pretending to be an abandoned orphan. His eyes were dulling over with bewilderment, or perhaps distress.

The dark silence which he carried around with him, and unpacked at least as frequently as the accordion from its case, threatened to drape around the stoop of his shoulders. But then his sombre eyes fell again upon the still unfinished chopped steak and its attendant dollop of as yet unsoaked ketchup.

He bent over the food once more, and filled his mouth with renewed urgency.

7

By the time dusk had fallen on the flat lands, and the accordion man had sought out his resting place, the rain no longer descended in torrents from a sky which stretched a couple of hundred miles back in a melancholy drizzle of anxiety to Arthur's neat little house in Chicago. Here, his pretty wife Joan, trying hard not to twist her hands together like she had seen troubled ladies do in the movies, was unsure whether to look with accusation or supplication at either the clock or the telephone. The one ticked loudly into greater worry, and the other remained ominously silent.

Arthur's savagely dismissive 'Three guesses!' kept bouncing about between the bones of her head. She saw him, for the hundredth time, delaying his turn back in response to her regular little wave, and then, when he at last *did*, the coldness in his very stance. Three guesses? She wished, how she wished, that she knew exactly where he was and precisely what he was thinking.

Joan was right to suspect that the answers would have given her no comfort. Arthur's trusty old Ford was at this moment bumping and lurching along the narrow dirt road that led to the small farmhouse where dwelt the magical Miss Eileen Everson.

It had been an easy piece of detection for him to find out where she lived: he had simply questioned a raucous group of seven-

36

year-olds swinging on some railings outside the school, and, gleefully avuncular, handed out cheap candy in return for accuracy.

But Arthur, apparently so decisive in this, had no plan of action, no ready sequence of honeyed words to greet the face at the opening door (ah! that face!), and little sense of the real meaning of this speculative journey off the beaten track. It was simply that the pressure steadily building in him, the feeling of restriction in his chest, the urgent grab at his throat which made him want to swallow, insisted that he aim his sights toward wherever Eileen Everson might be found.

And when found, wooed.

The wavering car headlights settled unexpectedly in a swift dazzle upon a small, shack-like building humped into an obstacle at the end of the track. At first, Arthur thought it might be an outlying barn on the Everson's land, but then realized that it was almost certainly the farmhouse itself.

For some reason, the obvious poverty of the place encouraged him. At least, he reasoned, there would be no justification for that snooty, nose-in-the-air brush-off he had occasionally encountered when trying his luck on his journeys. Even so, he still did not know how, or whether, to approach the dingy little cottage. He couldn't simply stroll up to the front door and announce himself, now could he?

Arthur switched off the car headlamps, and stared with ruminative anxiety at the darkened hump up ahead.

He was getting more not less uneasy now that he had reached first base, so to speak. What the hell was he going to do? What the heck was he going to say? 'Pardon me, lady, but I clapped my peepers on you in the music store in Galena this afternoon, and – ' Every single damned thing after the 'and' degenerated into a nervous gulp, a dry throat, and the kind of sideways swivel of the eyeballs which would make a cop arrest you on sight.

He lit yet another Lucky Strike. The match flared momentarily in the poor light. And he saw a sight to make his heart go bump.

It was Miss Eileen Everson!

She had come out of the little farmhouse in a way that seemed to show that she was upset about something. She stood thoughtfully for a few seconds, isolated. Arthur, with a buried gasp, leaned forward to examine her. Yes, yes, she was *the one*. He watched intently as she picked up the laundry basket and crossed to the clothes-line. There was the same lilt about her movement that, for Arthur, separated her from the rest of the human race.

Without knowing quite what he was doing, Arthur opened the car door.

Eileen had gone beyond the clothes-line and into a small copse on the edge of the darkening fields. She was wearing a quietly thoughtful expression, and it was not a particularly contented one. The books she read and the life she had grown into failed to make harmony. She knew for sure that beyond this farm and the little school and her inherited as well as her acquired obligations, there were places and people and things and ideas which would better answer her needs, let alone her dreams. She was not even sure what her dreams might be: but she was increasingly sure that this place was stifling feelings inside her that would expire altogether if they did not soon struggle free . . .

Gradually, and with a flutter of alarm, she became aware of the crunch and rustle of too cautiously approaching footsteps. It was as though someone, something, was creeping slowly up on her. Her own thoughts trying to get back into her head.

She whirled round, scared. And saw a man in the thickened dusk, who looked, from the gleam in his eye, to be almost as afraid as she was. Or something worse.

'Oh!' she gasped.

'Don't – don't be scared . . .' he whispered.

Eileen stiffened, preparing to run or to call out. But there was a familiarity about him, a sense that he had in some way been a part of her thoughts or . . .

'Who are you?' she said, her voice tremulous with an anxiety that had as much to do with the faint apprehension of a dread beyond this present moment. 'What are you doing?'

'Eileen,' he said, in a subdued croak.

The way he said her name, the fact that he had possession of her name, made her begin to panic.

'What do you want!' she raised her voice. 'How do you know my name?'

He was putting one foot forward towards her like a blind man who knew that near by there was a hole in the ground.

'Eileen,' he implored, hand outstretching in a plea. He did not know what else to say, and there was nothing in his head except her name, which he wanted to repeat over and over again.

'Go away!' she trembled. 'Leave me alone!'

She was ready tilted to run, to scream, or do something that would put her out of his reach. Her eyes were wide with fear, and they glistened in the dark.

'Don't,' he begged with quiet urgency. 'Oh, please . . . please.'

The desperate, yet unthreatening intensity of this supplication served to calm her. Her mind started to work again. She was able to look at him properly, and the figure who had loomed up behind her in the congealed light, a shape that had jumped into her imagination as the displaced or dislodged embodiment of one of her less than happy dreams, took on the outline and then the detail of a real person.

'I – I've seen you,' she searched with her words. 'I've seen you – in the music store.'

Her hesitant recognition hung for a fraction of time between them, a space in the air that was full of tension. He did not want to speak.

'There's a song,' he found himself saying, in an awed whisper. 'Like in the song . . .'

Arthur knew that what he said would not make sense. It was a foreign language shaken on to the tongue of the stranger by a startled exclamation, betraying that he came from another land.

She stared at him, and was unable to translate.

'What?' she asked.

He tried again. He had to put into words that she might understand, the true significance of this encounter in the rural dusk.

'They tell the truth, songs do,' he asserted, and stepped nearer, the assertion releasing his muscles. It had always been a self-evident proposition in his book.

But the movement made some of her fear come springing back. It was, in all circumstances, a pretty nutty thing to say. And a million miles away from the truth. She tensed again, ready to fend him off with clawing fingernails.

'Stay where you are!' she commanded, and then spoilt it by adding, 'Please!'

Arthur did not move again. He stood rooted, and looked extraordinarily humble, a penitent, a man who wished to change his life. He wanted to explain.

'I heard you say you were a teacher,' he said. 'I asked some of the kids where you – where you lived, and – '

He stopped, as though the rest were superfluous.

'Why?' she asked, in a troubled, and yet astonished whisper.

There was scarcely time to swallow. One part of his imagination could see the two of them standing face to face in a softened darkness, like figures drawn on the cover of one of the song sheets he knew so well. It was this glimpse that allowed him to speak to her without guile.

'I've been looking for you. All my life I have been looking for you, Miss Everson.'

'I d - don't understand – ' she stumbled.

'You've been in my head, Eileen. And in my heart. In my soul.'

So much without guile, indeed, that it was as simple as a catechism. Arthur had never before spoken to anyone in such a manner since the far side of his adolescence. Words of love and courtship had previously been, for him, counters to play in a contest that ought more accurately to be called sex and seduction. There was scarcely ever a time when he was not able to hear, and so to edit, the phrases which came out of his mouth.

And as for her, it was, again, only the small children who spoke to her with such unadorned fervour. She recognized 'truth' when she heard it precisely because of these daily experiences in her little classroom in Galena.

She waited, and, in doing so, gave him permission to move closer.

'I want to talk to you,' he said earnestly. 'Please let me talk with you.'

About to nod or to smile, eyes still fixed upon his eyes, she stiffened instead as a man's voice bellowed her name from beyond them in the direction of the farmhouse.

'Eileen!' it yelled, crudely breaking the spell, as effectively disturbing the pool of feeling between them as a rock thrown into calm water.

'Who is that – ?' hissed Arthur, startled.

She could see his eyes darting with alarm, and knew instantly that he had a cowardly streak in him. There was a danger that, caught out, he might run away, disappearing as quickly and as strangely as he had arrived. And she wanted him to stay.

'My brother,' she said to him, in a hurry of reassurance. 'It's my brother.'

Arthur could feel the space available to him shrinking very rapidly. He did not want anyone else to intrude. He did not want to have to watch his words. He did not want her eyes to settle on anyone or anything else. Even now, as the goddamned voice shattered the suspense between them, her eyes had flicked away from his face, and he picked up agitation in them.

He clutched at her, trying to call back the mutual awe.

'But I've got to talk with you – ' he almost cried.

'Eileen!' bellowed another voice, from the same direction.

It looked as though she was embarrassed by these raucous yells from the little house beyond the straggle of trees, and as though she, too, realized that the space allowed had diminished into nothing more than a gabble of potential misunderstanding.

'I – I don't even know who you are, or . . . ' she quavered, not wanting to protest.

'Arthur. I'm Arthur,' he said, with awful deliberation. 'And I love you.'

Love you? Love you? *Loves* me – ? Me? She could not take it in. She could not close her lips together or shorten the span of her eyes to make any kind of response which made any sort of sense.

Love you? Love you?

Loves *me*? And standing there, just standing there, as earnest as a preacher.

'We – ' she gabbled, in a rush of panic. 'We've had a family row and – and I . . . '

Two men were coming into view, walking towards them through the trees. It looked as though they had been out hunting. One of them, sour and already wizened, was Eileen's father, and the other her brother Jumbo. There was, to Arthur, a kind of malevolence about them, magnified hugely by their hunting garb. He saw at once that he, too, could be numbered among their prey.

The two of them stared at Arthur. The suspicious stare of

41

rough and poor men who knew that Eileen was the unexpected pearl of their toil. A pearl not to be messed with by any smarty-pants who did not value her. They could see at once that Arthur, in his suit, was that most odious type of all in their extensive vocabulary of cuss-words: a city slicker.

'Who the hell is this – ?' demanded the one they called Jumbo, right to the point. And Arthur saw that the man's fist was already low and clenched, ready to swing.

'Are you all right, Eileen?' asked her father at almost the same time, in a voice that could hardly have been more suspicious so far as Arthur was concerned.

Eileen made a small, submissive gesture which said a great deal about her relationship to the rest of her family.

'Yes, Dad,' she said, nervous. 'Yes – this is – '

Arthur plunged in. 'Good evening, sir,' he said boldly, with more confidence than he felt, and in a tone that sought to mark out a crucial distinction between himself and the type of fellow her father could too easily take him to be.

'This is – Arthur,' Eileen said, unsure of what to add. 'He's – '

She darted him a quick appeal, and he relished the complicity implied by her look. It enabled him to straighten his shoulders and stick out his chin, the way that he had always wanted to behave in any threatening situation. Two pairs of sullen eyes were aimed like arrow-heads at his precious new sense of himself, and he knew exactly how to deflect their barbs.

'I'm a friend of Eileen's,' he said, with an open smile and an extended hand. There could be no doubt that he was her gentleman caller.

8

Today, Arthur was thinking, his entire being marinating in wonder, today is the first day of the rest of my life.

Today is the beginning of the New Age where the lyrics of the songs, and their joyous syncopation along the line of their meaning, the emphatic swing which brings their melodious undertow back up on to the surface of the clean and glistening stream, where they provide the Testament that at last allows him to breathe, to expand, to discover . . .

Oh, her face. Her eyes. The lilt of her body. The way she moves from the hip. The flow of her legs.

The complicit looks she had given him.

The promise that shimmered briefly in each one of her swift, puzzled, sidelong glances.

Arthur sat at the roadhouse bar enumerating hidden gifts as though they were the secret names of God.

He was hardly aware of what was going on around him, though he had earlier greeted Ed and Al with the normal wry effusiveness that the fraternity of travelling salesmen kept for each other at their roadside watering holes. They showed friendly faces to each other because the outside world so often shook its head or closed the door upon them. They were warriors snatching a rest away from the front.

It was closing time. A tired waitress was clearing up. Ed was discontentedly playing on an elderly pin-ball machine. All the other customers except these three had sloped off into the night, leaving overflowing ashtrays and too many cubic feet of stale, yawning air. The evening had worn itself down to the stub.

Oh, her face. Her eyes. The lilt of her body. The way she moves from the hip. The flow of her legs.

'We're never gonna get out of this depression,' Ed was saying, right in the middle of this entrancing dream, his voice as morose as his face was heavy and tired.

'The hours I put in, door to door, for *nothing*,' assented Al,

43

staring gloomily at his Fuller Brush case. 'Peanuts. Selling what is *in fact* a very good set of brushes.'

Faith in the goods. That was it. Keep your faith in the goods. Doubt showed through like a sag of wrinkles behind the greasepaint. So no matter how weary, and how disappointed, you had to keep this faith, for apostasy would slam the door all the harder against your earnestly stretching grin.

'It's the goddamn territory, ain't it?' said Ed.

The way she moves from the hip. The flow of her legs. The complicit looks she had given him. The promise that shimmered briefly in each one of her swift, puzzled, sidelong glances. Oh, her face. Her eyes. Her eyes! The parting of her lips.

Ed had put his finger on it, of course. The territory. It was always the goddamned territory which broke your salesman's heart.

'They just slam the door in your face,' said Al, filling his mouth with peanuts. The ball bounced inside the pinball machine, clicking and buzzing with robot refusal. 'Some guy nearly broke my foot in two yesterday,' he snarled, glaring at the uncooperative machine.

The late hour had brought them to the unwholesome stink of dejection revealed at low tide on a mudbank. The one consolation behind red-veined eyeballs, exhaustion, slack flesh and booze that had lost its kick, was the collective and necessary assent that, yes, these endless flat areas of Illinois were the most difficult in the land within which to turn a commission and talk up a bonus.

'It's the territory,' Ed agreed, with the air of a man advancing a new proposition. 'No doubt about it. We'd all be smarter bumming the roads. Eh? What do you say, Arthur?'

'Hard times, ain't it, Arthur?' added Al, as part of the ritual.

She had turned her head and looked at him and an understanding had passed between them. She had . . .

'What did you say?' Arthur asked, barely surfacing out of an ecstatic grin.

The mournful pair stopped chewing the peanuts, virtually in unison. Something wasn't quite right here, their eyes seemed to indicate as they settled in potential accusation on the third of their number.

44

What the hell was he grinning about in *that* sort of way?

'Don't suppose you're doing very well neither, eh, Arth?' asked Al.

Arthur looked at them. He could not understand the question. He could not take in the surrounding mood of peevish or belligerent depression.

'Not doing very well?' he asked, and his bewilderment showed.

She had turned her head and looked at him and her eyes were like . . .

'Ah, but that's not the Real World,' Joan had been saying. Vinegar Joan. And Bert had said much the same, hadn't he? What the hell did they mean?

'Not doing very well?' Arthur must have asked, incredulity in every pore.

The two other salesmen looked at each other, jaws stilled.

'Wake up, old buddy,' said Ed, speaking for both of them.

'I'm doing very well,' Arthur announced. 'Very, very well indeedy!'

They could not have been more shocked had they seen the Pope coming out of a brothel with his vestments all awry. This was not simply a breach of ethics, it was shameless blasphemy.

It was a moment before either of them could get his mouth around the right words. The stupid grin on Arthur's face was not helping.

'Heading for the cuckoo house, are you, Arthur?' asked Ed at last, too surprised to jeer properly.

Arthur did not bat an eye.

'Me?' he said. 'No chance! I'll tell you guys something. Everybody who has ever lived in the entire history of these here United States would wanna be *me* if'n they only knew what I felt like inside.'

It wasn't just that you could have heard a pin drop. Nobody would have dared to drop one. The only possible sound was the rapid scuttling of nerve-endings across the skins of each of two stupefied listeners.

'What's wrong, Arthur?' asked Al, as shaken as a fundamentalist who has just been shown Darwin's notebooks. He was suddenly ape under the skull.

Arthur batted an eye.

'That's the trouble with youse guys!' he snorted, in contemptuous parody. 'You walk around with dirt n' ash in your eyeballs!'

'Hey!' protested Ed and Al in one voice, too astonished to open their throats any wider.

Arthur rounded on them passionately, and the fervour in his voice, the conviction on his face, was as upsetting as anything they had yet lived to see.

'You just can't *begin* to see what a fan-tastic world it is we live in!' he glowed.

'No – c'mon! Get your goddamn chins up off the floor! *Beautiful*. It is! Shining, the whole darn place *shining*! Can't you see it? Don't you feel it?'

In the shocked silence which again followed these terrifyingly evangelical questions, and the implication of their even worse answers, each of the two listeners subsequently confessed different things to himself in the intimidating silences of their three-o'-clock-in-the-morning thoughts.

Ed had a sickening fear descend upon him which whispered in his good ear that somewhere along the road between one music store and another his old pal had been visited like whosit on the road to whatsit and *found God*.

Al, less haunted, believed that his old pal had somehow in one miraculous transaction persuaded a drunken storekeeper to take his entire stock a dozen times over. Either that or his old pal had a temperature of 105° and shouldn't eat and drink in a dump like this again.

It was Al, therefore, who was the first of the pair to muster a suitably compassionate response.

'Sounds like a crate of eggs to me,' he said, his lips writhing.

A benediction, which, to a degree, lifted them out of Arthur's thrall.

'Sliced baloney, more like,' sniggered Ed, in gratitude.

'Yeh – it would be to *you*, Ed, wouldn't it?' Arthur smacked back, aggressively.

It wiped the smirk off Ed's face. 'Waddyamean?' he snarled.

Arthur wanted to share his joy with them. He didn't want to argue, or to call them names. He didn't want to spoil anything.

'Because – ' he began, 'Because – well – ' and he shrugged, helpless in the face of the radiance of his vision, 'because you don't know *the young lady in question*, do you?'

The long rounded and buttery 'A - haaa!' which proceeded in rich unison from Ed and Al was not one of mockery. It was the purest kind of relief, as natural to them in its merciful extension as letting go a full bladder in the men's room. It was an 'A - haaa!' of thanksgiving, as sweet as a Q.E.D. to a mathematician, or the slap of the fondling hand on a nice piece of ass.

'A - haaa!' *This* they understood! No reason to worry about good old Arthur after all!

'It's impossible to explain,' said Arthur, sheepish. 'It's not the sort of thing you can put into words.'

'Oh yes it is!' chorused Ed and Al in raucous delight, the dreadful gleam of old back in their eyes; a couple of tattered farmyard cocks who had caught sight of an even scruffier little hen come peck-pecking into their own patch of dung and grit.

Arthur looked at his knowing old buddies with a troubled frown. The oddly avaricious glee in their transformed faces reminded him of all the dirty jokes and grubby yarns they had swapped in the past at the beer-swilled butt-end of evenings such as this. He did not want any lascivious comments or dirty-minded ogling to sticky up his perfect image of the beloved Miss Eileen Everson. She *was* a farmer's daughter, when all was said and done.

But no. Please God, no. His dear old buddies wouldn't be such vandals, would they? They would acknowledge at once, his dear old buddies, that Miss Eileen Everson was not *the* farmer's daughter of a hundred and more of their chortling, far-fetched anecdotes.

They could surely see, good old Ed and good old Al, the difference between the salacious fantasy and the REAL THING?

Did not their wide smiles and their broad winks indicate their pleasure at his stunning good fortune? And wasn't there a happy, toe-tapping number they really and truly wanted to perform to show just how well they understood the miracle that had happened on the previous night?

IT'S THE GIRL!

As Arthur's suspicious frown was chased off his face, it was as though an olio curtain had crashed to the floor behind the stale and littered roadhouse bar. Here, ready and waiting in the sunshine of his dream, was a stage ready set for singing and dancing . . .

IT'S THE GIRL!

The long bar was certainly as good as any vaudeville platform in that gaudy little theatre which bobbed along on top of Arthur's shoulders. His two good buddies, dear old Ed and dear old Al, could join him up there under the glittering, gliding circles of vivid spotlighting. They would hoof into the sort of cheerful, bouncing, upbeat number which by its very exuberance cleans out the last nasty trace of salaciousness from the boy-meets-girl encounters.

And Arthur, Ed and Al, feet tapping, hands slapping, fingers clicking, banjo plucking, grins stretching – delight made manifest – would harmonize their way into properly tuneful celebration of –

– of that oh-so-wonderful, oh-so-sweet meeting in the soft light of the wooded dusk –

IT'S THE GI - I - I - IRL!

Sure thing. It wasn't anything else, was it? There was nothing else in the whole world which began to compare with the wonder and the vivacity and the hope which collided inside a man when he saw her. The one. The Girl.

IT'S THE GIRL! IT'S THE GIRL – !

'Get your hand up her skirt, Arthur?' Ed was asking at a bar which was just a bar.

The spotlights clicked off. The dance was stilled. The song died away.

WHAT DID HE SAY?

'Get your hand up her skirt, Arthur?' asked Ed, with a wet mouth.

'Lay her in the back seat?' asked Al, the leer spreading from lobe to lobe.

WHAT DID HE SAY?

'Has she got big tits?' This was Ed again, goddamn him, winking hard enough at Al to splinter walnut shells with his lids.

What were they saying?

Arthur lurched to his feet, struggling to get words up through clogged pipes. He could scarcely believe his burning ears. How *dare* these bums talk about the pure and undefiled Miss Everson

48

like this? Didn't they see that she was not like that? She was *different*.

'You filthy – you dirty . . . !' he gasped, quivering with outrage. 'As if you – guys like you – ach! You disgust me!'

Ed and Al reacted as though a rabid dog had charged frothing mouthed into their midst.

'Hey – hey – easy, boy!' they said. 'Easy!'

But Arthur was choking with grief. He had to pound his chest to shake the words out into the sob that was rushing into his throat.

'Everything I've –' he began and had to start again. 'Everything I've ever dreamed,' he managed to declare, ' – hoped for – longed for – deep inside me – here, in my heart – everything!'

Al and Ed were as embarrassed as though they had farted at the funeral of their own mothers. They looked at each other, stiff-faced and stricken.

'We didn't know, Arthur. Now, did we?' said Al, spreading the meat of his hand.

Arthur was swaying in his shoes, so moved, so desirous of expressing what was new and bright inside himself. It wasn't really necessary that these stupid, leering oafs he had thought were his pals should know the truth: but it was necessary to express it. He had to testify while the fervour was upon him. It was his *duty* to get it out into the sullied air . . .

'Years and years I didn't really know what I was selling,' he said. 'The songs! What they are all about! The way they *do – really* do – tell the truth, the honest-to-God truth. And they do! They do! Goddamn it, they do!'

'What? Them songs?' protested Ed, incredulous. Them silly toons? Molasses in the moonlight. Horse-shit under the stars!

Al didn't say anything. He couldn't. His mouth was locked open.

'Somewhere the sun *is* shining,' Arthur insisted, brushing aside the dirt that had fouled up his vision. 'And do you know where? Inside! Inside yourself. Inside your own head – in the spaces in between! That's where the blue and the gold is. On the other side of the black! I learned that last night.'

'Ah - aaaah!' said Ed and Al, in unison again.

It was perfectly clear, once more, what had happened to good

49

ol' Arthur last night. He was simply letting himself be carried away by what must have been an exceptionally enjoyable lay. They exchanged complicit sniggers.

'What are you goddamn *winking* for?' Arthur exploded. 'Oh, I won't mention the lady's name. Not likely! It's what she's sparked off inside me – Put the real meaning into them songs! I knew, I always knew they told the truth. But until last night – '

He stopped, abruptly. His ability to hear and to monitor what he was saying had returned to him at the wrong moment. He could see this comically inappropriate picture of himself as one of three travelling salesmen who had trespassed far beyond the protective boundaries of their normal way of speaking. He imagined how *he* would have received the impossible words that had just issued out of his new state of grace.

Arthur was embarrassed. He could not say another word. Let them wink. Let them snigger.

There was a deadly little pause. Ed and Al had had enough.

'By the way, Arthur,' said Ed, with nasty precision. 'How's your wife?'

9

For all his fine words and his breathless testimony, Arthur did not know with any certainty what Eileen had made of *him*.

True, she had not disowned him as an insolent stranger to her menacing father and even more menacing brother. Certainly, she had shot him a glance that seemed to share an emotional resonance with his own simply expressed feelings. But they had not kissed, nor brushed hands together. They had not arranged to see each other again. Whatever promise there was of things to come had not been put into words.

Eileen Everson had thought of Arthur with as much bewilderment as pleasure when alone in her bed on the same night that he had sought to show a world newly cleaned and polished to his justifiably cynical buddies in the roadhouse bar.

She did not know what to make of him. She was, in any case, nervous of men, or of certain types of men, and found it hard to keep her eyes still if any of them ever talked to her. Several had tried, of course, but there was something too threateningly demure about her, too much the school-marm, for their comfort.

She had not travelled far beyond Galena, and although she had read a lot, it was mostly a shallow kind of stuff, and she did not know much of the world. Her classroom was truly the centre of her life. She did not need to keep her guard up with her young pupils – and they, in turn, saw her as nearer to themselves in speech and in spirit than any other adults, including their parents.

Most of all, they loved it when she told them stories.

She made the classic old fairy tales come alive in their heads. The princes and the dragons, the princesses and the frogs, the giants, ogres and Little People, the severe morality not very distant from that which held sway in the playground. It transported them far from Illinois to the forests and castles of old Europe and then back again into the turmoil inside themselves in the here and now.

They loved Miss Everson.

Anyone who happened to be passing along Bench Street in Galena on this particular afternoon, and who lingered for a moment outside the little school, would perhaps be able to pick up the suppressed joy and excitement coming out of Miss Everson's classroom. Under the fluttering stars and stripes over the entrance, and past the swings and the slide on the presently deserted playground, and beyond the reach of the less fortunate kids from another class who were in view cleaning the blackboard erasers, Miss Everson was in the middle of a wonderful old tale.

'And so the handsome Prince – '

The upturned faces were shining with rare concentration: the kind scarcely ever brought to six-eights-are-for-ty-eight or seven-sevens-are-for-ty-nine.

'And so the handsome Prince,' she was saying, 'stepped out

from behind the trees and looked up at the tiny window at the top of the tall, tall tower that had no door. "Rapunzel! Rapunzel!" he called. "Let down your hair!" And thinking it was the old witch, Rapunzel let down her hair.'

Eileen took a beat, and looked at their expectant faces.

She knew, instinctively, how to pace a story, and did not fully realize that when she told them what the wicked old witch said, for instance, that her own face twisted and snarled in chilling mimicry.

Today, though, the fairy tale was being delivered with an even greater immediacy than usual. When the handsome Prince spoke, was there perhaps a touch of the man who had also stepped out from behind the trees the other night? Was it possible that the small room with a little window but no door, a room from which the beautiful lady could not escape, was achingly close to a certain poor farmhouse at the end of a narrow dirt track?

Whatever the reason might have been, the teacher was giving the story a resonance that sounded very personal to the listening children.

'Long, shining, golden hair all the way down, down, down to the ground,' she continued, a small smile at her lips. 'And. And then . . .?'

She looked around the class in invitation.

'The Prince climbed up!' they responded in a chorus of delighted voices. The best stories were always the ones you already knew.

Eileen smiled and nodded, entering into their pleasure. 'Just as he had seen the old witch do!' she confirmed. And then her voice dropped, and her eyes rounded themselves, and the hush came back upon the children.

'But when he came to the window, Rapunzel stepped back in fear. Oh my, she was scared! She had never seen *a man* before!'

At which some of the boys at the back of the class giggled and tittered behind their hands. They didn't quite know why, but it seemed necessary.

'Yes – some of you boys can laugh!' Eileen said. 'But, his face was so nice, his eyes were so kind, his voice was so gentle, that she . . .'

Her own voice had gone beyond her normal skills of simulation. Indeed, for the moment, she had actually lost focus on her young listeners.

'His face was so nice, his eyes were so kind, his voice was so gentle.'

She had built for herself another glimpse of Arthur as he had looked and looked at her and into her.

The children were staring at Miss Everson in astonishment. In the middle of the story, so to speak, she had fallen into a hole. She was fully there in front of them, and they could clearly see her, but she had disappeared into the land of princes, witches, doorless towers and mythic forests.

A buzz of delighted speculation went round the class. The children were whispering and giggling. And, as is the way with a collective of kids, they plucked the substance of her reverie out of the air. Eileen might as well have had a little bubble of 'she thinks' ballooning out of her in the style of the cartoons in the funnies.

The seven-year-olds, led from the story into their teacher's sudden, small reverie, had made a deduction already one step ahead of Eileen: the teacher is in lo - o - o - o - o - ve! Miss Everson is In Love! Miss Everson Is In L - O - V - E.

They knew the word to be a potent one. In the fairy tales they had listened to, it was Love that turned the nasty frog into the glittering Prince, or the weeping girl into the radiant Princess. And on the radio they heard the same word celebrated over and over again in sugared rhythms and candy kisses.

Love, the song said, *Love Is Good for Anything That Ails You.*

'They tell the truth, songs do,' he had asserted, stepping closer. One part of her imagination now (so much later than Arthur) saw the two of them standing face to face in a softened darkness, like figures drawn on the cover of a song sheet.

'I've been looking for you. All my life I have been looking for you, Miss Everson,' he had said.

'You've been in my head, Eileen. And in my heart. In my soul,' he had said.

Yes, she was thinking. Yes, it was as simple and as direct as the words in the story she was telling.

But the noises her children were making broke through. She

looked at them in dismay. If the Principal were to hear . . . well, it would be a thunderous Fee, Fi, Fo, Fum!

'Quiet!' she commanded, severely, rapping a ruler on the desk.

The unusual harshness in her tone was an admonition to herself. The children, however, were so used to seeing her as a fairytale Princess, shimmering in the sequins of her own gentleness, that they were dismayed to find that she could also be a wicked old witch.

10

The children of Lincoln Junior School burst noisily, gleefully out into the corridor from their various classrooms, their lessons over for another day. Some of the teachers tried to silence their charges; but the level of exuberance was too high in the neck to be easily corked down. As soon as the kids got out of the school doors, they would outdo the charge of the Light Brigade: meanwhile, the corridor – the escape passage – provided a spontaneous rehearsal.

A door opened, and those nearest to it fell into immediate silence. It was to no avail, however. Savage old Mr Warner, the Principal, was already storming out like the dangerous wild beast many of the children considered him to be.

He did not need to yell 'Quiet!' at them. His authority was so unquestioned, his power was so feared, that he did not have to bellow to get a hearing.

'Never have I heard such a commotion!' he said, and the anger was terrifyingly evident. 'Where on earth do you think you are! A fairground?'

The children stood rigidly at attention, scared. They would as soon be seen to disobey Mr Warner as refuse to accept a candy bar from a visiting aunt. It is unfortunately the case, though, that fear of this sort makes many a child want to giggle in a dreadful panic: you can feel the horrendous laughter bursting out of you, and your cheeks go red and your nose itches and your lips tingle and your throat implodes with the huge effort needed to remain silent.

An effort too great for one unfortunate lad. He giggled. Out loud!

Instantly, Mr Warner descended like some pitiless avenger upon the poor child. There was no escape, and nowhere to hide. Without a word, Warner took hold of the boy by the simple and cruel expedient of pinching his cheek with one hand, and slapping him hard with the other. One blow – but a painful one, and, with so many quaking witnesses, an especially humiliating one, too.

The boy burst into tears.

Eileen, too, had held her breath when Mr Warner had pushed his avenging way into the throng. She knew that he was a hard man, even though he was also a just one in his own lights. But the smack was *too* brutal, and it distressed her.

'Mr Warner . . . !' she protested.

Warner took no notice whatsoever of her, and she realized that the teachers could not be seen to show dissent between each other in front of the children.

'One word,' said the Principal to the corridor of pupils. 'One sound. That's all. One further *sound* from any *one* of you – and – '

The 'and' hung threateningly. There was no need to say any more. Each tensely quiet and very frightened child could provide the rest of the sentence according to his or her own imagination. The sound of one boy's weeping left them in no doubts about the direction their thoughts should take.

Warner looked at the scared pupils to let the threat sink in. Then he nodded curtly at Eileen, in belated recognition of her unwise interjection, and went back into his office.

Eileen and the children looked at each other in a mixture of sympathy and accusation. She turned her head away, upset. She could still hear the weeping from the humiliated boy. The pupils filed out, quietly, very subdued.

As soon as they reached the safety and freedom of the open air, their exuberance returned. They bubbled in a torrent out of the school, some part of the stream diverting in a small eddy round the candy man, and another flow temporarily dammed by the crossing policeman.

There was another man outside the school building, leaning against his car. His eyes watched the flag being taken down from over the main entrance, and then switched back with hopeful intensity to the door itself.

Arthur was waiting.

Back home in Chicago, still hoping for a call, or the sound of his automobile, Joan, too, was waiting. The telephone silent. The parlour clock ticking. And fear deepening, widening, inside her being. The taste of being alone was ash on her tongue.

Arthur stared and stared at the school entrance, his throat drying but his eyes brightening.

He saw Eileen come out into the air, and all the best tunes chimed together in his inner ear. He straightened, especially alert, wanting to watch her movements, the way she held her head, the way she walked. To be able to measure someone like this, before she knew that she was being examined, was to gain a secret knowledge of them, and so a hidden power. He hoped.

Arthur *was* able to look at her for several seconds, before, lifting her eyes, she realized that he was there.

As soon as she saw him, she stopped. She smiled, uncertain, shy. Then the hesitant little smile grew bigger, making her beautiful.

Arthur and Eileen moved towards each other. But mutually shy, oddly overwhelmed, they stopped again, standing a little apart, examining each other.

'Hello,' he said.

'Hello,' she said.

And their eyes explored each other, as though they were the only two creatures in the entire universe.

But no, someone else was also looking.

Mr Warner, apparently savage old fellow, could see Eileen and Arthur through the window, back in the school. He watched her closely. He observed the quick, almost excited way she had moved towards the man who seemed to be waiting for her. He

56

noticed how the man straightened up from leaning against the car, a snap of tension which bespoke excited anticipation. And when the man said hello to Eileen, and she said hello to him, Warner sighed to himself. His hard and lined face registered signs of pain, or of regret. He looked at the pair outside the school once more, then turned away, abrupt, and alone.

Arthur and Eileen were still examining each other, unaware of any other scrutiny.

'I hope you don't mind,' he said, finally, ' – but I had to see you again, Miss Everson.'

She dropped her eyes, and when she spoke, it was barely audible.

'I don't mind,' she said.

'I thought maybe a little drive – ? I – I could take you home and – '

Arthur swallowed, as overcome with confusion as a youth at his first dance. She lifted her eyes, encouraged by his awkward respectfulness.

'That would be – very nice,' she smiled.

All but bowing from the waist, in what was not meant to be a comical parody of costume-movie manners, and beaming happily, Arthur opened the car door for her.

'Your carriage awaits, madam,' he announced.

Her shy, pleased little tinkle of a laugh was the sweetest sound he had ever heard, not excluding the dance bands on the radio broadcasting direct from the Coconut Grove.

The songs were really coming true. At last!

They had called in at a gasoline station and each had for a while stared straight ahead. The silence between them became harder to break the longer it went on. Arthur had looked across at her several times, trying to think of something reassuring, or at least not too alarming, to say. He was also hoping that she would be the first to talk. But, aware of his strained, sidelong glances, she had looked down at her hands, clenched together in her lap.

Arthur could see the outline of her legs in the fold of her skirt. He was warmly conscious, too, of the smoothness of her skin, the flow of her neck, the soft swell of her breasts, the closeness of her arm . . . and all these wonders caused a familiar order of thoughts to marshal themselves in his head and in his loins. But he tried to control them, for fear that she might be able to sense the pulse and pressure of them. . .

'I haven't offended you, I hope?' he blurted, suddenly.

She did not know what was in his mind, and could not really understand the question. She had wanted him to start talking, and she had tried to make herself respond eye-to-eye to his increasingly frequent, obviously anxious, sidelong glances. There was something about him which made her feel as though she were between floors in a fast elevator. She could not think properly, and she did not know how to assess what was happening to her.

'I'm not very – at ease – with people,' she said. 'Men, I mean.'

'That's all right, honey,' he responded, with evident relief. 'I've got enough moxie for both of us!'

His laugh was just that little bit too knowing, and gave her a sudden and unwelcome glimpse of another Arthur beside the man who had addressed her with such direct simplicity under the darkening trees.

An insight that was enough to make her ask, with a touching vulnerability that wiped the suspiciously brassy grin off his face, 'You won't tell lies. Will you . . . ? Arthur?'

The gap between his real situation, his proper status, and the dream that had started to unfold like the road along which they were now driving, opened up in a terrible wound in Arthur's conscience.

'Not if I can help it,' he asserted, the two of them unaware, or unwilling to acknowledge, the ambivalence or ambiguity coiled into the answer.

She looked at him, sweetly, and earnest, willing more reassurance.

'And you're not married?' she asked. 'You promise?'

His hands were gripping the steering wheel too tightly now, and his laugh was harsh.

'Do I look like a married man?' he chortled. 'Why, I even got a hole in my sock!'

Neither of them saw the dead bird, feet up, lying on the rutted road. They were not looking at anything else except themselves. That is, Arthur was seeing Arthur, wriggling at the bottom of his own words, and Eileen was seeing Eileen, dismissing the possibly false note in his laugh and in his joke, and yet half-sensing that she was somehow complicit with him. No. No. He was *not* married.

As for the dead bird, the maggots had already attacked it, apparently from within.

11

The one thing you can say with certainty about hogs is that they are wholehearted in their appreciation of food. It was Eileen's job to feed them each evening, and this one was no exception, Arthur or no Arthur. The two of them had arrived later than her usual hour, as the surly displeasure of her father made clear. There was no room for a leisurely politeness, or the chink of afternoon tea cups. A bucket of swill – mostly slops and potato peelings – was thrust into her hand. Wordless, she had taken it out to the penned hogs, and Arthur, feeling more than a little out of place, had followed her into the squelch of mud beyond the little hovel of a farmhouse.

Eileen emptied the bucket of swill into the trough. She did it with a suppressed rage. Her family had embarrassed her.

'You oughta let me do it,' Arthur said, unhappily.

'Oh, no. I'm used to it. You'll spoil your suit.'

With squeals and grunts of a greed so full of relish it became utterly pure, the hogs were thrusting their soft pink snouts into the slop in eager search for the bigger lumps contained in the grey soup of the swill.

Arthur looked down at them with an urban astonishment.

'Look at them *eat*!' he gasped. 'Ain't they *pigs*!'

She laughed, and looked at the animals with a fresh eye. The crunching, munching, grunting voraciousness of their enthusiasm was so splendidly uninhibited that it had the power to shake up the sense of appetite in a human onlooker. A new thought threatened to form in her mind, and her expression changed. There was a hint of her latent but strong sexuality in her eyes, and in her voice, as she again looked at Arthur in the fading light.

'They eat up anything,' she said, nervously. 'Almost – almost any old thing you can imagine. . .'

Her voice had trailed off. The pigs grunted and slurped. Arthur was staring at her. He wanted to touch her, to hold her, stroke her: and she knew it.

Grunt, slurp, munch, squeal, crunch, grunt.

'I don't want to talk about hogs,' said Arthur, strained.

She half-looked at him, then kept her eyes on the greedy animals, a faint smile compounded of both apprehension and encouragement on the paleness of her face in the soft evening light. She could not quite bring herself to say, 'What *do* you want to talk about, Arthur?' but it was as though she had.

Arthur slowly and tentatively reached for her hand. He knew it would be soft and yielding. Joy was ready to burst through his ligaments, his veins, and the marrow in his bones. His fingers were almost touching, were about to close on her waiting hand –

'Are you coming on in, Eileen?' bellowed her father from the bedroom window of the little farmhouse.

Arthur quickly jerked his hand away. Eileen stiffened a little.

'Yes, father,' she called back across the dusk. 'In a moment.'

'Lock up when you do!' he growled, and pulled the window down with a crash.

Eileen looked at Arthur, obscurely ashamed. She imagined that the moment of hand-holding had passed, and would not easily return. She saw Arthur as a man with a car and a suit, a man from the city who did not work with a hoe or a shovel or a bucket of hogswill, a man of so much more sophistication than the two men in her family. He would surely scorn the way her father snarled and her brother glared. Jumbo even chewed tobacco, and sometimes spat it out in an evil brown juice.

'Dad and my brother have to get up at five in the morning,' she said, by way of an apology. A prickle of threatening tears stung at the corners of her eyes.

'*You* don't, though. Do you?' he shot back at her.

She answered with a timid little laugh. 'No. Not that early.'

In fact, Jumbo and her father expected her to get up when they did to fix their breakfast. She might have a job to go to at the school in town, but now Mrs Everson 'had crossed over Jordan', as Eileen's father put it whenever he mentioned the death (which was not often), she had to be the woman of the house. That is, to cook, to wash, to clean, to help out around the farmyard, light the fires, make the beds, mend the work clothes . . .

The awkward pause lengthened between them as the hogs snouted about in the messy remnants of their swill.

'So I'd better get going, then?' Arthur said, or asked, with a glum expression.

Eileen did not reply at once. She was looking at the farmhouse. He turned to follow the line, and the tension, of her gaze.

The light went out at the top window from where surly Mr Everson had shouted down at her. And then the light died at a second window.

The hump of the farmhouse was in complete darkness against the lowering evening sky.

'They're both in bed,' Eileen said, practically in a whisper. 'My father and my brother.'

Arthur considered that this near-whisper gave him a certain licence. She had re-created a delicious sense of some conspiracy between them. And the rapidly gathering darkness, in which rooks were coming home to the distant trees like premature blobs of night, placed a mantle of intimacy over the land.

He put a finger to his lips and dared to wink at her.

'Not a sound, eh?' he said, as softly as she had spoken.

She did not hesitate for more than a fraction of a second.

'All right,' she whispered. 'You can come in for a little while.'

They moved off together towards the safely darkened house, not quite touching each other. Behind them, the hogs continued to grunt and slurp, disposing of all that was left in their filthy trough.

At exactly the same time, it so happened that Joan took yet another look at the clock. Then, with a heavy sigh, she opened her purse, and took out her lipstick holder.

'Sometimes – !' said Eileen, in the farmhouse.

'What's the matter?' he asked her, gently.

She looked at him, steadily, unsure whether he would understand what she scarcely dared to say of her feelings about her life in this little house marooned in the fields beyond the town.

'I feel as though I'm suffocating in this house,' she told him. 'I don't feel I can stick it out much longer.'

'I know what you mean!' said Arthur, with too much conviction.

The manner in which he so readily agreed with her made her feel disloyal. It is one thing to criticize your own family by implication, but quite another to allow an outsider the same privilege. The last thing she wanted was for him to show by a snigger or a derisive aside what it was she had little doubt he thought about her apparently churlish father and undoubtedly rough-mannered brother.

'Oh, they're good, really, my family,' she said, quickly. 'But since my mother died – it's not the same any more. And we're all very different from each other.'

Eileen wanted him to understand that she was not like the other two men, who, she could see, intimidated Arthur. But she also did not want him to express the difference in too demeaning a fashion.

'It's hard to believe that fellow is your brother,' he agreed. And although he had near enough put it in a way she did not want to hear, she could not help feeling pleased.

'Is it?' she asked him. 'In what way?'

She had given him an opportunity he was not about to let slip.

'There's something delicate – no, yes, but – sort of – hesitating about you, Eileen,' he began, trying to describe the effect she had upon him, but lacking the right words. 'No, not in that way. I don't know how to describe it. It's not any one thing, it's everything, all together. Specially when you look sideways.'

'Do I look sideways?'

'Not exactly sideways. I mean, you ain't got a squint,' he corrected himself. 'You don't see *two* of me. Though I wouldn't mind seeing two of you. My wife says – '

He stopped dead. The last three words had burnt a hole in his mouth.

Oh, God. Oh, Jeezus.

He sucked in his breath, and dropped his head.

'Arthur?' she said, faintly.

He was rocking gently in his distress, almost hugging himself for comfort. His mind was not so much blank as filled with an angry red turmoil, like the swirling shapes sometimes to be seen on the inner side of tightly clenching eyelids. For a second, he could not think. His stupid tongue had cruelly betrayed him, and the game was up.

Except –

'God rest her soul,' he croaked.

'Arthur?' she said again, as tense as she had ever been since bending to listen to her mother in moments before the end.

'That's why I hate motor-cycles!' he said, with the passion of genius.

'D - do you mean – ?'

He nodded, and the gulping fear within him, the violent panic, made it all the easier for him to burst into tears which were so heartfelt that she could not doubt their authenticity.

'Three years ago last – last Tuesday,' he sobbed, throwing in a clinching detail, his mind now searching fast for the appropriate pictures. 'When I – oh, God! – when I think about the senseless waste – her broken young body. . .'

'Oh, don't cry, don't,' she said, instinctively rushing to put her arms around him.

'She was looking in a butcher's window,' he sobbed, clutching at her for dear life, fresh inventions shaking into his mind. 'She knew how I liked a lamb chop. This motor-cycle – out of control –'

Arthur could see Joan, face open in horror, whirling round from a window full of meat as the motor-cycle reared up on to the sidewalk, coming straight for her.

The man with dark goggles was himself, face merciless over the bucking handlebars. He buried his face in Eileen's soft body, weeping. She stiffened, virginal and scared. Even as he cried, his fingers were probing at her, cupping her breast, and then, remorseless, undoing her buttons, one by one, along the length of her torso.

'Oh!' she gasped.

And then, 'Oh. Arthur . . . no – I –'

But he was busy. Half her buttons had been released already.

'My darling – my baby,' he sobbed and murmured, his fingers not resting. 'This is the first time I've felt *anything* since that day. . .'

'I've never – I – I'm scared . . .' she half-heartedly tried to still his foraging hand.

But there was no stopping him now. His passion could not be turned back, and he himself had no more control over it.

'Dear God, Eileen,' he sobbed, or panted, or both. 'Take the pain away! Please! Please!'

Her own passion had been contending with her fear, and now it triumphed. She had no thought for her father and her brother up the narrow stair in the rooms above, nor for her own inexperience, nor for the patch and darn on her underwear. She simply wanted to pull this man into her.

'I'll try – try to – ' she moaned. 'Poor Arthur – dear Arthur – '

They sank to the floor, coiling together. He was pulling at her underclothes, and soon her thighs were bare. She was clenching her body, helping him to loosen himself and then plunge into her, and both of them were gasping with the force of their own urgency.

Love Is Good For Anything That Ails You?

Arthur was in no condition to turn the title of the song into a question, and neither was she. Their passion, now, had taken them beyond *his* favourite syncopations, and just as far from *her* tower in the woods. The one which had a window but no door.

12

Arthur had let himself into his own dark house. Moonlight filtering behind him made menacing shadows. He looked furtive. The stair creaked under his step.

His wife appeared at the top of the stairs. She was frightened, but she was also hopeful. If it was not the especial nightmare of a passing, leaden-footed rapist, then it might be. . .

'Who . . .' she called. 'Arthur?'

'No,' he said harshly, climbing towards her. 'It's Dracula.'

In truth, he *did* feel like grabbing hold of her neck. He was guilty, scared and exhausted. Several times in his long and over-due drive home he had stopped his car, got out into the rural night and lit a cigarette. He could not make sense of all that had happened to him in the last few days, and had eventually arrived home as much because he did not know where else to go as for any more respectable domestic instinct.

Arthur was not a brave man, and he was quaking at every step.

'Arthur, oh, Arthur!' Joan was saying, with enormous relief. 'Thank God! Thank God you've come back!'

The warmth in her voice astonished him. He had expected a sharp-edged tongue and a barrage of accusations. He knew that he would not have been able to maintain his own rehearsed aggression for longer than a few minutes. The bowl of dog biscuits, he thought, was to be his supper for many another day after this one.

'You trying to be funny?' he growled at her, uncertain how to react.

She was back in the bed where she had waited with increasing desperation. The fact that here he was back at home, standing puzzled at the foot of the bed with that wary expression she knew so well, was for the moment all that mattered to her. The life of an abandoned wife was too hard and too bitter for her to con-template, and she had turned the events of their last morning together over and over in her mind, and found herself wanting.

'I thought you'd gone for ever!' she almost cried, eyes filling with the misery that might have befallen her.

'I have! I've gone!' he insisted, encouraged by her expression. 'What do I get here – in *that* bed of nails.'

'I'll try again, Arthur,' she said quickly – and he had never before heard such fear and humility in anything she had ever said to him. 'I'll try harder! I've – I've even . . . put lipstick on – !'

Because he was still trying to digest the astounding impli-cations of her tone he did not notice the tiny shudder of revulsion which twitched at her shoulders. He took in the words. Was he

65

absolutely sure there was not mockery here? A prelude to worse invective?

'Waddyamean? You *always* put lipstick on – !'

She could not stop herself turning her face away a little, the blood pounding in her cheeks.

'No,' she said, with difficulty, 'on my – on – '

Incredulity was rising in him faster than he could manage. He found it impossible to keep his lips on the edge of his mouth.

'What? On your . . .,' his voice was tremulous. 'On your nipples, Joanie? Have you?'

She pulled her head back into place to look directly at him once more. She gave him a frightened little smile, and nodded quickly.

'You said – you said you wanted me to . . .,' she half-whispered, as ashamed as ashamed could be.

He was too thunderstruck to move for a moment. Then he sat on the bed, so excited and overcome that he was a man transformed. He could not keep what was, for her, a terrible awe out of his voice.

'But how did you know I was coming back *tonight*?' he asked.

'I – I've been putting it on *every* night – hoping and praying you would come back to me,' she said, on the verge of trembling again.

He saw none of her struggles and nothing of her humiliation. It was, for him, enough that she had somehow or other managed to remember, from years back, an at the time unwisely expressed fantasy of his about the ideal marital life. She had told him, then, that he was little better than an animal, though Arthur had never seen anything on four legs which used lipstick.

And glory on high, here she was with scarlet nipples!

'Lemme see!' he gurgled, growing hard at the loin and damp at the lips. 'Show me, angel. Show me!'

But as he reached for her with a predatory claw, she instinctively put up her hands to the top opening of her nightdress. His disappointment, and his contempt, came immediately.

'Oh, I see,' he sneered. 'Still the same after all.'

'No, Arthur,' she said, struggling with herself. 'Not the same – but I'm shy . . .'

'But I'm your *husband*, Joan!' he emphasized, and the sense of sexual proprietorship was as nasty as he made it sound.

Their eyes searched consequences and powers, briefly. And then slowly, excruciatingly, she exposed her breasts. The nipples were vivid with lipstick.

'Do you – like it?' she asked him, nearly in tears.

His eyes were wide and bright with wonder. He could not easily believe it, and, as though to make sure it was not a mirage thrown up by the heat of his own sexual fantasies, he tentatively reached out to touch her nipples, for all the world like someone nervously daring to touch a priceless work of art when the museum attendant was not looking.

'You *was* listening! All the time!' he breathed out his awe. 'Jeepers, Joanie. What lovely, lovely little rosebuds!'

She was both pleased and ashamed, proud and humiliated.

Are they? she meant to say.

'Are they – are they as nice as *hers*?' she asked instead, unable to help herself.

Arthur reacted as though he had been shot. He reared up from the bed, quivering. In the same instant, he had a picture of Eileen turning her face away, weeping.

God almighty, how did Joan know?

'What do you mean – ?' he asked, trying to be indignant and failing ignominiously. He sensed that the lurid red nipples were a mockery, a trap, designed to make him lower his guard. He knew that Joan was a clever woman, brighter by far than he was, and he mortally feared the sharp cross-examination he was sure would follow.

Where could he go? Where could he hide?

But no – look! – Joan's eyes had not taken on the dangerous old glint. She seemed as nervous as he was . . .

'It's – just something . . . I felt it, Arthur – ' she was saying, and it sounded more like an apology than an accusation.

'Well, you're wrong,' he said, emboldened into emphasis.

She looked up at him from the bed. She wanted to believe him, and was encouraged by the vigour of his denial. She thought she knew by now what it was that Men wanted ('all that stuff') and her time of doubt and anxiety had slowly filled up with disgusting images of Arthur doing to other women what he sometimes did and more often tried to do with her.

'Arthur?' she appealed, not willing to put these dirty pictures into words in her own mouth.

'Wrong! Wrong!' he shouted. 'May almighty God strike me dead on the spot!'

A tiny sideways flick of the muscles of his eyes was the sole acknowledgement of the possibility of an Omnipotence that might not greatly care for such an avowal, and hence be tempted to take it too literally.

But Arthur remained alive and well on his feet, his face hot with spurious indignation.

He saw Eileen, again, turning her lovely head aside in shame. And Joan's eyes fixed upon him in entreaty.

Oh God, oh God, he thought, why am I such a shit? How do I get into these messes?

'But – but you *have* wanted to?' she was asking.

Arthur was able to acknowledge to himself that the tone of her questions was of an utterly different order from what he had expected. She sounded, now, as though she really wanted to know, and would use the answer for some purpose other than punishment.

The anger and the fear drained out of him. He felt exhausted, a mental tiredness and confusion reaching into the weight of his limbs.

Arthur, at this moment, wanted to tell her everything. The telling might enable him to see what was happening to him. But he could not, dared not, bring himself to utter the truth.

'Wanting to is not the same thing as doing it,' he said instead, his voice dull and flat.

'Tell me why you *want* to, Arthur?' she asked, quietly.

The gentleness of the question puzzled him. What was going on here? The implications might be even more terrifying than the kind of intimidation he had been arming himself against. Honesty was too dangerous to contemplate.

Was it?

'Perhaps – men,' he said, dragging himself along a cutting edge inch by inch, half-expecting his blood to flow. 'Perhaps they aren't the same. Perhaps? As the ladies, I mean. Do you think?'

It was a universal truth, so far as he was concerned, that whereas Men Wanted It all the time, and with sauce on it, Ladies

Hardly Ever Wanted It, and then politely, without gymnastics.

'But *most* men – ' she began, in rather too much of her old tones.

'Are dead inside!' he snapped back, ready for combat again. 'Yeh – and outside!'

She fell silent. They looked at each other, unsure which frontier between them had now been reached, or breached, or retreated from.

But the fear she had so recently endured fluttered again at her mind, and she began again.

'So I've been thinking about it – ' she said, hesitant, but conciliatory.

'And?'

She looked at him, wanting to scream.

'Perhaps it's my fault,' she said quietly.

This was so unexpected, so open, that it triggered a great yearning in him to try to make clear to her what his own life felt like inside his own dream. He didn't want to tell her about the songs because they had gone over and over all that in the past – and it invariably finished with him having to concede his own stupidity. He didn't even want to bring up the subject of her father's money: that could wait until he was more certain of the lie of the land, and had got himself on the leeward side of it.

Instead, he wanted her to get some idea of the compulsions of his sexuality. He wanted her to know – to acknowledge, to *comprehend*, and so to act upon – the thought – that – well – gulp – well –

Fucking was the most important thing in life.

It was the hidden code in the songs he tried to sell. It was the secret power on the billboards and in the movies. It was the light that leapt out of a pair of sparkling eyes. It was the rhythm that put the colour into things, the flavour into food, the sugar in his tea, the cream in his coffee, the spring in his step, the spread into his smile, the – lipstick on her nipples . . .

Wouldn't it be incredible if he could 'talk dirty' to her?

Wouldn't it be fantastic if he could suggest that she – *diddum, diddum dee dee.*

Characteristically, and with his tongue feeling for the edges of his mouth, Arthur went about it by a circuitous route.

He looked at her, saw the intensity of her concentration upon him, and launched himself.

'I heard a true story the other day,' he said. 'In a band, dance band, they are. This man and this woman singer. They – '

He stopped, his confidence wilting.

She was, of course, puzzled by such a beginning.

'Arthur?'

He swallowed, and decided to continue.

'This man,' he reiterated, 'and this woman singer. They – well, at the hotel where they were playing, see. They gave the elevator man twenty dollars to stop the elevator between floors and – turn his back.'

Again, he stopped. And he waited, watching her intently, almost fiercely.

'Why?' she asked, despite herself.

'So that they could make love in the elevator.' And as he spoke he stayed looking at her with the same challenging ferocity.

Her face was collapsing into contempt and disgust. For an instant, she had thought he meant that the couple in the elevator were just kissing each other, but she saw, from his expression, from the angle of his words, that he was talking about something much, much more horrible.

'Then they are just animals, Arthur,' she said. 'And you know they are!'

He would have been shocked into elation by any other reaction from her, whether her nipples were scarlet or not. Nevertheless, the disappointment was so big that it became a pain. He could feel his throat tightening with an old misery, and tears of despair – as well as of shame – leaked into his eyes.

'Are they, Joan? Are they?' he asked her, defenceless.

The disgust she felt was now at full flood. A torrent of polluted, sewage-thickened water that had broken through its muddy banks and was washing over the entire contents of her mind.

'It's disgusting!'

His disappointment and regret was similarly at the flood, rising too fast and too high for him to do anything other than choke and gasp in his own drowning head. He saw the man and the woman in the elevator, and tried, as the air left his lungs, to grab hold of them, and share in their joyful, funny, guiltless coupling.

'I wish – ' he choked, as the elevator plunged downward, 'I wish – '

'You wish what?' coming out of a face tightening even more with still growing horror.

The elevator had plunged so far downward in its shaft of wistfulness that he had lost sight of any image of it, or of the sexual novelties it had displayed behind its lattice-like doors.

'You wish *what*?'

'Nothing,' he croaked, shaking his head in heavy distress. 'Nothing.'

But she was staring at him with a sickened fascination. The repulsion she had felt about the exhibitionist fornication of the filthy man and the filthier lady in the bizarre story he had told her gathered together in her mind in one angry, festering, suppurating boil and now it burst its odious, stinking pus over her imagination.

'You wish *you* were that man, don't you!' she vomited the thought at him.

My God, my God, I've married a pervert. I've lived with a monster!

And yet it was as though he had not heard her hissing accusation. His face had gone as blank as a head on a mortuary slab, and there was not a trace of colour in it. His eyes, so often the windows on to his turmoil, were now still and dark, seeing nothing, showing nothing. He seemed unable to move a single muscle.

Nausea ebbed from her as she stared at him, and her hysteria fell away into a new apprehension.

Perhaps – and please God, yes – perhaps he had only let such filth out of his mouth because he was *ill*. Perhaps her poor husband did not really know what he was saying. Even her upright father, the poor, dear man, had uttered a single, nightmarish obscenity when the nurse with the big bosom had leant over him to plump up his pillows on the day before he passed over.

Maybe all this time, during all these awkward and embarrassing nights in the creaking double bed together, Arthur had been in some sort of slow and complicated *fever*. Which now, at last, by the looks of him – by his stupefied pallor, his dumb exhaustion, and the bleak see-nothing deadness of his eyes – had finally burnt itself out . . . ?

He began to sway a little on the balls of his feet, like a beaten boxer.

'I wish . . . ,' he said, again, and left whatever desire it was hanging as a threat in the gaps between them.

She waited. Holding her breath.

'I wish I could play the saxophone,' he said, with grief in his voice.

'*What?*'

Really – he was going crazy, she thought. He was going out of his mind! No wonder he had disappeared in the way he had, causing her such torment. No wonder his own burgeoning lunacy had made him *make* her *degrade* herself into using the lipstick on her nipples!

Saxophone? Saxophone? Saxophone . . . ?

'What?' she said, unable to hear its sobbing blue rhythms as they caressed the dance floor. 'Arthur?'

'Shhh!' he hissed at her, urgently.

And then he did something so weird that she was for the moment more than ever confirmed in her diagnosis.

He sighed so deeply that it was as though desolation beyond any hope of repair had spread itself in dark shapes about him in every direction and for the rest of time. He sighed, and looked down at his hands. Her mouth dropped open in fearful incredulity as, slowly, with what seemed to be an ominously meticulous precision, he lifted his hands and began to beat them up and down in the air with a steady, slow rhythm which had a vague resemblance to – what? Something she knew, something she had seen elsewhere . . .

The rhythm of his hands was quickening even as she watched.

Arthur was weary to the bone, and his mind was in the worst turmoil he had known. In front of him, in a bed, and with lipstick on her nipples, was the woman he had sworn to love and to honour until death did them part. Away across the night was another woman, as lovely as the blue flowers on the edge of the fields, who was sweeter to his soul than anyone he had ever known. The bank would not give him any money and the store-keepers scattered across his territory would not yield to his entreaties. He knew that he lied, that he boasted, that he cheated. And that even the crystal-pure vision he had vouchsafed to his drinking pals in the roadhouse was somehow warped and sullied by the seduction which had duly followed on the parlour floor.

He remembered the way the greedy hogs had squealed, grunted and slurped at the trough. He thought their skin was near enough human. And their behaviour . . .

His face, then, had gone dead. The disgust flowing towards him from his wife was threatening to seep into his own mind. So near to telling her the truth about himself, he had ended up knowing that never, never, would she be able to understand. Not in a million years.

Eileen tilted her head at him, and a couple enjoying themselves in an elevator had momentarily beckoned him, but to no avail . . .

'I wish,' he had managed to say, 'I wish I could play the saxophone.'

'What?' she had gaped at him. 'Arthur?'

'Shh!' he hissed at her.

Urgently, because no matter how ridiculous, his beloved music was at last coming to his rescue. He had summoned it up out of the void which had threatened his annihilation.

The dance band he was conducting – with white gloves, and a polished ebony baton – slid smoothly at his command into *Let's Put Out the Lights* as he remembered Rudy Vallee singing it on the radio.

It transformed the theatre on his shoulders back out of decay and silence into a glittering palace. The bedroom became the best sort of dance hall, with coloured lights glistening and twinkling, their refractions caught in the myriads of mirrors in a revolving dome suspended above the gleaming floor.

The baton in his hands continued to conjure up release and delight. Was it not, this stick, the direct descendant of the magician's wand in the stories that Miss Eileen Everson told to her class?

At the insinuating, insistent thought of her – and of his betrayal both of her and Joan – the music in his head wound itself down, and the magical baton slipped from his fingers.

Arthur lowered his arms.

In the music-less pause which followed, the silence without wonder, Arthur and Joan looked across their mutual misunderstanding at each other.

'What were you doing, Arthur?' she asked him, carefully.

'Pretending,' he replied, without animation.

She watched him, and saw the sigh rather than heard it.

'But what – and why?'

'That I got my own dance band.'

She could see now that he was totally and completely sane. She was also able to acknowledge, again, and just in time, that if she were not to lose him altogether, she needed to make yet more of an effort to understand him. The self-accusation came back to her. She should not have let her disgust well up so quickly.

They were examining each other, and, as her expression softened, he put his hands over his face, deeply upset.

She felt confused, and her love for him, always closer to the maternal rather than to the erotic, flared up into a puzzled compassion. But she did not speak. She did not know what to say.

Arthur took his hands away and turned his face back towards her.

Half-smiling, and half-crying, he sent out a small supplication.

'You won't wash it off, will you?' he said.

'What?'

And almost in a whisper he told her. The lipstick. It was an important sign for him, her scarlet nipples. A token of brazen vulgarity to set against her ignorance and her physical coldness.

'The lipstick,' he said, eyes moistening again.

Joan put her hands to her breasts, protectively. Then she realized that she had better not. Reluctantly, she lowered her defences.

'No,' she assented, with a smile that could not hide distaste. 'I won't wash it off.'

13

Many things had happened during the remainder of the night in Joan and Arthur's double bed. Her anxious compliancy had exacted a greater punishment upon her than she had thought possible.

She felt now as though she were covered in pubic hair.

His demands had grown with his excitement, so that each concession she had made had taken her to the edge of yet another one. There had been, it is true, several moments of struggle, but, increasingly emboldened, imperious even, he had more or less *threatened* her with the dire consequences of his disappointment. She had remembered each time, but only just in time each time, the way in which, full of cold fear, she had looked at the silent telephone, the ticking clock, and back again to the silent telephone.

Arthur had little idea of how much, in her order of things, he was abusing her. Nor could he properly admit to the buried or subdued rage which was in him as he demanded more and more energetic sexual callisthenics from her.

Eventually, when satiated, and mistaking her silence for the calm of quiet satisfaction, he had begun to talk about what he wanted from his business life. An unbidden desperation gave an unusually sharp and eloquent edge to his discourse.

You don't like me being away from home so much, he had argued, and she had not disagreed. After all, he had continued, with a glint, you never know when I might take it into my head not to come back. Her silence on this point encouraged him.

I don't want to travel the roads talking my head off to dumb storekeepers, he had insisted. We'll never make money that way. And she could not argue against an increasingly obvious fact.

Arthur had long had the debilitating sense that the days of sheet music were coming to an end. People did not so often gather around the piano in the parlour to play and sing their way through the popular songs of the day. They switched on the radio. They bought themselves wind-up phonographs. He had seen for himself on his travels how the sales of phonograph records were on the up and up.

Now, if he had a bit of capital behind him . . .

Depression or no depression, some people were still doing well. And there was always a need for entertainment. Especially when the times were troubled. Eh? Eh? Excited by his own logic, he had reached across and tweaked at her still scarlet nipples, enjoying at last his sense of sexual proprietorship.

Eileen was beginning to fade from the surface of his consciousness.

Almost as though she knew that a rival woman was losing grip, Joan, listening, thinking, reviewing, had put her hand on his genitals: the first time she had done so solely on her own initiative. The light was already trickling through the drapes as he mounted her again. And this time, in the grunt and the thrust of his expiring energy, he had at the same time, in staccato urgency and with brutal insistence, made her agree that Daddy's money be put to proper use . . .

Joan could hear again the words of her own assent as, in the morning, she made the bed.

There was something cold and abused in her eyes as she straightened the sheet and plumped up the pillows. Arthur, shaving, could not see her expression. He was looking at his own lathered face with chirpy satisfaction.

'Y'see!' he called to her. 'A bit of capital and a bit of affection. That's all a guy needs. That's all *America* needs! Some capital. Some carrot. My own store! Selling records. That's where the money is today!'

She paused in her work. She could not keep the anxiety from peeping through. A fear that, to lathered and beaming Arthur, was like a sudden glimpse of the face of a sick ape glowering out of the bars in its cage at the zoo.

'But – it'll be risky,' she was saying. 'Arthur – wouldn't it make more sense to – '

The razor stopped dead in the creamy track along his cheek.

'You won't let me down, will you?' he said. 'You *said*. You promised.'

It wasn't much of a pause, but Arthur held his breath.

'No. I've agreed,' she replied, in a dull voice. 'You can use Daddy's money.'

The razor resumed its crisp glide through the stubble. A beaming face in the steamy mirror.

'Amazin' what a bit of lipstick will do in the right place,' he chortled. 'Eh, Joanie?'

'Yes,' she said, in the same flat tones.

He was too full of himself to pick up such a warning resonance. His little record store was practically building itself in the seconds between one stroke of the razor and another.

'You won't regret it, honey,' he called to her. 'Honest.'

And as he slushed the water, he became too insistent, too careless of the false notes an idiot could have picked out of the glug-glug of soapy water.

'I love you, Joan, I really love you, doll!'

The expression on her face as she heard his over-emphatic declaration could have been orchestrated into one of his own favourite tunes.

IT'S A SIN TO TELL A LIE.

Arthur was not out to break any hearts. But even if she had tripped delicately into the words of the song he would not, for once, have heard them. He could only see the shiny black records, polished by the store lighting, as the big round metal head bit into the magical grooves.

Playing *It's a Sin to Tell a Lie*. And many other less apt songs. He thought that, yet again, he had found the salve to minister to his old wounds. The patch of blue was now as wide as the heavens themselves.

But if Joan *had* sung the words of the song, she would have been holding sharp scissors in her hand. To plunge into his back on the final crescendo. . .

14

Time does not pass as quickly as a montage in the movies, but the consequences of previous actions – though extended and weighed by many long days and nights – can present themselves with much of the same dramatic brutality.

Winter had come to Illinois. The trees were black and gaunt, without life. All the land around had forgotten the verdant seasons, and was apparently dead. Yet somewhere under the hard soil, or beneath the drifting snow, or at the heart of the sombre, stripped trees, protected from the winds which howled down from the frozen stretches of the north, life was stirring in the bud.

And so it was with Miss Eileen Everson, the teacher, and teller of tales about princes, witches, imprisoned maidens.

She had awoken to an unfamiliar nausea several mornings in a row. Her period had delayed and delayed . . .

And Arthur, the man who had spoken to her with such touching simplicity under the shadowy trees, the man who had wept so bitterly for the broken young body of his poor slaughtered wife, Arthur had not returned, nor written her a line.

Eileen had been unable to prevent herself thinking of him, at first, as a kind of prince who had come out of nowhere to awaken her. She had looked around and about and found herself in a new kingdom. Her entrancement had lasted longer than reason itself should have allowed – reason, the sour old republic made of barren stones, at the bitter heart of every dreamland.

But, gradually, inexorably, and with the taste of real bile at the back of her throat, she had at last come to accept that Arthur had disappeared from her life as easily as he had come into it.

She wept quietly into her pillow at nights, and dreamed of the Prince in Rapunzel. He had fallen from the high tower without a door, and been blinded by the sharper thorns of the bramble which grew at the bottom. When she awoke each morning, it was her own eyes that felt the pain.

Eileen had forced herself to go to the doctor in town to have her worst fears confirmed. He was severe with her. His lips had gone tight, and oddly white, in the sanctimony of his disapproval.

She wondered what on earth was going to happen to her. There were no visible signs of her pregnancy yet, but when the baby started to show, she knew she would be in desperate trouble.

The children in her class had already noticed that all was not well with their teacher. It was not because she gave them any less attention, or had stopped leaning over their drawings or exercise books with an encouraging smile and an improving finger. They had seen the sigh on her face at moments when she thought they were properly busy. They had picked up the occasional wandering thought in the middle of one of her still rapturously received stories. And a blessed collective instinct had made them solicitous of her welfare. They rushed to do things for her. She remained, even more than ever, the kindest and brightest adult in their small, secret lives.

At this moment, for instance, one of the boys from the back of the class was lingering behind after the last lesson to see if she wanted him for anything. She had smiled a no and a thank you, and began to dust the chalk off the blackboard. Oh, were it as easy to wipe away the stains of the past!

The lad turned to go, a little disappointed, but in a hurry now. He all but collided with the stern Principal, who was coming through the same doorway.

'Steady there!' barked Mr Warner.

The boy jumped back in genuine fear, expecting a slap.

'Ooo – sorry, sir,' he gulped. 'I . . .'

'Look where you're going, boy!'

'Sir!' quavered the boy, backing out with great caution, and feeling himself lucky not to receive the meaty weight of the old devil's hand.

Mr Warner looked at Eileen, and an especially alert witness would have been able to testify that the Principal's harsh, worn face softened a little.

Certainly, there was an uncharacteristic hesitation in his speech.

'I – ah – you aren't rushing away for a few moments . . .?' he asked her.

'No . . .?' she said, a little surprised.

He made sure the door was shut. He hesitated, and his eyes flicked around at the children's drawings on the classroom walls, their pictures celebrating Thanksgiving Day.

'I've – ah – I've known you a very long time now, Eileen,' he said, in much the same way that a nervous man might clear his throat.

'Oh, dear,' she said.

The sharpness came back to him. 'What's the matter?' he darted at her.

'That's the sort of sentence that usually spells trouble!' she smiled back at him. But her heart was beginning to beat faster with the anticipation of threat.

He did not deny the observation. Indeed, the quick, shrewd gleam in his eyes confirmed it for a fraction of a second. But then, palpably awkward, he made his glance slide away from her waiting tension, and he simulated an attentive examination of the drawings on the classroom wall.

One of the oldest pictures settled his eye.

'*That* one,' he said with a sudden emphasis, picking it out with a plunge of his finger. 'I haven't looked at it, I mean *looked* at it, for – oh, almost thirty years when I taught this class.'

She did not follow the line of his eyes or the stab of his finger. She knew that something was very badly wrong, and the tension made her body as still as her voice.

'What did you want to say, Mr Warner?' she asked.

He looked at her, and seemed about to tell her. The words, whatever they were, failed to make it to his tongue. Instead, strangely, he covered his eyes with one hand, like a pupil taking a memory test, and began to intone the lines of doggerel from the twelve-oblonged picture he had pointed at.

> 'January snowing,
> February rain.
> March with winds a-blowing,
> April sun again.'

He took his hand away from his eyes, not so much in acknow-ledgement that he had so quickly reached spring, but in order to

80

stare at her in a disturbingly challenging manner. He continued, eyes still upon her:

> 'May a world of flowers,
> June with dancing leaves,
> July long lazy hours,
> August golden sheaves,
> September apples redden,
> October winter's near,
> November, skies all leaden,
> December, Christmas cheer!'

The year had whipped by in his mouth, and the silence which followed seemed to be longer than the rhyming, chiming months. *Skies all leaden. All leaden.*

'Yes,' she nodded in a tight voice. 'It's strange how long little things stay in the mind.'

'But you see, Eileen,' he said, moved, 'I can remember *you* saying those lines as one of my little girls. Standing right *there* – with a bit of blue ribbon in your hair.'

He had indicated, with that familiar (and, to many a child, dread) thrust of his forefinger the place where, in fact and in his mind, pretty little Eileen Everson had stood to recite. He knew then that she had an especial grace – one which would grow with the years.

The older Eileen, without the flop of bright blue ribbon, but with much the same look of anxious concentration on her face, knew for sure now what it was the old man had come to talk to her about.

There was no escape in the pretty pictures on the classroom wall. Her nerves shrieked suddenly in her skin, like the squeak of chalk, when, on a downward slope or an upward loop, it scraped the blackboard and set your teeth on edge.

She consciously controlled her voice, and her face.

Oh, Arthur, leapt into the chasm of her mind. *Oh, Arthur. Where are you?*

'Doctor Bartholemen is on the school board, isn't he?' she said. 'He has told you about – about my – condition. Hasn't he?'

81

Warner took the measure of her question, and probed at the shame and desperation bravely hidden behind it. Then, in an oblique tribute to her own courageous self-control, he nodded, crisp and to the point.

'He asked me to contemplate the picture of Miss Everson, the teacher, and her illegitimate baby,' he said.

'Yes,' she sighed.

A picture which the guardians of Galena would refuse to countenance. Canting minds and luridly enflamed imaginations would see her as a cesspool of corruption, not to be allowed near the innocent children.

It would be better if she were to breathe tuberculosis germs over them than inculcate in their unformed minds the degrading idea that a young woman who had not married was nevertheless capable of bearing child. Yes, the picture of Miss Everson, the teacher, and her baby, must be trampled underfoot, or flushed away as the nastiest of waste matter. The very flag over the school entrance, stretching and flapping in the cold wind, would droop in shame should such an image be allowed to come to life.

Mr Warner turned away in pain to pretend to look at those other and sweeter pictures on the wall. She was surprised to see that there was the hint of moistness about his averted eyes. He was surely the last man in the whole of Illinois to have the smallest particle of sympathy or understanding for her plight.

'Where does it all go to, I wonder?' he said, mysteriously, but in a thickening diction.

Still half-expecting a lecture on personal morality, larded with the ample grease of standard humbug, she was puzzled by his tone and his manner. There was such gentleness in him at this moment, and so many not quite hidden signs of a warmer human emotion than she had ever known him to possess, that Eileen did not know how to respond.

'Mr Warner?' she asked, with a frown.

'These children,' he said in that old abrupt voice of his, still looking at one of the drawings pinned to the wall. 'Look – here is a tree one of them has drawn. And it's like a diamond. With different kinds of fruit on the same branch. A tree out of the Garden of Eden.'

He turned back to her – and the regret upon him was like the ache of the Fall, the most ancient of wounds for which there never could be a bandage.

'That's how they see things, you know,' he continued. 'I think they really do see things in a way that – in a way that they eventually lose. Not only lose, but forget they ever had.'

She was astonished. Never before had she heard him speak like this. Not once in her experience of him, whether as his pupil or as his colleague, had he so much as ventured any word about the children or their work which was not utterly prosaic and utilitarian. Discipline was almost the be-all and end-all of his teaching philosophy. What was the longest river, where was the highest mountain, when was Abraham Lincoln born, and stand to attention when I'm talking to you. *Quiet!*

Did he realize that the picture which summoned up wistful dreams of a permanently lost paradise on earth had been drawn with quiet concentration, tongue poking out at the corner of the mouth with the effort of putting a rosy red apple and a bright yellow pear on the same bough, by the boy whose cheek he had pinched and slapped on the day that –

On the day that Arthur had met her outside the school?

Eileen wanted to remonstrate with the harsh old man. No one who had such a sadly beautiful conception of the lost land of childhood should then permit himself to break into it with terror and violence.

'Yes,' she began, 'So why do you – ?'

She stopped herself from asking the question. This was not the time nor the place. And anyway, *she* was the one on trial, so to speak.

'You were going to ask – why, if I understand *that*, why do I *hit* them so often?'

'Yes,' she said, quietly.

'So that they can learn enough to bend their backs in the fields, Miss Everson,' he snapped. 'Or endure the wearing out of their bodies and their spirits on the assembly line. What do they want with visions, or trees shaped like diamonds? Or any memory at all of the Garden of Eden? Cheap music will do. Cheap music. And beer. And baseball.'

Cheap music? *Love Is Good For Anything That Ails You?* Yes? No?

Songs tell the truth, songs do!

The declaration that came swooping back on her, words spoken by the plausibly honest Arthur, gave the real dimension to Mr Warner's account of human inadequacies.

'Life isn't very grand – sometimes. Is it?'

He looked at her with sadness, and replied gently.

'Not when you break the rules, my dear.'

The Rules. The Rules! Break them, and they break you. That's what he meant, and that's what he lived by. She knew how severe the consequences of her passion were going to be. But she had no plans. Against reason, Eileen had hoped to be able to carry on with her job for at least another couple of months. She would face outrage when it came, but she wanted to delay it as long as possible.

But now she knew that the Principal was here to tell her that she had to go away immediately.

'This is the worst day of my life,' he said, and his head was lowered in what looked to her to be genuine grief. He really seemed to mean it. She felt a stab of guilt for his distress.

'I'm sorry – ' she stumbled out her apology. 'I'm very sorry about everything.'

Mr Warner had the manner of one trying to deflect a heavy blow as she said this. He blinked rapidly, intolerably moved. It was more than he could do to keep the tears from his eyes and a wobble from his voice. A secret that he had been content to keep locked away under a forbiddingly harsh exterior was demanding release.

But still she did not see it. The gap between her experience of him at the school and the knowledge he himself had of the covert joy in his own heart was as yet too wide for her comprehension to leap.

She simply thought that he was being very much nicer than anyone would have imagined to be possible.

'Something, very, very special indeed – very very bright and – ' he seemed almost too moved to get the words into an ordered sequence, 'will go out of my life when you leave this little school of ours. I won't want to come here myself.'

'Oh, now,' she protested, astounded by such excess.

He let his moistened eyes settle upon her, and, before he

spoke again, a bolt of amazement jolted her into the disturbing realization of what it was he meant.

'No. You don't understand,' he said, even as she grasped it. 'And you'd be horrified if you did.'

They held glances for just a moment. He knew, then, that, almost inadvertently, he had finally given expression to his most cherished secret. His oblique declaration of love had not, after all, been too obscure for her to fasten on to it. At any other time, in any other place, she would have been horrified to the point of nausea. But now, in the welter of her own distress, and because of his own remarkable delicacy, she could accept the meaning of what he said.

It was both a sweet and shameful moment for him as he saw the understanding, the acceptance, in her eyes. He gave her a wintry little smile, then turned away.

He pulled himself up short, in the act of turning away. And, as though it were an inconsequential afterthought, he took out his wallet.

'Please don't be offended,' he said, taking some dollar notes out of the pigskin.

'No! Don't do that!' she cried.

But he grabbed hold of her protesting hand, and thrust the money into it, adamantly. She was prepared to take the offence he had asked her not to feel, but found instead that she was moved.

An act of pure kindness when its recipient is in misery or doubt can be too much to bear. A sudden gleam of light hurts eyes that have just got used to darkness.

'I – oh, Mr Warner,' she choked. 'I'll always remember this – always'

She clenched the money in her hand, and knew it to be the token of an undefiled love. Arthur's betrayal of her cut all the more sharply. She had to twist her head away in a vain attempt to staunch or to deflect the strong flood of her emotion.

And as for Warner, his secret out and not contemptuously thrown back in his face, the tears were glistening in his eyes. The fierceness was nowhere in evidence.

'I know trees that are shaped like diamonds,' he said, so softly that it was almost a whisper. 'I've never forgotten.'

'Nobody ever stops yearning, Mr Warner,' she said, gently, letting him know that he need never be ashamed of the secret he had nursed and nourished for so long.

But he did not want her to say anything sympathetic. Much of the old no-nonsense briskness sprang back into his face. No wishy-washy sentimentalist he.

'Then they better had, Miss Everson,' he announced, stiff and abrupt. Yearning was not useful. Yearning would not help. And that, he seemed to say, was the sensible way of the sensible world, so don't you forget it.

Or: look what your yearning brought *you*, young lady.

He thrust out his hand, immensely dignified.

'Good afternoon, my dear,' he said, as he closed the door.
Oh, Arthur! Where are you?

15

Oh, Arthur – where are you?

It did not matter how many times she framed the question, or in how many ways Eileen put it to herself – angry, pleading, wistful, contemptuous, incredulous or dully mechanical – she never got an answer.

Oh, Arthur: where are you?

He was safely ensconced in one of the lands of his dreams. Except he wasn't too safe, after all, and the Dream had taken on the same drear shape everyone else insisted on calling Real Life.

Joan had honoured her word about her father's small legacy. Against her better judgement and, so to speak (or to speak of it in what she would prefer to be a furtive behind-the-hand whisper), on her back and with lipstick on her nipples.

Arthur had grandly surveyed possible properties in the grandest streets of Chicago. He had ridiculous visions of his phonograph record store spreading the polished bend of its immaculate plate glass on one of the corners feeding on to swish Michigan Boulevard. Next door to the bank that had rejected him, perhaps.

He had blanched when he was told the price.

Ah, well, he had shrugged, start small, and build up. He would soon be able to spread his wings. Eventually, there would be another of his record stores, bigger and better, elsewhere in Chicago. And then in other towns in Illinois, putting the hick storekeepers who were his old enemies out of business. Soon, Arthur's record stores would be all over the country, and he might even set up his head office in New York. He would shift millions upon millions of records. All good dance-band music. All his favourite songs.

Maybe. Soon. Perhaps . . .

At about the time chagrined Eileen was staring nervously at Dr Bartholemen's brass nameplate back in Galena, Arthur had bought the small box on the Loop which was to become 'his first store'. You had to begin somewhere, he conceded. So he ordered a large amount of stock to mitigate the disappointment about the size and position of the store.

Stock which, so far, was diminishing at a rate nearly too small to measure.

So here is Arthur Parker in his little store. The decorations are still new. There is a plant dying in the window, the 'good luck' ribbon now limp. Outside, the snow was drifting down lightly, the crystalline flakes dissolving into damp anonymity as soon as they touch the sidewalks.

To say that business was bad would be like adding that Everest is high.

Arthur, alone, forlorn, drummed his fingers, a dream crumbling as each cold day slid icily into another.

'Come on. Come on,' he was muttering. 'Where are they all?'

'They' were the customers who scarcely ever stepped over his threshold. His displays had not seduced them. Just as he had had 'the wrong territory' when not selling sheet music, so he now had 'the wrong position' now that he was not selling phonograph records. It wasn't *his* fault!

Bored, and worried, he wandered over to the window to look

out on to a street full of passers-by who would not break stride, pause, enter and go out again with armfuls of brown-paper-sleeved records.

If they would not look in, he would look out.

Outside, unexpectedly, there were some girls modelling fur coats for a photographer. And, inevitably, as Arthur looked across at these beautiful creatures, the dull grey defeat or anxiety in his eyes began to give way to his old yearning.

It was not simply that there was now a lascivious gleam in his orbs, his peepers, or whatever the novelty numbers called them. Nor only that he wanted to call across *Hey, Hey, Good Looking* at the models. No, it was more like an unidentifiable but pleasant taste remembered by the tongue, forgotten by the brain. There was *something* on the tip of his imagination, on the very edge of his nerve, which he knew he wanted but could not quite identify.

What was certain, it was not merely a female body.

The girls in their luscious furs, girls with slender long legs, and hair made for stroking, were placing and besporting themselves in the lightly falling snow. They were living puppets for the photographer. Store mannequins brought out into the air and given human flexibility.

One of them tilted her head back in an instructed smile. And, for some reason, maybe because of the configuration of light and mood and stance and female grace the image of Eileen Everson darted back to sting at his mind.

Eileen. Eileen. What did I do to you?

Oh, Arthur. Where are you?

Neither knowing that the two thoughts occupied the exact same moment.

There was a third person intruding upon the coincidental union. One who had the means to make a more direct physical connection.

The telephone jangled, to prove it.

'Loop Records. Hello?' said Arthur brightly into the mouth-piece. It *might* be an order. You never can tell in the music business, can you?

But it was Joan. O God, it was Joan.

'Oh, hello Joan,' his voice went flat. 'Depressed? What, me?'

He made an effort, daubing colour. Every day he went home

from the store she insisted on looking at the day's returns. Every evening she looked across the table at him with troubled anxiety. Small columns of figures were mounting up not to optimism but to an epitaph. Depressed? Too damned right!

'Depressed? What – me? No - o - o!' he falsely chirruped into the telephone. 'Had a very good day, in fact. No, that's true! Don't be so ne – ga – tive.'

On the other end of the line, Joan was refusing to accentuate the positive. She had had more than enough of bouncy promises and false prospects. It was her duty to make Arthur face up to Real Life again.

And he knew it was *his* task to pull as much wool over her eyes as there were sheep in the universe.

'No, that's true – a very good day!' he was insisting. 'Well – not so bad as last week, not nearly. Joan. Will you *stop* saying I told you so. I'll make it pay!'

He masked the phone in desperation, twisting his head aside, to call out, with a lack of conviction she could surely hear –

'One moment, madam. With you in a moment! Yes, sir, of course sir, one second sir!'

Arthur pushed his mouth back into the threatening telephone, seeing Joan's tightening face at the other end of the line, and speaking in a rapid gabble which gave no space for her to interrupt with either a question or an accusation.

'Must rush. Yes. Usual time,' he said. ''Bye, pigeon.'

He put the telephone down on its cradle as though it were a live bomb. She would see the returns, anyway. Four records so far this morning. That was all. Four records and two small tin boxes of phonograph needles, one soft and one loud.

And a cretin who came in out of the softly falling snow and wanted to know if he had any military marches.

Arthur would rather be seen dead than stock such *oompah-oompah* rubbish. So far as he was concerned, the customer was only occasionally right. Like when asking for *Roll Along Prairie Moon* or *Pennies from Heaven* or *It's the Girl* or –

Love Is Good For Anything That Ails You?

Arthur looked glumly around his customer-less store. The ladies modelling fur coats out on the street, Joan's depressing telephone call, the sense of impending doom about the whole

grand enterprise of owning his own record store, the slowly
spiralling snow flakes – everything, all of it, merged into the beat
of the song.

Love Is Good For Anything That Ails You –

Suddenly, decisively, Arthur went back to the door. He turned
the sign round from OPEN to CLOSED (was there much difference?), and went out into the gentle snow.

Softly, softly.

16

Arthur's old car was on the road again.

The land was white and sparkling with the virgin purity of
freshly fallen snow. Its clean expanse seemed like the promise of
yet another new beginning. Arthur's resilience was reasserting
itself in the familiar form of a whistled tune as he clutched the
steering wheel of his trusty old chariot, his passion wagon.
Whistle while you work.

Once more, the lyric of *Prairie Moon* was helping him along on
his *chug-chug* journey through Illinois.

O.K., so they don't have cowboys in Illinois – so what?

He didn't have to elbow his way into someone else's store and
fast talk through the virtues of the sheet music. Not any more.

He thought briefly about Joan, and quaked inside. He pushed
the image out of the way. He would think of some explanation
for his absence. If he ever went back, that is. If he ever went back
. . . If.

Hello, Eileen. How are you?

No, that wasn't going to be so easy, either.

Another little difficulty was pushed away. The snow lay round
about as though it were in the middle of a carol. But Arthur,
deeply unsure of himself, did not feel regal enough to be a
Wenceslas.

Roll Along Prairie Moon. That was more like it.

He was whistling jauntily again, as happy as the birds. And as the simple song beat out in his mind, the white land scudding past, he saw a cowboy twirling a lariat. It was himself, free of all restrictions. Rope 'em, steer 'em, brand 'em. When a man could be a man, and –

'What *are* you doing?' an alien voice cut into the fantasy.

The cowboy with the lariat, the happy cowboy, went the way of all dreams – which is a lot quicker to the same place as the way of all flesh.

Arthur realized that his own voice had said something out loud.

'What are you doing?' he said to himself.

Fearful, he slowed, and pulled in off the road. There was a billboard by the wayside, announcing to no one special the Carole Lombard film. *Love Before Breakfast.*

Arthur did not look at the billboard this time, but he knew it was there, like a gaudy warning.

He got out of the car and, brooding, went into the murk beyond the Carole Lombard billboard. Somewhere to think. Or maybe even somewhere to hide, between the soggy patches in the clean snow.

Arthur lit a cigarette. It was the last one in the pack. Ruminative, anxious, he pulled the blessed smoke into his by now well-blackened lungs, and threw the empty Lucky Strike pack away.

'What am I doing?' he said to himself. 'What *am* I – '

His puzzled thoughts trailed off.

Coming slowly towards him, along a path through the murk, a young girl was carrying what looked like a basket of eggs. The first thing he noticed was that she was exquisitely beautiful.

She was coming towards him, and she was as lovely as the flowers in May.

The second thing he noticed was that she walked in a strange, slow, steady gait. It was like seeing a piece of film that had been subtly slowed in its motion. She might have been at the beginning of a slow and graceful dance . . .

Arthur waited with bated breath, entranced, as she slowly approached. He set his face in a friendly smile of greeting as she came alongside. But she showed no sign whatsoever of acknowledging him. It was just as though he was not there. The smile wavered on his face as she seemed to glide past, and would soon be beyond him.

'Good morning, miss,' he said.

The lovely girl seemed to start with alarm. She stopped, and turned cautiously about, not quite looking at him.

'What do you want?' she said.

The way in which she walked, the manner in which she had passed alongside him as though he were not there, and, now, the look that was not exactly looking at him, the speech addressed as though to someone standing half a yard to his right, came together with a bump of pity in Arthur's mind.

'Excuse me,' he said, with awe in his voice. 'But you can't - um - you can't *see*. Can you?'

The exquisite blind girl hesitated.

'Not really,' she said. 'No.'

'Do you need somebody to walk with you, miss?' Arthur asked, affected by both her great beauty and her appalling affliction. 'It'd be a great honour.'

She was firm and instant in her refusal.

'That's very kind. But – no. Thank you.'

Arthur wanted to help her. He especially wanted to be able to hold her arm. Chivalry and lust contended in him, and both might yet triumph. You never knew, did you? If he was nice, especially nice.

'But you ain't got a stick!' he protested. 'The ground is very rough, miss. It's not safe!'

'I come here every day,' she said, in a voice as steady as her elegant, slow walk. 'I know my way. Good-bye.'

He looked at her sadly, wanting to say more.

'Good-bye, miss,' was all that he could say.

Slowly, and carefully, she walked away along the path, as graceful and as mysterious as a figure in a dream.

The combination of her beauty and her blindness touched Arthur to the quick. And as he watched her go so slowly away from him, genuine pity tightened at his throat.

'I'll never forget this!' he called after her. 'Never!'

She stopped. She stayed absolutely still. Her back was towards

Arthur, but something in her stance seemed to show that she had perceived the emotion in him.

'I think you're a very beautiful and a very brave young lady!' he called, again.

The blind girl smiled a small, sad smile to herself, but she did not turn around. She continued on her way along the path, putting her feet down with measured care.

'Please pardon me saying that! I couldn't help it!' he called again, louder, so that the receding figure could hear.

Arthur watched her go, and the sight of her made his eyes prickle. As ever, he was a man easily moved.

'I'd cut off my right arm if I could make you see again,' he said out loud, but far too quietly for her to hear. 'I don't know what I'd do if I could – if I could . . .'

Alas, his expression changed.

'*If I could get into your pants,*' he added, *definitely* to himself.

Well, she was lovely. Her face. Her figure. So delicately made, as though God had given her compensation for lovely eyes that would not let in the light.

A spurt of shame caught up with and overwhelmed Arthur's lust.

'Be careful!' he yelled across the space between them. 'Be - careful!'

The blind girl was now out of sight. Moved, ashamed, Arthur sighed and went back to the car he had parked by the billboard at the roadside.

There was nothing to show for his encounter with the exquisite blind girl except his own mixed emotion, her sad smile, a few words, a crushed and discarded cigarette pack, and his own footprints.

17

Late in the same afternoon, Arthur had reached the dirt track which led to the small farmhouse where Eileen lived. He knew that this had been the inevitable destination of his impulsive journey. But now that he was here, his courage was wavering.

'I haven't been able to get down this way. Business, you see,' he said grandly. It was only a rehearsal. He was speaking only to himself.

He waited and watched. The two men did not seem to be anywhere in evidence.

'Couldn't come and see you. Been very busy.'

The words sounded all right when he said them, to nobody, in the car. He began to persuade himself that Eileen would find them all right, too.

After all, why shouldn't she? They didn't own each other!

'That's O.K., Arthur,' she ought to say, with the loveliest of smiles. 'Why don't we lie down?' Already beginning to unbutton her dress.

He went over the sequence again in his head, reassuring himself that they *would* happen, in exactly the same fashion. Her breasts gleamed encouragingly.

Yes. Yes. Why not? He had only to speak, and they would be in each other's arms.

'I - ah - I haven't been able to get down this way,' he stumbled out the words under the actuality of her steady gaze in the little parlour. 'Business, you know.'

'Or to write,' she said, flat.

Arthur shifted uncomfortably. He had been a fool to persuade himself that he could get away with it. They were sitting well apart, with no prospect of touching. It had even looked, for a while, as though she were not going to let him set foot inside the door.

'No,' he said, beginning to get scared.

'Why not, Arthur?'

The question was steadily matter-of-fact. This was worse, in its way, than shrill accusation, which at least signified the presence of an explosive emotion. One kind of strong feeling could be made to feed another. There was no hand-hold, no place of purchase, in this dreadful, flat, unemotional questioning.

'I'm here now – aren't I?' he said, pathetically.

The steady gaze she gave him did not alter. It forced him to lower his eyes.

'And what are you here *for*, Arthur?' she asked him, in the same relentlessly cool voice.

He did not know what to do with his face or his eyes or his hands or his legs. Her tone, and her gaze, stripped him of all pretension, and so of all defence.

'You, my love,' he said. In supplication.

'Am I?'

'What?'

'Your love,' she said.

Arthur looked at her. This simple exchange had released him from his own disastrous furtiveness. The sight of her there in front of him was once again triggering in him the extraordinary, and vital, response he had felt the first time he had set eyes upon her.

'Now that – I know this doesn't sound very nice, Eileen,' he heard himself saying, 'but now that I can see you, sitting there – I – yes. My love.'

'And when I'm not in front of you?' she asked, in the same disturbingly direct manner.

He could not detect any softening in her tone, and she was as far from smiling as a stone sphinx. The only thing he could do was to make a similarly direct appeal to her, and throw himself on her mercy.

And what if her father or her brother were to come back?

And, God, how lovely she looked, even when questioning him like this. He swallowed, and shifted again, aware of time running out, and of a loss he had not until now known how to measure. If he didn't say something soon, she would be for ever beyond his grasp. And, suddenly, now that he was here, the thought was too desolate to contemplate.

She was looking steadily at him, waiting for his answer. The clock was ticking, the fire was fluttering, the light was fading, and his heart was missing a beat.

'Don't let's talk like this, Eileen,' he implored her in a thickening voice, and uselessly.

She pursed her lips a little.

'What way shall we talk then, Arthur?'

There was an edge in her voice, and almost an amused contempt in her eyes, as she spoke.

'What *do* you want to do?'

He tried a cheerful, cheeky little grin. Oh, come on, his face said, as near to a wink as he dared to go, come on. We both know what I'm talking about, don't we?

'Kiss you,' he suggested.

'Is that all?' she asked, and there was no doubting the mockery that snickered cruelly at him from behind the question.

His smile died. He did not know what to say. He realized that he did not have the slightest idea of how to handle her. His tongue had become as heavy as lead, fixed inside the soft cavern of his mouth in punishment.

'To tell you the truth,' he gulped, feeling the pain of it, 'I haven't – '

'The truth, yes,' she interrupted. 'Please tell me the truth.'

It pulled him up. He opened and closed his mouth. He could not even think of an answer, let alone say one.

She waited. And, this time, there was tension in her. She was like a spring coiled and about to be released. It frightened him. He got ready to ward off the blow.

'*Are* you married, Arthur?' she asked.

Do I look like a married man? Why, I even got a hole in my sock!

You won't ever lie to me, will you, Arthur?

Not if I can help it.

Only now, so to speak, could she see the dead bird in the road, eaten from within by maggots.

'*Are* you married, Arthur?'

'What d'you want to go and ask me *that* for?' he spluttered, with every semblance of genuine indignation.

She did not answer, but kept her eyes fixed steadily and evenly upon him. He tried to hold her gaze, knowing how important it

96

'Life is just a Bowl of Cherries'
Jessica Harper (Joan), Bernadette Peters (Eileen) and Steve Martin (Arthur)

'Pennies from Heaven'
Steve Martin with Vernel Bagneris (the Accordion Man)

'Love is Good for Anything that Ails You'
Bernadette Peters

'Yes, Yes, My Baby Said, Yes, Yes!'
Steve Martin

'Pennies from Heaven'
Vernel Bagneris

'Love is Good for Anything that Ails You'
Bernadette Peters

'Let's Face the Music and Dance'
Bernadette Peters and Steve Martin

'Let's Misbehave'
Christopher Walken (Tom)

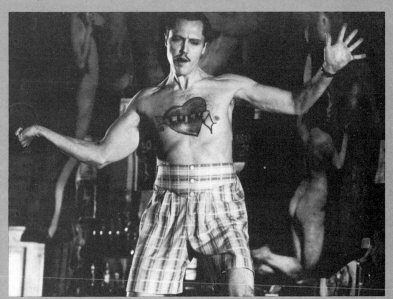

'Let's Misbehave'
Christopher Walken

'It's the Girl'
Tommy Rall, Steve Martin and Robert Fitch

'Have You Ever Seen a Dream Walking?'
Steve Martin and Bernadette Peters

was for him to do so. But it was too much for him. If she had looked away just once, for the tiniest fraction, if she had moved a single muscle, he could have kept his face steady. She didn't.

His eyes slid helplessly away.

'Yes,' she said, with flat certainty. 'Yes. You are.'

The little room ached with silence. A silence which stretched and stretched like the thinnest membrane. It became unbearable. There was no virtue in the fact that he did not again attempt to deliver up a brazen lie. He simply could not get it out under the calm of her gaze, and the flat certainty of the answer she had herself provided.

He had not said a single word, nor made the smallest sound to suggest that such a word was possible. But his silence was eloquent.

She nodded. And still she waited. And still he could not speak.

But the silence could not stretch into eternity. The membrane broke at last, with a piercing rip of pain.

'You - you haven't gotta dr – ' he eventually said, almost choking. 'Do you think you could make us a cup of coffee?'

The very ordinariness of such a domestic question was moving in its admission of defeat – his defeat, and hers. Misery came pressing in on her from every side, and every corner of the room.

She was besmirched and polluted. Her life lay in ruins. Yes, one might as well chink a cup of coffee against one's teeth . . .

Eileen's eyes filled with tears. Not all at once, not in a passionate gush, but slowly, and terribly. Arthur, watching her intently, could not bear it.

'Oh, don't do that,' he appealed, his own voice breaking, 'or you'll set me off.'

'What have you got to cry about, Arthur?' she asked him, with just sufficient control to speak properly.

'I dunno,' he choked. 'But it feels like *everything*.'

She watched him for a moment, almost clinically. He was obviously profoundly upset. He was crying. But her own tears had stopped welling so slowly into her eyes. Brave, and matter-of-fact, she had somehow regained control of herself.

Getting up abruptly, she began to make the coffee.

The room was filled with peaceful domestic sounds. The water agitating itself in the hot kettle. The chink of cups and saucers.

The tinkle of spoons.

'I'm going to have a baby,' she said, in an ordinary voice, to complete the picture of domestic harmony.

He was shocked out of his skin, his everyday skin. He was shocked out of his tears, his everyday tears.

He was shocked into dumb silence.

And then the trembling started, at the end of his nerves.

'How – how do you know?' he quavered. 'I mean – I mean, is that definite?'

'Quite definite,' she said. Then her eyes narrowed. 'Have you already got children?'

'No,' he swallowed, feeling as though he were lying even when he wasn't. 'No – I – no.'

She measured him, evenly, and as steadily as ever. She did not raise her voice or lift her hand. It made what she had to say sound totally chilling. Lacking apparent venom, it came at him with absolute passion because of its cool passionlessness.

'*If you tell me any more lies, I will stick a knife in your back.*'

'Christ, Eileen,' he quivered.

'The truth. Please,' she commanded.

My God, a secretly commentating part of himself was yet able to say, my God, isn't she great, isn't she a magnificent woman, doesn't she look marvellous – ?

'Cross my heart and hope to . . .' his voice trailed off as he realized, in time, just how inappropriate such a childish oath was at this moment. 'No. Eileen, no. We haven't got any kids.'

The change in his voice allowed her to accept that, in this at least, he was telling the truth.

'But do you live with your wife?' she asked.

'I – ' Arthur began, tempted to spin out another story. She had not been killed by the motor-cycle outside the butcher's window. But he had got his lamb chops that day. She had been so very badly injured that she was a vegetable . . . so mutilated or damaged inside that, despite all his devoted care, his angelic ministrations, his continued fidelity, they had from that day on been unable to have sex together . . . and . . .

'I – ' And he stopped. Helpless.

She would stick a knife in my back. She really would!

Oddly, too, he did not want to lie. He really did not want to.

Even as his native sense of invention flashed invitingly before him, even as the details so readily formed themselves, he recoiled from them.

'I – '

'I see,' she said, calmly.

A calm which, in its evidence of quietly endured pain, jerked him to his feet in a cry of anguish.

'What are you going to do!'

'There's nothing very much I can do,' she answered, remaining calm. 'What are *you* going to do?'

'Me?' he said, surprised. Then the terror boiled up inside him. 'Yeah. What the hell am *I* going to do?'

'You can write down your address.'

The terror stayed on the boil. He saw the consequences. He saw her calling at the house on South Campbell, a baby in her arms. He imagined the way in which Joan would have opened the door, her expression friendly or neutral, and then the transformation that would happen to her face. The cry of rage and bitter humiliation –

'What?' he asked, oozing fear.

'Oh, don't worry,' she said, with that shrivelling trace of contempt and bleak, controlled self-sufficiency, 'I won't mess you up. But I've lost my job and I've got to leave home – '

'Oh, God. Oh, Christ!' he moaned, as he saw how much damage he had inflicted upon her.

' – and if I – well, *really* need help or – Arthur? Won't you?'

This was the nearest she had come to any sort of appeal. He had to give her that.

Arthur looked at her, and nodded. A manly nod.

He took a piece of paper from his inside pocket, tore a bit off, looked at it, then, like one taking the plunge, scribbled something rapidly.

Arthur folded it over, hesitated, then folded it over again. He was fighting against himself. Fear had risen up inexorably to swamp his finer sensibility. The address he had written down for her was not his own address, nor anywhere near it. Perhaps it does not even exist.

He hesitated again as he handed it over.

'I'll do what I can, Eileen,' he said, with as much due solemnity as he could indecently muster.

She took the scrap of paper and folded her fingers around it, as though it were a token of love, a precious gift. And yet there was also the barest hint that she did not truly believe it to be made of anything other than fool's gold.

'I *believed* you, Arthur,' she said wryly. 'Silly me.'

'I believed myself,' he mumbled, in a sort of apology that was also a kind of explanation. He lowered his head.

There was a glint of knowing amusement on her face as she studied him. She now accepted the full degree of his villainy towards her, and the acceptance was not wholly sterile, nor totally embittered. His miserable 'I believed myself' was, in part, true enough, and she could see it. And had she not, in turn, been complicit with his own earnest lies?

'Yes. I know you did,' she said.

As the implications of this complicated half-absolution sank in, astonishment rose into his throat.

'You mean, you understand – ?' he asked.

She did not answer, but her eyes did.

'My God,' he all but gasped. 'I think you really do.'

The conversation between them had suddenly shifted gear. Her steady, virtually expressionless, matter-of-fact questions, and his evasive, eye-sliding procrastinations and prevarications, had together shaken out genuine emotions and – even for him, with one crucial exception – a kind of honesty that had a keenness about it which made the air between them thin down to such a measure that their lungs were hurting.

Their eyes again explored each other. Her sexual hesitancy again insufficiently hid a sexual urgency at least as great as his.

'I wanted you, you see,' she said.

Arthur brightened considerably, and his share of the air became breathable again.

'Did you, darling?' he asked, with a lot of the perky bravado back in his voice.

'Oh, yes,' she said, simple and direct.

This lack of coyness, and its absence of any of the movie-mimicking female mannerisms (such as a tilt of the head or a flutter of the eyelids or a slight, inviting purse of the lips) touched him with wonder.

'And you still do, don't you, Eileen? You – still – do!'

She held his excited gaze, and then nodded, not as one confessing a shameful admission, but as a woman making a proud assertion of her own unsullied feelings.

'Yes,' she said, 'I still do. Very much.'

He could hardly believe the manner in which she spoke. Ladies were not supposed to acknowledge their sexuality in this unadorned way. They were expected to hide any such yearning in something of the same fashion in which they obscured their real skin with paints and powders, and their real smell with exotic perfumes. Decorations that, when too lavishly applied, showed their 'availability' – at a price. The only directness of expression that was ever encountered was in the language of the gutter, never in the parlour. From bar daisies, not domestic primroses.

Arthur could not help but make the connections the world he lived in had decreed to be appropriate for the coupling of men and women. He was not especially clever, and he was certainly not very brave, but he knew, somehow he knew, what most people somehow knew but did not so often admit, that sex was not a covert, dirty, sinful urge.

And yet, and yet. To get it, to enjoy it, to celebrate it, he knew, or thought he knew, that he had to cheat and lie and crack dirty jokes with his similarly embattled buddies. The only women they ever met on their travels who talked openly about, well, about, um, fucking, were the 'ladies who made their living on their backs'.

'I – never in all my life. Not once,' he let out, in absolute awe. 'I've never heard a woman talk like that. Just like that.'

Eileen lowered her head a little. But it was as much with a sense of irony as of shame.

'It's not decent. Is it?' she said.

Not decent? Decent? Nine times out of ten he would have been compelled to agree. Ninety nine times out of a hundred.

'It – it,' he stuttered with excited wonder. 'It's marvellous!'

She lobbed a single word at him. The single word that stands like a high wall in the path of every easy dream.

'But,' she said.

And she waited for his face to change, to lose its eager, astounded anticipation.

'But what? But what? Eileen – ?'

'But you went away.'

He frowned, and his face closed in on his thoughts.

'Yes,' he said. And sighed.

And waited.

'So that's that, then,' she said, like one wiping up the spilt milk. 'Isn't it?'

Oh, no, it isn't! he wanted to yell back at her apparently final dismissal of his excitement and his pretensions. She couldn't simply announce the end of it with such matter-of-fact vale-diction. There must, must be some other way of prolonging things. Some other means of getting her back down again from the tall tower in the now darkened forest.

He was staring dumbly at her, trying to formulate something.

'Say we were married, me and you – ' he began, unwisely.

'And if pigs had wings!' she snorted in amused derision.

'No. Say we was! Eileen – ?'

'Well?' Oh, so very crisp. So very deflating.

What could he say?

Arthur began to shift about again, both in actual physical movements and in his mind.

Say they really *were* married – would it turn out to be of the same order of struggle he had had with poor Joan? Would Eileen put the lipstick on her nipples out of fear rather than enthusiasm, as he now (belatedly) knew to be the case? Would the directness, the simplicity, the *marvel* of her avowal of physical desire ebb away into mechanical, mundane, ever-weary acceptance of the regularity of his appetite? The sigh of the head on the pillow. The half-reluctant turn of the body under the probing, questioning caress of his hands. Would she, too, insist on putting out the light? Would she, too, regard novelty as perversion?

And – hardly daring to bring the thought to the brink of thinking – and would she, too, be as disgusted, as hysterically appalled, as the near-screaming Joan when he tried to feed her mouth with his own p——, and he swallowed. Better not think of it. Better not expect anything quite so thrilling, so –

How the hell to find out what Eileen really, truly felt about the things which he spent so much of his time thinking about?

'Well?' she said. So crisply. So deflatingly.

102

Arthur now knew the way to do it, and it made him nervous.

'There's a story I – ' he began, then immediately broke off, dry-mouthed. 'Do you mind if I smoke?' he asked her instead.

'No.' Oh, so crisp. So deflating.

He fumbled nervously at his pack of Lucky Strike, wishing that her eyes would leave him alone for a minute. Every little movement he made, in thought and in deed, felt heavy and awkward and guilty.

Arthur managed to get the pack out of his pocket and the cigarette out of the pack.

'Do you want one?' he asked, trying to deflect her gaze.

'No,' and her eyes did not move.

He dragged the smoke into his lungs with hungry relief. It made him able to speak behind the blue column he expelled into the air.

'In a band,' he said, in a tone not dissimilar to the way she enunciated 'Once upon a time' at the beginning of the tales she used to tell her class. 'This man, and this singer, this woman singer – '

'What's this got to do with – ?'

'Shhh! A minute. A minute,' he said, urgently. 'They – at the hotel they were playing – they gave the elevator man twenty dollars to stop the elevator between floors – and then turn his back!'

He stopped, and he looked at her. And he waited, as tense as a stage prompter in a dangerously lengthened pause between one line of dialogue and another.

Eileen took her time. Almost too long. He was beginning to feel a strange, sinew-hardening hope flicker out in him like a guttering candle.

'Do people do things like that?' she asked, eventually, and there was no mistaking the quick glitter in her eye. What was it? Excitement? Curiosity? The flash of prurient disapproval?

In the corner of his mind, Arthur saw a man and a woman in an elevator, and he was the elevator man, turning to watch their raunchy thrashing and gasping.

'Like what, Eileen?' he asked, holding his breath, and trying to hold her breath, too.

'Well –' she said, not too sure that the picture she had in *her* mind was even half-way accurate. 'Well, make love in an elevator – ?'

'You mean *kissing* – do you?'

'Oh – is that all?' she said. And her *disappointment* was thrilling.

Arthur slapped his knee in delight.

'That's a good girl!' he exclaimed, in great glee. 'Oh, Eileen, Eileen. You knew what I was talking about!'

Her smile widened in complicity. Her eyes had brightened. There was a taut, sexual tensing in the angle of her body, the shape of her lips, the gleam of her skin.

Arthur was shot through with urgent physical excitement.

'Would *you* ever do that?' he propositioned. 'What *they* did?'

She looked at him with real provocation, her lips slightly parted, and a challenge near enough to the brazen in her eyes.

'Between which floors, Arthur?' she said. And it was just as much a proposition as his had been.

Arthur's eyes popped, and then, expanded by a still incredulous delight, he roared with excited laughter.

I Want To Be Bad!

The song that could so easily have illustrated the half-jokey, half-threatening sexual conflict, and sexual complicity, between Arthur and Eileen would have needed appropriately vulgar burlesque colours.

'Between which floors, Arthur?' was a line to make both of them sing and bounce in boo–pi–doo excess.

And a line that gave him the admission ticket to see her as a hip-jutting, leg-snapping, eye-darting, nipple-thrusting stripper. With every hot and tassled thing exactly the opposite of the demure. The opposite to Joan, who even now, with forehead puckering cold anger rather than the former anxiety, looked at the clock again.

'*Between which floors, Arthur?*'

No sooner said, with her provocative, inviting amusement, than done. It was, for Arthur, as though a splendid elevator had come gliding down in grand confidence slap into the middle of this poor little room, to take them out of the lies, the pain and the human dread that had been expressed within its narrow walls.

The elevator doors were opening to take them up and away

from the pain and the doubt, and the mood of bleak pessimism expressed, so to imagine, on the glum-looking mug of the elderly elevator man waiting at the opening doors.

Eileen, with her amused question, had in effect beckoned Arthur in. He was entitled, now, in the fertile lands of his curious dream, to give the glum guardian of the gates a twenty-dollar bill, and smirkingly to ask him to turn his bony old back –

And then –

Oh, boy, wouldn't that elevator shudder 'n' shake!

The thought, the image, was so vividly present in Arthur's eyes that Eileen did not need to transpose it back into the words of the peculiar little story he had told her.

'Between which floors, Arthur?' she had said, summoning up the pictures, the burlesque colours, the mockingly salacious rhythms, the descending elevator.

Even before his laughter had peaked, and even knowing what she was doing, she began, slowly, to unbutton her blouse.

Problems could always be postponed. Perhaps. But the flesh could not wait. No perhaps about it.

Their mouths and their tongues sought each other, so quickly and so violently, that their teeth clashed.

18

The cheap music that Arthur loved so much is more versatile than its sniffy detractors often allow. There are not many of us who do not have in our heads, however irritatingly, the remote or even half-forgotten tinkle of a popular song which can instantly carry us back on swift wings to a time, a place, a person, an event, significant to us.

Songs tell the truth, songs do.

No: they probably don't, unless by The Truth you mean some tiny, glistening sliver of it, a fragment of broken glass in the long grass of our overgrown experience. A jagged piece of waste which fleetingly, and mockingly, catches and refracts the rays of the sun.

The same Helen Kane song that could have been used to add zest and burlesque colour to Arthur and Eileen's sudden and unexpected grappling – *I Want To Be Bad* – might also have been overlaid on at least one or two heads as their owners looked down upon the ground in the field which stretched beyond a billboard telling the night, the snow, and any passers-by, of Carole Lombard's latest film.

If that were so, however, the beat of the music would by now be stretching into a cruel dissonance.

The field where Arthur had stopped to think about what he was doing, and had seen instead a lovely blind girl walking so slowly towards him with a basket of eggs on her arm, was not as empty as he had left it.

Darkness and snow had pressed down upon it, and a cold wind shifted in melancholy whispers of desolation across it.

Nobody should have been about on such a night.

But there were figures moving slowly outward from its edges, hunched and grimly attentive. Near the path through the field which bent to come close alongside the road, a man was taking a plaster mould of the distinct footprint where Arthur had stood watching the blind girl approach.

Beyond him, it was the police who were searching about. They had rigged up some sort of lighting in the field, and it was casting an oddly threatening mixture of light and shadow across this small stretch of an Illinois night.

A police lieutenant was pulling back a cover which had been placed over a figure upon the ground. His expression was difficult to read. It might have represented a solemn pity, or no feeling at all. But scarcely anyone else who did not share his trade would have been able to suppress a gasp of outrage.

The figure under the cover had been brutally snatched away from her already sightless life. Her great beauty was now hardly recognizable, because her tongue was out. The blind girl had been viciously strangled, and it was obvious that the life had been choked out of her with a pitilessly formidable strength.

A basket close to her had spilled out a mess of broken eggs, the yolk and slime of them curiously repellent.

She had been raped. In her death-throes, she had been further abused. And it seemed that only darkness itself could now cover or soften the horror that had swooped down claw-fingered upon her slow grace, her dancer's step.

It needed, this scene, a deal of weeping. Two elderly people, standing to one side, broken, were the only ones there who could not stop their tears from flowing. They were trying to speak to a tight-faced policeman about their daughter, but they found it hard to insert even a few stumbling words into the surge of their grief.

Another policeman straightened up suddenly, and called out something to his colleagues, who quickly gathered around him. The cop who had called out was holding an empty pack of Lucky Strike cigarettes by a small pair of hand-tongs.

And Arthur's discarded bit of litter was being put into a cellophane bag, tagged and labelled in the same manner as the plaster cast of his footprint. Poor Arthur had left more behind, after all, than a wistful call to a receding figure.

I'd cut off my right arm if I could make you see again. I'd –I don't know what I'd do if I could – if I could . . . If I could get into your pants.

Be careful! Be – careful!

What would Arthur not do to make her *live* again? He who would cut off his right arm just to give her back her sight.

Not that he was at the moment preparing himself to make any such painful barter. The thoughts in his head, as he drove back from Galena and the yet again betrayed Eileen, were solely of the girl he was once more leaving behind in the poor little farmhouse at the end of the dirt track of his yearnings.

The moon above was bright and silvery. The flat land on either side of him eerie and endless.

Arthur's car shug-a-lugged along, splashing light, like a lonely voyager in the vast space, the vast night. At the wheel, the driver, feeling the chill enter his bones, was not in the whistling mood which so often accompanied his journeyings. There was no lariat

107

to twirl in his essentially innocent fantasies. Instead, there was the recharged memory of Eileen to sting at his mind, at his eyes, and at his loins.

Oh, God above, oh God, she was so passionate. She knew and understood his own passion and his own cowardice. They had left each other an hour or so ago with hugs and kisses, reassurances and declarations, and a mutual pain in the soul which he knew would haunt him for the rest of his life. He loved her, and she him. The fact astonished him and lifted him up.

But it also scared him, and cast him down.

He did not know what he was going to do. He knew well enough what he would *like* to do, but . . .

Fear spread all about him, as flat and as eerie as the white land under the silvered moon, and as short on vision against this endless expanse as the splash of his headlights. It was a night when, formerly, before this land was tamed, the wolves used to howl in animal desolation. And Arthur heard the miserable cur hidden in a canine cringe deep within himself imitate the same sound . . .

Lost in bitter introspection, he came out of himself as his lights picked out the Carole Lombard billboard up ahead. Another, more pleasant, but equally culpable thought licked out at him at exactly the same moment –

'I'd cut off my right arm if I could make you see again. I don't know what I'd do if I could get into your pants.'

Be careful! Be careful! For even as he unconsciously lifted his foot off the accelerator, Arthur saw, all at once, two police cars parked in line by the field. He could see a light in the field where he had met the blind girl. And, as his car continued to slow down, almost of its own volition, he saw a policeman by the roadside, chewing gum, and looking – *hostile.*

For a moment, Arthur and the cop looked at each other. Their eyes met and held. Arthur's eyes flicked aside in a swift, puzzled anxiety.

What the hell was going on here? What can have happened?

He pressed his foot down hard. The car suddenly picked up speed. The gum-chewing cop stopped chewing gum. He stared after the rapidly receding vehicle and then, just in case, with a little of the same order of premonition that had made Arthur jam his foot on the pedal, the policeman noted down the car number before it disappeared from view.

The lieutenant of detectives would now have available to him one discarded cigarette packet, one plaster cast of a very distinctive footprint, and, much more speculatively, of routine interest only, the registration number of an automobile.

You never can tell. Little things such as these can be, for a detective, pennies from heaven.

But as Arthur continued his journey towards Chicago and home, starting to think now of the hostile or at least uncertain welcome which awaited him, he had no reason to be aware of any of these coincidences and juxtapositions. The unexpected and puzzling sights on the road and around the field near the Carole Lombard billboard had already drifted slowly out of his mind.

His hands were relaxed on the steering wheel. He was looking where he was going, but his thoughts were mostly elsewhere.

He was not, in short, ready for what now happened.

A ghoul, an apparition, a dark and evil spirit, was suddenly leaping out upon him! A tattered, gesticulating monster with a weird hump on its back, waving tentacled arms at him, right in front of the car, right out of nowhere except the cauldrons of hell.

The fear jumped inside Arthur at the very same time. Not the usual, subdued throb of anxiety buried beneath his surface jauntiness. He had long since accustomed himself to that. No, this was the fear that leapt and burned, the ghastly panic that singed the edge of every nerve, that screamed like a banshee in the sudden terrible vacuum which was all that was left of heart or reason.

Arthur tried, in his shock, to brake and to swerve to avoid the gruesome apparition.

Somehow, as *the thing* screamed and gesticulated its dank evil at him, Arthur found himself on the far side of it, and still intact. He might even have passed right through it, and yet avoided capture from its infernal, clawing, clutching grasp – its hunchbacked venom.

Trembling, Arthur made himself look back.
There was nothing there!
The road behind him, scudding away into darkness, was empty of vehicle, of human, or of demon.

The grotesque, evil thing which had swooped and flapped at him out of nowhere had returned to nowhere.

'Je - sus Christ . . .!' hissed Arthur to himself in trembling dread.

It was a warning, if ever there was. A vivid and horrible demonstration compounded of sulphur and madness, of what would happen to him if he did not change his ways. The lies and the treachery, the waste of his own fluids in wicked adultery, had summoned up the apparition as a last dire warning of the hell that awaited.

He continued on his way, his own lights ahead of him, and a fearful intimidation pressing hard against him: he had to be different. He had to be *good*. He must stop making his own bed on the far, black side of Paradise.

But the humped-back demon had spiralled off the road as Arthur's car threatened to run it down. It had spun itself off into the banked-up snow. The moonlight of the crisp and clear night picked out the gasping figure in the snow.

It was the accordion man. The player of turgid hymns.

There were deep and bloodied scratches scored into his cheeks, made by a wildly struggling girl's fingernails. His cracked lips were flecked with a foamy-white scum, and, sprawling helplessly into the snow which could not clean him, he was plunging down and down into a near catatonic void.

The accordion man, face besmirched by the merciless yet driven outrage he had visited upon a blind girl, rolled his eyeballs up at the silvery moon. There was no sense or forgiveness in the vast and spangled heavens. The moon glimmered down without pity or understanding.

And his eyes, scrabbling vacantly in his head, went milky white. His mouth opening wider and wider in a scream that was as anguished as any that had ever been heard since the hungry wolves ceased to prowl.

Except that there was no sound. The soft and silent snow, the cold silver moon, the aching darkness, were not pierced.

The apparition had become soiled human flesh again, torturing out of itself a terrible silent scream. The hump on its back was the piano accordion in the battered old case, the keys packed away so that the fingers which had tightened around the soft

110

white neck could not dig into *The Old Rugged Cross* or any other remembrance of the blood that had washed away the sins of the world.

By the time Arthur arrived home and had crept as silent as a mouse into the marital bedroom where his obligations lay fretfully sleeping, the message he had seen in the lonely night was burned deeper than ever into his already troubled sensibility.

It was not his arrival, but his sobbing which awoke Joan.

She reared up in the bed.

'Arthur? What is it? What's *happened*?'

Surprise had displaced her anger. Arthur stared at her, and she had never before seen such dread and such misery on his face.

'I've seen – ' he was choking, 'I've seen a – a *message* – '

'What are you talking about?' she exclaimed, a little scared herself now. 'Where have you been?'

'I gotta change. I gotta change,' was all that he would answer, the horror wrenching the avowal almost bodily out of him.

'Arthur?' she quavered.

'Put your arms around me, Joan,' he begged. 'For God's sake. Put your arms around me!'

As sure as Christ, he had to change!

19

A train clacked and clanked along the stretch of the Elevated above South Wabash Avenue in Chicago. Already noisy, it excelled itself on the bend in near-animal squeals of protest as the brakes slowed its passage. For the moment, the pedestrians on the sidewalks on either side of the girdered parapet could not hear themselves speak. No matter: they were used to it.

As the noise receded, another sound claimed precedence. An accordion was faltering its way through *Rock of Ages*, ever cleft for whomsoever might pause to listen.

Except, apparently, for the hobo who was playing the hymn.

No one passing would fail to hurry his or her steps when looking at the man on the sidewalk with the old piano accordion. People stepped around him, far more troubled than amused by his appearance. His fingers were probing without conviction at the keys, more by rote than in invention. His lips were dry and cracked. But, worst of all, the eyes of the street musician were without question the eyes of someone crazed beyond human recall.

The strains of the old hymn, if amplified only a little, would have reached the little store where Arthur was still failing to pack in the customers. Even at this moment, he was once again drumming his fingers in irritation and anxiety.

Life Is Just a Bowl of Cherries signalled its optimism at him from one of the brown-sleeved records. And, yes, still Arthur was hurting his teeth on the hard bit at the middle of the soft and pulpy fruit.

Bored, he began to spin the yo-yo that he had bought the other day in a novelty shop on the Loop. A run-down jumble store which seemed to be doing a damned sight better business than he was. Well, he shrugged, if people wanted to waste their money on silly toys, he might as well join them.

But no toy spinning at his fingers was capable of diverting Arthur's gloom for more than a minute. The so-called apparition, as he now thought of it with rather diminished respect, may well have modified his behaviour over the days and weeks which followed. Nothing, though, could substantially shift for long the sense of disappointment that had now settled upon him as a permanent blight.

He thought of Eileen with a dumb, nagging pain for too much of the time.

It was not a memory he deliberately conjured up. Indeed, he was trying to put her out of his mind, pushing the image of her away almost with anger: an anger made out of shame and longing so mixed up in his heart that he could not separate them.

What had happened to her? Where was she, the woman he knew that he loved?

Suppose she had turned up at the false address he had scribbled down for her?

112

He recalled – trying not to – the way she had folded her delicious long fingers around it, taking possession of his lie.

Between which floors, Arthur?

He winced away her baby voice, her challenging smile, and his betrayal. The yo-yo span. A man came in to buy a box of phonograph needles, and then, shuffling dubiously through a stack of records, chose one. Every time this happened, Arthur was just about able to persuade himself that the cherries were still up there on the tree.

But where was she? How was she doing?

Miss Eileen Everson, pregnant ex-schoolteacher from Galena, had packed a small case and caught the train to Chicago. She had virtually been driven out of the place where she had been born and bred, loved and honoured, then betrayed and, as sure as God made sour little apples as well as those big red ones, eventually reviled.

She had arrived at the La Salle railroad station with a great deal more hope and confidence in her step than both the hard times and her situation could possibly justify. The big city had always attracted the waifs and strays of its huge hinterlands, and then, by brutalizing degrees often too slow for the victims to recognize, turned them into an urban flotsam and jetsam.

Eileen had no premonition of this – and no experience to justify such an anxiety – when she located a tawdry hotel that seemed to her to be cheap enough until she could find herself a job and then move on to better things. She did not intend to seek out Arthur at the address he had given her: not for a while anyway.

Her room was not much bigger than a cubby-hole, and a sparsely equipped one at that. It had a narrow bed, dirty curtains hanging in a state of exhausted depression at the grubby little window, and a notice on the inside of the door which insisted that GUESTS ARE NOT PERMITTED TO ENTERTAIN VISITORS.

A nasty little old hotel keeper had shown her into the room and taken her money with what she thought was an unnecessarily churlish warning that, when this had gone, settlement had to be

113

one day in advance. At least – the emphasis made with poking finger – at least One Day in Advance.

When he had shut the door and left her in sole and undisturbed possession of her first home away from home, Eileen had not been distressed by its grubby inadequacy.

She had actually smiled with pleasure and excitement.

The grubby window was partly open, acknowledging that the worst of the winter was over. The sounds of a piano accordion were rising up from the street below. *Onward Christian Soldiers.* It reminded her a little of a strange and somehow both sweet and threatening man she had once seen playing at an intersection in Galena. On the day that she had first seen –

Arthur. He was here somewhere. He lived and breathed in this great city.

Eileen was smiling to herself, the sense of anticipation, her venture into the unknown, tingling not wholly pleasurably at her senses. She went to the window and pulled aside the filthy curtain in order to look down on the street below.

She saw a drunk and a couple of obvious hookers.

If she could also have seen a little further, and a little more forward, the slight crinkle of self-doubt in her eyes would surely have darkened. There would be sign after sign for her to encounter which said, baldly, NO HELP WANTED. She would have seen herself, in dejection, coming out of the pawnshop, having traded away her paltry assets.

Worse still, the face staring in so hungrily through the window of a cheap café was her own. It was to be Eileen, her hope dwindling as fast as her tiny reserve of money, who looked vainly in her purse outside the café before sighing and turning away.

She all but walked her shoes off her feet in her search for a job, any job. The mean and grasping hotel keeper had waylaid her in his own miserable apology for a lobby and, with threats yet more obnoxiously emphatic than before, taken what were almost her last few cents.

Good Times were being heralded around nearly every corner, but here and now, in 1934, they had not reached the pregnant girl from Galena. Life was not a bowl of cherries. It was scarcely even a dish of scraps. There was no music in her ears, and little food in her stomach. Soon, her shape would be dramatically different,

114

and her prospects – wretched though they already were – would be dramatically worse.

While a bored and worried Arthur idled in his empty store, she saw disaster coming straight at her. And there was no way that she could think of stopping or deflecting it.

Except –

Did she not have Arthur's address?

Arthur, at his real address, was not the less worried, even though his predicament was not so harsh and pinching.

He could not easily go to sleep at nights, and he was not grappling at Joan with anything like the old fervent urgency. Life, for the while, had lost its salt and pepper.

Joan was fast asleep, dreaming of herself as a little girl with pig-tails and a wooden-handled skipping rope. But, beside her, Arthur's troubled eyes were still open, and gleaming in the dark.

The alarm clock ticked along as though it were a fat man in a hurry.

'Joan?' Arthur turned to her with a sigh. 'Joanie . . .?'

She did not wake. *Tick-a-tock-a-tick-a-tock-a-tock*.

'Nobody's buying, Joan,' he said, very quietly. 'Nobody. I made a mistake. . .'

Joan became dimly conscious of words being softly spoken. She stirred. The word 'mistake' registered over the downward beat of the skipping rope. Her eyes struggled open, and she turned to Arthur to hear what he was saying to her.

Arthur pretended to be fast asleep.

Eileen, in her desperation, and swallowing her pride, had looked for Arthur's house and failed to find it.

She was now more than ever worried and miserable, wondering what on earth she was to do to survive in this callous, windy and cavernous city.

The hookers she had seen from her window returned, insinuatingly, again and again to the tormented edges of her mind.

She had heard one of them laughing on the street below. A furtive exchange of words about money between such a woman and a man with a gaudy waistcoat had taken place within her earshot.

Money. Money. Money. The measure of all things.

Wandering alone in the night, a half-formed, half-suppressed plan flickering like the lick of a hot flame at her shrivelling consciousness, Eileen found herself in a drab street of a dank physical depression perfectly fitting her present mood.

The accordion man was approaching her on the same side of the street, pulling himself along in a wretched, zombie-like shuffle. He was walking in the way she felt *she* wanted to walk: that is, as though the world was too heavy a weight for any poor human to bear.

As he came alongside, he looked at her, his expression going at once from glazed vacancy to sharp accusation. He stopped.

'Noooo!' he gasped.

'What?' she said, startled.

He peered at her, eyes widening, a crazy man.

'I thought you were *dead*!' he spluttered at her in awe and dread.

'What?' she said again, astounded.

The crazed musician was peering even more closely at her. His face was thrusting into hers, and she stepped back in alarm.

'Ca - a - can you see me – ?' he stuttered in terrified incredulity.

'Leave me alone!' she shrieked, ready to beat him off, and looking around for help that clearly was not there.

He recoiled in horror, as jerkily abrupt in the movement as though he had been violently pulled back on the end of a rope.

'You can! You can!' he screamed. 'You can see - ee!'

'What – ?'

'You're dead!' he yelled, pointing a dirty-nailed and trembling finger at her, using it as a weapon. She evaded it, her heart throbbing with fear. But she could not escape his thrusting face as he peered even more closely at her with hot, mad intensity.

Her stomach tightened.

'What do you want . . .?' she managed to ask.

The crazy flame seemed to gutter out in his staring eyes.

'I thought – ' he whispered, brokenly, 'I thought – '

'What?' she said yet again, for want of anything else.

The flame leapt up again, rekindled by a gust of cold air. His voice raised again in a passion of justification.

'The D - Devil had put out your eyes! He t - told me to pup - punish you – !'

He grabbed claw-like at her arm, and the contact with her flesh changed again the beat and the drive of his derangement. The crazed expression softened a little into a desperate longing.

'Give me a kiss, lady,' he leered, trying to pout his cracked lips in hideous semblance of a caress. 'Kiss. Kiss.'

'Go away! No – !' she screamed at him, struggling free. But he would not let go and she smacked out hard at him.

The accordion man staggered back, holding his face. And almost at once let out the weirdest and most forlorn howl she had ever heard. It was the agony of a soul in hell, or to be more mundane, the cry of a tortured animal.

It was so hauntingly desolate that she lost her fear.

'Oh – I'm – don't – ' she appealed, stricken by the sight of someone in such appalling distress.

But he stopped making the noise. Abruptly. As though the sound had been mechanically switched off.

He looked at her, and straightened himself. He pulled the last remnants of his human reason around himself, as one might an inadequate piece of clothing in the teeth of a bitterly cold wind.

'I've got my dignity, you know,' he said.

'Yes. I'm – yes,' she swallowed, rather taken aback, and made to feel obscurely ashamed. 'But you mustn't – '

He was not listening.

'The streets belong to everybody,' he announced, hanging on to the shred of affronted sensibility he had once more, and momentarily, discovered in himself.

With that, he hoisted up his battered accordion case and strode off with a poignant imitation of a stiff seigneurial dignity.

Eileen watched him go. The encounter could not be anything other than upsetting. She had the strange feeling that she had met him someplace else – but already her life in Galena, ordered and secure even when narrow and claustrophobic, had become too remote for her thoughts to inhabit with any sure purchase.

Her eyes, following after the crazy man who had accosted her, took in the neon sign of a bar.

They narrowed speculatively.

20

The bar was not the sort of place where a man would wish to take his grandmother.

It had a roughness in atmosphere worse than in décor, an acne of the spirit. An early juke was quivering its own brand of music. A dozen or so men and two ageing whores were scattered about, as though specifically positioned by a malignant wit to make the place seem even more untidy.

A heavy-faced, morose individual was playing a desultory game of pool in the rear, clicking striped and dotted balls about, apparently at random. There was a smell of strong liquor, cheap perfume and tired bodies in the stale air, perfectly in tune with the boxing posters on the wall.

Eileen entered with uncertain resolve, hesitated, hardly daring to look around. She imagined that the tentative odiousness of what she was still only half-thinking was instantly recognizable in her every configuration. Perhaps every man in the place would suddenly turn and point at her, uttering foul and lascivious remarks.

She more or less sidled up to the bar. One of the whores looked at her sharply.

'Excuse me,' Eileen said with faint gentility to the barman.

'Yes?'

'How - how much is a - glass of lemonade?'

He looked at her with amusement. 'It's so long since I sold one, I don't know. To you – two cents.'

Eileen was keeping her head down, determined now not to look around and about in case she inadvertently crossed glances with another customer.

Client. Wasn't that the word?

The barman examined her quizzically.

'Oh. Yes. Then – yes. I'll have a glass of lemonade, please,' she said in a sudden nervous rush.

'You sure you've come to the right place, sweetie?' he said, not entirely without sympathy.

She lowered her head again, and did not quite reply. She

sensed, now, that many in the bar were indeed looking her over. The pool balls, for instance, had stopped their ivory clicking.

The barman gave a small shrug – none of his affair – and got her the glass of lemonade.

'Have a drop of gin in it, honey,' said a man's voice at her elbow. A confident, showy kind of voice, very sure of itself.

Eileen visibly stiffened.

'Pardon?'

'That's a very nice drink, for a lady,' the man who had been playing at the pool table said. 'Gin and lemonade.'

'Leave her alone, Tom,' growled the barman, who knew what manner of man he was. His rarely called upon sense of chivalry was mustering itself in what was to be at least a token demonstration.

'I'm only offering to pay for it,' sniffed Tom, more amused than offended. He did not, however, stop measuring the girl.

Eileen was cautiously lifting her eyes.

'This one's on the house, honey,' the barman leaned in to her, speaking gently. 'Just drink it down and go home. Like a good little girl.'

He slid the gin and lemonade towards her, with so little conviction that it seemed as though he wanted to pull it back.

Eileen looked wildly at Tom and the barman, seized hold of the glass, and, with the bravado of panic, swallowed down half the contents in one gulp. The gin splashed into the lemonade came as a shock to her tongue and throat. It had a heavy, dull, vaguely perfumed taste.

'Ugh,' she shuddered. 'It tastes like poison.'

'Then don't try another,' urged the barman, still anxious to warn her. 'There's some girls it doesn't suit.'

'You never know what you like until you try it.'

It was Tom again, at her elbow, full of confident innuendo. His was the hiss of the articulate serpent in the Garden, and she was the Eve already inclined to listen. But whereas the oldest tale ended with the woman putting clothes on, this one was meant to leave her stripped naked on a feather bed.

Eileen looked hard at Tom. She thought she could pick up the innuendo. The fierce hunger in her stomach had been made worse rather than assuaged by the bite of the gin.

'That's true,' she said, with a lift of her chin.

A number that some sang at the time was the latest variety of the old, serpentine invitation. *Let's Misbehave* told a girl there was no percentage in being 'good'. If Tom had warbled it to her, he could not better have expressed the look in his eyes as he sized her up: a mixture of lust and avarice that made her skin crawl.

On the other hand – well . . .

She made herself hold his gaze. And return it with interest, an imitation of the way that, in her abandoned home less than two months ago, she had looked at Arthur and said, 'Between which floors, Arthur?'

'What do you want to do to me?' she asked, faltering a little, but still holding him eye to eye.

Tom allowed himself a flicker of amusement. Trouble was, it also held more than a touch of the disdain he was never able to obliterate altogether when talking to a woman.

'You must be joking,' he said, deadpan.

They were already a bit apart from the others in the unsavoury bar. She had already gone one step too far. But *Let's Misbehave* was only a song, not a positive injunction. And before she gave herself up to the dark unknown, or the nausea, Eileen made one more stab at the good fortune which was so determinedly eluding her.

'Can you lend me five dollars?' she asked him, miserably.

'Lend you? You *are* joking?'

'I – I'd give it to you back.'

He did not know whether this was genuine humility or complicated sarcasm. Both would have pleased him. He probed at her, saw that it was the former, and that she was helpless, and smiled.

'We'll think about it. There's no hurry.'

'No,' she agreed, in a tiny voice.

He's not so bad he's not so bad he's not so bad.

'Caught a little short?'

'Sort of. Yes.'

'That's nothing to be ashamed of, baby. Not nowadays.'

Eileen wanted to coil her hands. She needed to look anywhere else but at his face. A decision had to be made, and it had to be made soon. Either it was the hunger for food she was enduring, or the strong maleness he was exuding, the obscure sense of power and menacing physicality, but something was making her head swim and her mouth go dry.

She made herself look at him again, and was caught by his hard, small smile.

'What's your name?' he asked.

Eileen waited a fraction too long.

'Lulu,' she said.

Tom began to snigger, but then held it back. 'That's a very – nice name,' he said.

'I don't like it very much,' she said. 'Makes me sound cheap.'

Between which floors, Arthur?

'Oh, nobody'd ever say that, Lulu. Look at that fat whore over there – now that's what I call cheap.'

Eileen looked. The fat whore, as gaudy as a carousel, and about as wide, bounced the look back with no compunction. 'Who are you looking at?' she yelled across the bar. And Tom curled his lip a little in amused disdain for both of them.

Eileen turned away quickly. She closed her eyes, shame spurting into her mouth like bile.

'Here – are you all right?' Tom asked.

She did not know how she could go on. Her face, now, was blanched of all colour. The hideousness of her plight, and the nausea for what seemed the only possible way out of it, was crippling her spirit.

'I feel a little sick,' she managed to say.

'How much have you had to eat today?' he asked.

'Nothing.'

He stared at her. The line of her delicately small limbs, the shape of her face, the softness of her throat, the baby-like voice. Plus that touch of elegance, or delicacy, or class – call it what you will – which always made a man want to turn his head. And which always made Tom want to subject, then debase, humiliate, and put to work. On her back.

'A girl who looks like you shouldn't go hungry,' he said. 'You know you're very nice looking, Lulu.'

This time, she did coil her hands. What he said both flattered and frightened her.

'Thank you – ' she murmured, barely audible.

For once in his life, with a woman in a bar like this, Tom found

121

himself on the edge of nervousness. There was something so different about her he couldn't get to what it was. His lips suddenly needed to be moistened, so that he could sneer.

'What did you come in this place for?'

She didn't answer. She didn't look up at him.

'Do you think some guy was going to give you five dollars just like that?' he asked her, with a hint of anger in his voice which showed how puzzling she was to him. 'For *nothing*?'

Eileen could feel the pressure, the potential violence. She did not want to answer. Every exchange between them now, however small, was like the preamble to a contract. He was no frog at the side of the pool who, once accepted into her bed, would turn into a gentle prince. More like, it was she who had to undergo the transformation –

'Nowadays,' he was insisting, 'that's almost a week's wages for some girls.'

And he was looking at her intently, waiting for her to wilt. The tension of her body in anxiety presaged to his mind the clench of her limbs when he got her into his bed. *If* he got her into bed . . .

At any moment she might run back out into the street, and he knew it.

'Yes,' she said, agreeing to nothing.

'I mean, you've got to give something back in return. Don't you?'

'Yes,' she said.

'I mean . . .'

'Yes,' she said, agreeing to everything.

And now, again, she looked him full in the face. Almost despite himself, he felt his insides turn over. She was going to be a pleasure to violate. He might even keep her exclusively to himself. For a while.

'I know how you feel, and – ' he began, unctuous, and falsely solicitous, preparing to put his hand on her in a signal of ownership.

'Do you?' said Eileen, sharply.

It pulled him up short. A little more caution was in order. Even down as much as she appeared to be, even in her obvious desperation, he saw that this woman had an edge to her. An inexplicable independence.

'Well, I can imagine it,' he conceded. And then looked more openly at her, trying to be encouraging. 'I'm not such a bad guy when you come right down to it.'

'Are you married?' she asked the pimp, solemnly.

Her question was totally unexpected, to both of them. The tone of his would-be encouragement had momentarily caught at a cadence which she had heard before. Arthur was still very much in her mind, even though she knew by now that the address he had given her was not where he had ever lived.

And you are not married. You promise.

Do I look like a married man? Why, I even got a hole in my sock!

But she blinked. What had this hard-faced man got to do with her betrayer? Did not all men tell lies – did not they all want one thing?

Tom simply found the question ridiculous. It bore no relation to his way of thinking about the world. This girl might be even more green than he had dared to hope. The fresher the flower, the sweeter the bloom.

'Married?' he laughed. 'What – *me*?'

'Yes. I thought you were.' And she said it combatively.

The snap in her answer was, in truth, meant for the someone else who also lived in her thoughts. Embittered by desperation, she revoked or reordered the sequence of deception (and, yes, she was able to admit, self-deception) which had brought her to this condition. What on earth was demure, shyly hesitant Miss Eileen Everson, schoolteacher in a small Illinois community, doing sitting in a bar with a man like this Tom? Why was she so poor, so hungry, and so wretchedly alone?

Do I look like a married man? Why, I even got a hole in my sock!

There had been a harsh note in Arthur's laugh which even at the time had aroused her suspicion. But she had deliberately put it down. She wanted him.

'Married? What – *me*?'

'Yes. I thought you were,' she had snapped.

'Oh, I see,' said Tom, nastily. 'You've been around, haven't you?'

'I've had dozens,' she said, as brazenly as she knew how.

The claim enabled her to put a sharp and hard brightness into her eyes. She had had enough of this. Her sense told her that she was going to be more, not less, humiliated if she dragged out this encounter in order to avoid the crude, the explicit, and the bargaining that would at least, the very least, get her something to eat and drink.

Eileen drained her glass.

'Well, then,' he leered. 'What's the fuss about?'

'No fuss, baby,' she said, imperiously giving him her glass. 'Here. Get me another.'

Her dramatic change of tone was not altogether pleasing to him. Tom liked to think that he could work people out. Especially women. But this one looked too good, and talked all wrong. Her shifts of mood were too volatile.

Tom's eyes seemed to go as hard and as black as chips of malachite embedded in his skull.

'You're not a tease, are you?' he said, with a voice to match.

'A tee - ee - ese?' she mocked, too unsure to get her alleged confidence at the right pitch.

He frowned and glared.

'I mean, I'm not spending a goddamn cent on you if – '

'If what?' she interrupted, trying to be pert, and succeeding disastrously.

The expression on his face brought her back with a lurch of fear to the true nature of this conversation. She had never looked into the eyes of a snake, but imagined that it would look like this man's cold, alien hostility. The pictures in the big-print, coloured story books she had used in the classroom gave the monsters, wicked stepmothers, cunning elder brothers and flesh-greedy giants expressions like this.

'I'll cut your face,' Tom said, after he had looked at her. His voice did not sound in the least angry, and so it chilled her to the bone.

There was a tiny silence in which she could capitulate. Perhaps in most new conversations between two people there is a moment when power sets up the pulse, when each discovers who is the stronger of the two in the area at issue.

When Eileen next spoke, it was as though she had placed her neck under his smart, laced-up shoe.

'I'd like another drink,' she said, politely and submissively. 'Please.'

The cold brutality left him at once. He simply switched it off. Her change of tone allowed him to play the smoothly masterful role which pleased him most, because he thought it represented his true nature. He liked to look at himself in the mirror. He knew the film star who reminded him most of himself.

And he regularly cut the little hairs from the inside of his nose.

'Certainly, darling,' he said, oiling his own smile as he took the glass from her now properly submissive hand. 'Same again?'

'Yes please,' Eileen gulped, trying to keep the tremble under control. 'Only not – but with not so much lemonade?'

Tom went back to the bar with a chortle, two glasses in his hand. He was also pleased that the sweaty mug of a barman would register his success with the lovely lady. Eileen, after all, was a better looker than he really expected to get.

Thank God for hard times. You never knew what a girl would do to earn a living nowadays. It gave entrepreneurs of his standing a chance to better themselves.

Eileen watched him go up to the bar, with hatred in her eyes. She knew the trap into which she had placed herself, and she knew that she would need the poison they called gin to help her through.

'Oh, Arthur,' she said to herself, for perhaps the hundredth time in the last, and worst, few days.

She looked up to find the voluminously large prostitute standing over her, and hissing at her. It was like being suddenly confronted by a funfair marquee with the wind in it.

'Why don't you get lost, Snow White!' it spat at her.

'What?' Eileen blinked.

'Get out of here,' snarled the fat whore, jerking her thumb for emphasis, 'if you don't want to get your head beat in!'

But the prostitute saw that Tom, at the bar, was looking around at her, and she waddled away as suddenly, and furtively, as she had arrived.

Shocked, numbed, Eileen closed her eyes for a moment. Revulsion was churning around inside her, and she thought she was going to be sick. The faint, metallic taste of hunger, or of gin and lemonade, and certainly of her own bile, was coating the back of her throat. Thinking of what was undoubtedly going to happen between Tom and her, she had a momentary and inappropriate anxiety about whether or not she had bad breath. It certainly tasted like it.

When she opened her eyes, hoping now that her breath *did* smell, she saw Tom go across to the fat prostitute, his face dark. But as he leaned in to talk to her, it looked as though he was being extremely amiable. He was smiling, exactly like a man delivering a particularly subtle joke with a hilarious punch-line.

Eileen could see, though, that the woman who had threatened her was herself being threatened, and far more effectively. She was quaking, and seemed to be saying that, no, of course not, she didn't mean it. Crude and vulgar and repulsive though this woman was, her evident fear told Eileen far more about her trade than imagination had yet allowed.

Tom was giving the fat whore a last, smiling threat, and returning with the drinks. Eileen wanted to get up and run. But she could not seem to move. He would probably catch up with her before she got to the door, and there was no one here likely to help. What about the barman? What about the –

He was upon her, and smiling at her.

'I'm not a prostitute,' she announced, abruptly.

'I didn't say you were, darling,' he said, completely unruffled, sitting beside her. ''Course you're not.'

The tears were threatening in her eyes and throat, at last. She urgently wanted to make something clear. She had to set up a rigid boundary for this man to see, a limit to the extent of her shame and her helplessness.

Oh to come to this! To come to this!

He was looking at her with curiosity rather than sympathy.

'I'm willing to – to – you know – ' she could not find a decent euphemism, and half swallowed, half nodded, acknowledging the word at the same time as she evaded it. 'For five dollars. But only once. Never again. Really.'

He waited in case there were any more such protestations. But she had finished and the plea in her eyes almost unsettled him. Alas, it also gave him an erection. She was going to be so delectable to take, and he was sure the abject begging would eventually fade away. Amateurs were always the best.

'That's all right, darling,' he said, as near to soothingly as he felt he could manage. 'That's what I thought. Look at me.'

Eileen tried to do so, openly. But somehow her eyes would not settle. They were looking what Arthur had called 'sideways' at him.

There's something delicate – no, yes, but – sort of – hesitating about you, Eileen. No, not in that way. I don't know how to describe it. It's not any one thing, it's everything, all together. Specially when you look sideways.

Do I look sideways?

Not exactly sideways. I mean – You ain't got a squint. You don't see two of me. Though I wouldn't mind seeing two of you –

'No – come on,' Tom was insisting. 'Give me the once over with them dazzling eyes.'

I wouldn't mind seeing two of you. My wife always says –

Eileen looked at him.

Oh, Arthur. Oh, God, Arthur.

'Now – I'm not a bad-looking guy,' said Tom. 'Am I?'

'No,' she said.

She pushed away all thought of the other man. She looked and looked at this new one. It was true. He wasn't a bad-looking guy. She could imagine his mouth searching out hers. She could imagine –

A little of the horror went out of her.

Tom was alert enough to see a slight relaxation in the tension of her posture. His last glimmers of uncertainty left him. A relief which made him seem infinitely warmer as he leaned in towards her. There was one line he had never failed to deliver at about this point.

And she was ready for it.

'So just pretend we're – you know. Friends.'

She took the line, almost eagerly. It was a way of accepting something new.

And so the handsome Prince stepped out from the trees and looked up at the tiny window at the top of the tall, tall tower that had no door. 'Rapunzel! Rapunzel!' he called 'Let down your hair!' And thinking it was the old witch, Rapunzel let down her hair.

So just let down your hair, she said to herself.

'Yes. Friends,' she agreed with a shaky laugh. 'Good companions.'

'Except instead of giving it away – well – '

'I get – you give me – the five dollars . . .'

Tom put his hand on her knee, caressing and yet also gripping.

'What are you whispering for?' he asked, with an amused jeer. 'Come on! You might even *enjoy* it, honey.'

Eileen scrutinized him, with her steady gaze of old. She forced hardness into her eyes.

'Yes,' she said. 'I might.' And did not look away.

'That's my little honey pie,' he grinned.

She hesitated, and then meticulously put her hand on top of his hand. A bargain sealed.

It made her feel sick, this touching of his flesh. This was no way to come down out of the tall tower in the dark woods. . .

21

Tall buildings made of brick, with fire escapes in black iron clinging to the sides like elongated spiders. Narrow alleys between them, leading nowhere. Shuttered doorways, cat wire, broken bottles, windows without glass. Drunks supine on the fragmented paving, or on all fours in their own vomit.

Life is just a bowl of cherries.

The shelters for vagrants were doing a roaring trade. A roaring, snoring, grunting, farting, belching trade. Oh, to sleep, to sleep, perchance to dream. Inside every man's head another scene, sometimes worse, often better. A field of buttercups, as golden as they were in childhood. Boughs heavy with orange blossom peeping over a high red wall, a dragonfly hovering over a pond. A woman with high breasts as perfect and as sweet as firm young pears . . .

Wood-hard beds were placed side to side and almost end to

end in a cavernous, bleakly Dickensian flop-house. High and darkened windows spaced out the melancholy.

The snorts and the grunts and the mumbles of the sleeping down-and-outs made a flop-house nocturne. Bed by bed, defeated or soured faces had shuttered themselves away for a few hours of safety.

Except the accordion man, wide awake. His instrument tucked under the bed, his face staring up at the high, cracked ceiling. And his reason scrabbling in his head like a rabbit in a noose. The more it struggled, the worse the pain, the tighter the grip, the more certain the end.

He was seeing again and again what the Devil had made him, forced him, to do. Or perhaps, p - pup - perhaps, it was God. Or the vengeful spirit of Rufus Solomon from his childhood, the man who had cast him out.

Or his own lust and wickedness.

The itinerant musician, receiving the accusation as his own finger turned to point inwards at the tattered remnants and broken shards of his own itinerant mind, sucked his breath in a shudder of revulsion.

He rolled over in the hard, narrow bed and found himself facing a cadaverous and fierce-eyed Irishman, not long off the boat.

'Can you play that thing?' the Irishman demanded.

'W - what?'

'Dat accory-dion. Know how to play it, matey?'

The accordion man answered yes, but abstractedly. He did not know what the Irishman was talking about.

'And me! And me!' insisted the other with emphatic, argumentative vigour. 'I know how to play it. By golly, I do. I do!'

An aggression which broke into the accordion man's confused thoughts.

'I ain't arg - g - guin' – ' he returned.

'Shaddup willya!' interjected another flop-house voice, angry at the noise of talking in the middle of the night.

'And don't you tell me to shut up, soldier!' snarled the Irishman, but to the wrong man.

'I d - dud - didn't say – wasn't me, sir.'

''Cos I'm a killer I am!'

When he had delivered what was, for him, a routine threat, the Irishman sank back in his bed, apparently losing interest in both the accordion and its owner.

The black man, however, did precisely the opposite. He stared and stared at his aggressive neighbour in the entrancement of wonder and fear.

Perhaps it was *him* who had done it?

Maybe many men, even all men, had done it?

And what did he feel like now, this man in the next bed? Was his head bursting, and his tongue rotting, and the sky rolling down upon him, night and day?

It was some time before he could get the question to order itself in the right sequence. First of all, he had to let a lady with a big red umbrella pass on high heels across the echoing threshold of his mind. Another, but mercifully fleeting, emissary from the infernal regions below his bed.

The accordion man blinked her away. The red umbrella disappeared. The words came up into his mouth, catching themselves on the browning stumps of his teeth.

'D - did you – ? *Kill* anybody? Did you?'

'Oh, I expect so,' said the Irishman, not very interested. His rhetoric was not meant to be questioned, and whenever anyone did, it usually meant trouble for himself, a lovely man for sure, for sure.

A moan escaped the accordion man: 'Don't you *care*?'

The Irishman took a renewed interest.

'It don't trouble me one bit, old pal. I swats them down like flies.'

'Did they bite?' asked so urgently. 'Did they scratch?'

The excited horror in the questions flared a further curiosity in the Irishman, but it also warned him. He turned away.

'Ach – go to sleep, you silly auld sod!'

But the exchange between the two had not been a whispered one. It awoke some of those who were sleeping, and irritated the few who were still trying to get to their dreams. Their own inviolate territory, their one prized possession, was being needlessly plundered and threatened. A chorus of protests and angry shushings arose out of the normal grunts and snores the length of the room.

130

'I keep seeing her f - face all the time,' the accordion man shuddered, hearing none of the nocturnal cacophony.

'Don't you shush me, you bugger,' snarled the Irishman, to the wrong man again.

It renewed the catcalls and jeers to 'be quiet', but a new thought meant that he, too, did not hear them this time. He leaned in once more to his shuddering neighbour, and an energetic enthusiasm lit up his face.

'Can you play *'Twas a Wild Colonial Boy*? I can! I can!'

But his declaration met with no response. The man at whom it was directed did not even seem to hear it. His eyes were raking the high ceiling, and his breath was making unwholesome noises in his hollow cheeks.

The Irishman turned on his side again, contemptuous.

'Ach! You can't play at all, at all!' he protested.

But the accordion man had slithered out of the reach of words, disappointed or accusing. The memory of his crime now demanded all the space that was left in his head.

She was for ever coming slow and sightless towards him along a path through a field where, hitching along the route he knew so well, he had turned off the road by the Pretty Lady Billboard and wandered into the field in search of – in search of –

What?

There was a message, there must have been a message. A purpose. He knew that when the figure had come gliding so slowly out of nowhere. He had talked, and she had not answered. He had smiled, and she had not smiled. He had looked at her, and she had not looked at him.

Perhaps he had not talked. Perhaps he had not smiled. But he knew he had looked at her, and that she had not looked at him.

'I c - can play you *Rock of Ages*!'

Why had she jumped out of her skin? If she had not started so. If she had not dropped her basket.

'*The Old Rugged Cross*! I'll play *The Old Rugged Cross*!'

Had she not given him a dime? Didn't he then get a meal? Chopped steak. Oh, oh chopped steak, with puddles of ketchup, richer than blood.

'Thank you very, very much, folks. Thank you. Thank you very, very much. Thank you – '

She had started to call out, to make noises. 'What's the mum -
m - matter? Why did you do that? I got my d - dug - dignity, you
know.'

It was very nice.

Pardon lady?

It was nice – a nice hymn . . .

Sh - shall I play you another one, lady?

Puddles of ketchup. The blood that washed away the sins of
the world. So why did she call out like that? Why?

When he clutched at her, she was so warm, and he was so
cold. And when he thrust his face close into hers, and put his
eyes hard upon her, he could see that she had eyes that were not
eyes.

The Devil had put her eyes out! She must have been as bad as
bad can be.

And yet she was so warm, and he was so cold. She was so soft,
and he was so hard. It was so strange to kiss her, but she wouldn't
keep still, she wouldn't keep quiet.

Kiss, kiss lady. Give me a kiss.

They were on the ground, and she was thrashing about. That
was how he had killed a chicken for Rufus Solomon back back in
the he didn't know when, a long way away and a long time away.

You had to break its neck and pull out its feathers.

It was hurting his face with its beak. Sharp beak, tearing his
flesh.

Kiss, kiss, chicken. Give me a kiss.

Chick, chick, chick, chick-en
Lay a little egg for me.

You had to break its neck and pull out its feathers. And the
feathers were so warm and so frilly, and the flesh beneath so soft
and so pink that you had to bite a piece out of it before it went
cold again, as cold as his own . . .

But when after a while he saw what he had done. when the
sticky fervour had gone off the part of his own flesh that also
belonged to the same Devil who had put her eyes out, he wept in
despair.

The spilled eggs were broken, and weeping too, weeping their
own slime.

It don't trouble me one bit, old pal. I swats them down like flies.
Did they bite? Did they scratch?
Ach — go to sleep, you silly auld sod!

He kept seeing her face now, all the time. Not as it was when she came near to him, and ignored him, but her face when he had finished with her.

Can you play 'Twas a Wild Colonial Boy? I can! I can! Ach – !
You can't play at all, at all!

A shaft of silvery-clean, cold, moonlight was spiralling through the dusty gloom. It came from a high roof window and, even as the Irishman turned on his side in disgust, it hit the wall opposite.

The accordion man, mind and memory racing totally out of control, saw the silvery beam thicken and become blood red. Blood splashing on the wall. He sat up in the bed, transfigured. His eyes fixed on the light.

For him, now, the flop-house had been seeped in the menacing red tinge, so that no shape, no space, no other colour could escape it. The lamb of God was pouring out His blood and calling him Home.

The vagrants were in line, and their gaunt, accusing faces were telling him what he had done. Even as he floated between them, looking for peace, his face sad and haunted, the blind girl was there, waiting.

He thought he had returned to his bed. He wanted to escape. But when he pulled back the blanket – there she was, as he had left her. Her tongue lolling out between her teeth and her blind eyes were not so glazed that they could not stare at him.

The accordion man screamed.

A scream that he could not stop, and had no wish to stop. A scream that went with him as a loving companion as he charged with outstretched hands at the huge window. And even as it died away with his tumbling, turning fall, it remained as all he had to say to the world he had left. The only sound it would ever understand.

22

An ambulance with a clanging horn and a speeding police car howling with urban alarm went hurtling past Arthur's record store. Curtains of rain had swept in from across the great lake to give the night in the city a million other glimmering reflections. Street lighting slid and slithered on the wet sidewalks, neon leaked imitations of itself in the nearest puddle or stretch of glass. Storefronts dripped and gutters swirled. It was difficult to read the posters in the windows.

SALE. HUGE REDUCTIONS.

The notice in Arthur's window told its own story. Stock he had bought high he was trying to sell low. The optimism of the first transaction dwindling, by degrees that Joan found inevitable, to the dejection of the second.

Coming out of his store, Arthur was locking up, his spirit disastrously in tune with the drearily falling rain. The proprietor of the adjoining store had chosen the same moment to lock and bolt his door. He looked sideways at Arthur. In other times, or other places, he might have said what almost anyone else would have said with the rain drenching down upon them, and puddles at their feet in the pitted sidewalk in front of them. He would surely have mentioned the weather.

Except that he was in trade, and the times were still not so hot.

'How's business?' he said.

'On the up and up,' said Arthur, savagely. 'I made five sales today, and it was only four the day before.'

His neighbour laughed, not with mirth but with unease.

Arthur did not wait for any more words, and splashed off into the wet street.

The night, the wet, and his own depression closed in around him. He had already been forced to sell his car, and he was trying to walk as far as he could to save some of the fare to his home. He was only too glad to delay his arrival, in any case. Joan had reverted to her old self with a vengeance. The books and ledgers were proving her right, up to the hilt. 'Daddy's money' was as good as gone.

She no longer put the lipstick on her nipples. It was easier for her to say NO.

Splash. Splash. Arthur's feet were padding along the puddled sidewalk with the heavy tread of his failure. He was trying hard to put a song into his heart, but it would always fade after a few bars. The number he didn't want to remind himself of was *Brother, Can You Spare a Dime?*

A distinctly worn old hooker was clacking towards him. She put on a token smile and hesitated.

'You wanna nice time, honey?' she asked him, mechanically.

'No. I *like* being miserable.'

Lifting his head to deliver the sardonic remark, he saw Eileen, or a version of Eileen, up ahead, illuminated in the rain by an old street light.

Eileen!

'Just around the corner, honey,' purred the old hooker.

Then she looked properly at her potential client. His face was transformed before her very eyes. It looked as though he was in the presence of a holy miracle. She followed the direction of his glance, shrugged, and teetered on her way in click-clacking heels.

Arthur simply could not believe what he was seeing.

The woman up ahead under the old lamp looked up, as though compelled to do so by the thrilled incredulity of the glance that had fallen upon her.

And she, too, was transformed.

They were both rooted to the spot for the moment, staring at each other through the night and the shadows. The traffic was shush-slushing by on the dull gleams of the wet street, but they could neither see nor hear it. There were people about, tilting into the rain, but they were unaware of them. No other sight, no other sound, no other movement.

But the song that Arthur tried to find came unbidden to both of them.

FANCY OUR MEETING.

The song had not allowed him to imagine such an encounter as this among the many encounters he *had* dreamed to be possible.

135

He had met her by the side of the lake. He had seen her through the coloured spray of the Buckingham Fountain. She had turned her head and smiled at him on the Elevated. They had collided with each other, near enough, when each was walking alone between banks of flowers in the park.

But never, in his imagination, had he again set eyes on her when it was dark and wet and miserable.

And she standing under an old street light.

Somehow, they were face to face. He had crossed the distance between without knowing it, for everything and everyone else in view had become as insubstantial as ghosts or wraiths, hardly there at all.

'Arthur.'

'Eileen! My God – what are you doing here?'

'Arthur. Oh, Arthur,' she said, so moved. 'You are such a bastard!'

'Eileen. I haven't stopped thinking about you. Not once!'

He was so full up to the very brim with emotion, so full that, at first, he had not even taken in the astonishing change in her appearance. Her clothes were provocatively sexy, her face over-coloured with make-up, her hair radically different.

This new sight of her came to him. He looked at her again, and his voice trailed off.

She surely wasn't, was she?

'What the hell are you dolled up like this for?' he asked, the anger already there, a *proprietorial* anger already there.

Eileen gave him a wearily pert, half-ashamed tilt of her head.

'Three guesses,' she said.

No! Surely not. She surely, surely wasn't – But yes. He could see that she was. Miss Eileen Everson, so delicate, so demure, so decently hesitant, had turned into a whore. A two-dollar screw.

'No!' he exclaimed, incredulity still working to block any words.

She kept her gaze upon him, and he could smell her perfume.

'No! But Eileen! – You're a *schoolteacher*!'

'And I used to tell them fairy tales, Arthur.'

'Eileen – ' he said again, hoarse, imploring. He saw the way she had come out of the school that day. The two pictures never, never, could go together.

136

'The name is Lulu now,' she smiled, tightly, mimicking the pert insolences of her new trade specially for his benefit.

The name is Lulu now.

He grabbed hold of her arm, angry and upset. He could feel silky stuff under his fingers.

'Come on. You're coming with me!'

'You want to buy?' she asked, with the same mocking and pained insolence.

'Shut up!' he snarled, almost pulling her off balance. 'Or I'll wash your mouth out!'

He was dragging her from this place, pulling her along the street. It was not that she was struggling, but his fury and his shame made her seem as though she were. She gave herself up to his angry determination.

Arthur did not know where he was going. When the shock had subsided, the vigour left him too. It was raining, and it was dark. There were accusations to be made, and accounts to be settled. Whatever had happened to her had clearly been his fault, or, he qualified, in a characteristic shift of the weight in his mind, *mostly* his fault.

But the feel of her hand in his grip, its submissive and helpless softness, made him aware that it was not just the rain in his eyes.

He knew that now, given his new chance, now he could not let her go. And yet Arthur did not know where to take her. He was willing to make renewed avowals to her but he did not know where to take this poor little girl for five minutes of talk!

They were in a café, like two nighthawks winding down the dance with the chink of coffee spoons against saucer and sugar bowl, ready to talk until morning's early light.

Arthur and Eileen had the place to themselves, apart from one other anonymous and lonely-looking figure, and the tired counter man. But it seemed to Arthur that there were others expected, too: expected, but not wanted. Eileen kept darting glances of apprehension at the window which looked out on to the street. It was steamed up, making people and traffic seen through it obscure and wetly shimmery.

And then he thought that she might be wanting to return to her post under the old street light, back to her beat, and her clients.

'It's not right, Eileen,' he was remonstrating. 'It's just not right! Not for a girl like you!'

She dragged her gaze from the steamy window, and looked at him with threateningly baleful eyes.

'You gave me the wrong address.'

'What?' he asked with a frown, even knowing full well that pretended bewilderment was no adequate cover for a proper embarrassment.

'There's no such place as you wrote on that bit of paper.'

He could not answer that. He sipped his coffee, but did not taste it. The automobiles were shushing and swishing outside in the wet street, and he could hear them. It was like listening to whispering rumours of his own squalid betrayals, and Arthur felt that his heart was going to break.

It didn't.

Because he was able to sip at his coffee again, and to speak: although when he did speak, his eyes were shifty, and looked less like a man burdened with the melancholy knowledge of his own inadequate soul than a pickpocket in the actual commission of yet another petty crime.

'Put yourself in my shoes, Eileen,' he said.

Which is to say: listen, I know I seduced you, and told you I was not married, and made you promises, and made you pregnant, then disappeared and eventually returned, made love to you again, heard about the baby, wrote down my address, promised to help but – well, you couldn't *really* expect it to be the real address, or *really* expect me to help out, could you, because I *am* married, and –

'Put yourself in my shoes, Eileen.'

'Oh, I have! I know I can't rely on you, Arthur. Not for anything!'

'That's right!' he said indignantly. 'Blame it all on me!'

Eileen had to laugh – almost.

'Oh, Arthur.'

'I know, I know.' He had the grace to be ashamed. His indignation was an affront to her sensibility and his dignity. 'I can hear myself saying things sometimes, and – oh, God. I'm a washout.'

And, then, as he hovered somewhere between a cleansing self-knowledge and a treacherously absolving self-pity, a dark new thought swooped at him. One that he should have had

138

before. One that he had many times prevented himself from putting to himself.

'What about the baby? What's happened?'

She did not answer straight away. It was not out of any delicacy for either her feelings or his. The answer had been blanked out of her consciousness. The crime had happened to someone else.

'It's been gotten rid of,' she said, when she did answer. And she said it abruptly.

Arthur stared at her, taking it in. Or, rather, working it out. The enormity of her plight, the scale of evil that had fallen upon her, bit with pointed fangs at his mind. No verbal device or emotional subterfuge could get in the way of the raw distress which welled up inside him like the tears now trembling at the rim of his eyes.

'Oh, God. Oh, dear God,' he choked. 'Why is it all so – ? Why can't the world be – ?'

His voice broke, and he could not continue. He was too upset to notice that, apparently unmoved, her eyes were again raking the steamed-up window, trying to decipher the wavery, shimmering shapes on the street beyond the glass.

'Because that's the way it is,' she said at the same time, brutally matter-of-fact.

Arthur already knew that she had a steadier resolve than he had ever been able to aspire to, let alone emulate. He knew that she did not shift her eyes about when she wanted to know something, whether it was painful or not. For all her shy hesitancy there was a directness and an honesty about her which, at times, was only the finest slither away from hardness.

It was his sense of Eileen's bleak acceptance of what could not be changed that made him expose his silly old dream to her, here and now, in an almost deserted café that ached with a big-city loneliness.

'But – but – I wanna live in a world where the, where the *songs come true*!' he insisted, the pain wrenching hard at him. 'I – why not? Why not? There must be *someplace* where the song is for *real*!'

What song?

Eileen looked at him, and she knew what he meant. It was the same thing that the writers of the fairy tales meant. The same

139

thing that the singer of the psalms meant. Except that it had degenerated into a tap of the feet and a sweet syncopation which sang trite thoughts along the line of the song.

What song, Arthur?

'*Happy Days Are Here Again*! Is that it, Arthur?' she asked him, wry, but not without pity.

Is *that* the song, Arthur? What song do you mean, Arthur?

> *O come, let us sing unto the Lord: let us make a joyful*
> *noise to the rock of our salvation.*
> *Let us come before his presence with thanksgiving, and*
> *make a joyful noise unto him with psalms.*
> *For the Lord is a great God, and a great King above all gods.*
> *In his hand are the deep places of the earth, the strength of*
> *the hills is his also.*
> *The sea is his, and he made it; and his hands formed the dry*
> *land.*
> *O come, let us worship and bow down: let us kneel before*
> *the Lord our maker.*

What song, Arthur?

Arthur and Eileen stared long and deep at each other, knowing that there was something better than this if only they could find it.

The traffic hissed in the rain, and the electric lighting hummed a little.

He could see now the glisten of unshed tears in her eyes. No, this was not the world of the songs, and they would have to manage as best they could in it.

Real Life was at their throats. It wasn't going to let go.

'I'm in trouble,' she said suddenly, looking first at the window again. 'Terrible, terrible trouble.'

He swallowed, not being a brave man, and waited for her to continue.

'I went into this bar. I – there was this man – he bought me a drink.'

'He would, wouldn't he? The rotten bastard.'

There was a pause. They could hear the noises outside again, telling them to be quiet. His eyes did not stray from her face. And she was trying to cut the story down to the bone, the narrative of her shame and despair.

'*And I did it with him for five dollars.*'

She did not tell him about the weary tramping about in search of jobs that weren't there. Nor of the small amount of money that slowly dwindled, nor of her face pressed against food-store and café windows trying to get nourishment from the sight rather than the taste of the food. She did not mention the grey-faced retching into a chipped wash-bowl in the mornings, nor tell him of her search for him, or of the thoughts of her own self-destruction in the slow and sleazy Chicago river, down where laden barges hooted her own melancholy.

There was no point in going over all that.

Just tell him the end result. He could guess at the decline which slid her body into it, stretched out on her back with a stranger pumping himself into her. Just tell him that, 'I did it with him for five dollars.'

Arthur was silent for a moment.

'Well,' he said. 'You got to eat. I suppose.'

She looked at the window again. He wanted to tap his spoon against the side of his cup. He wanted to make a noise.

In truth, he wanted to scream. But, instead, he waited.

'This guy – he paid to get rid of – ', she swallowed, refusing to say the word. 'He bought clothes and . . . Now he says I owe him two hundred dollars. And if I don't get it . . .'

Eileen left the threat unfinished.

'He's got you then,' said Arthur, chillingly. 'Hasn't he?'

The fear jumped into her eyes, and she looked yet again at the window.

'He's given me the key to a room on Rush Street. I can use it for . . . You know. And pay him fifteen dollars a week for it.'

'Jesus Christ,' exclaimed Arthur. 'This is supposed to be the greatest country in the world.'

'Or I can pay him back,' she continued relentlessly, not even noticing his qualified patriotism. 'But I have to do it tonight. By tonight.'

'What'll he do if you – *what's the matter*?'

He had noticed her looking at the window before, but this time her expression was changing as she did it. Catching her fearful

141

anxiety, and sharing her dread now that she had told him so much, he jerked his head around to follow her widened eyes.

Outside, discernible through the steam and the shimmers, a car was slowly prowling on the edge of the road. She knew that inside the car would be Tom, the pimp, his face mean and eyes narrow. Checking. Just checking.

Nobody in the Chicago of 1934 could afford to be indifferent about the many kinds of crook who so diligently polluted the city. Tom was small meat and potatoes, but there was a power in him to make any of his girls who crossed him wish they had never been born. He had told Eileen what he would do to her if she ran out on him, and he had enumerated the punishment in slow, precise detail. There was, to her, no question but that her fear was wholly justified.

And if she was frightened, then Arthur would be, too. He had little or no physical courage to begin with, and her sudden panic in the desolate café made him feel weak in the bowels. When she clutched at his hand and hissed at him that they must run and hide, it was as much as he could do to force one leg in front of the other. But, somehow, they found themselves running, panting, through the wet streets. The sound of her feet, and the gasp of her breathing, gave back to him all the urgency he had ever needed.

Arthur was aiming for his own shuttered record store. They had waited in a darkened doorway, and then under the girders of the looming Elevated rail, before crossing the still wet street to his little shop.

He was so nervous that he could not at first get the key to turn in the lock.

She was standing back, looking around and about, very nervous, and unsure whether this was a sensible place to go. Already, there was someone looking at them, down the street.

'Well, I don't know where else to go, do I?' he was saying between his teeth, all fingers and thumbs. 'This key is sticking.'

'Hurry up, Arthur!'

And the door swung inwards, at last, into a haven of unsold and silent music. Arthur's hand went automatically to the light switch inside the door.

142

'No!' she said, urgently. 'Don't put the light on!'

'Don't be so goddamn ridiculous!' he snarled. But he did not put on the light. Each of them thought, for the moment, and as his hand jerked away from the switch, that from now on they were condemned to live in darkness.

Arthur wasn't absolutely sure, but he had a pretty good idea that none of the songs he loved had allowed for that.

But he was wrong, of course.

23

Arthur's store did not have the overhead light on, but it was not at all difficult to see most things in it except the small print on the record labels and the tiny throb of the vein in Arthur's forehead as it fluttered out his fear.

A garish urban glow was seeping orange-backed into the store from the street outside. The looming El cast the long shadows of its manifold struts and girders to construct a weird, griddle-like pattern inside the store, alternatively suggesting prison bars in an opera set, or tombstones in a German pen-and-ink satire. Any place out of normal hours, when its everyday functions have been suspended, seems to have that which is perverse or uneasy about it. Nightwatchmen do not always soliloquize because they are bored.

The little store was no different in this respect, and the fear which had driven scurrying Arthur and Eileen into its shelter made even the display stands, the posters, and the brown cardboard jackets on the phonograph records take on other and less placid identities. The cash register might have been about to deliver itself of something ominously cryptic.

Arthur had to wait for more than a few seconds before he

143

could feel the familiarity of the place begin to reassert itself. He had endured much boredom and disappointment between these walls, but even so he knew every square inch of the store. It was his.

Eileen's eyes had grown accustomed to the light.

'Phonograph records,' she said, in a flat voice.

'Hundreds 'n' hundreds!' he beamed, suddenly inordinately proud and proprietorial. 'Almost any dance tune you can name! Any *good* dance tune. I tell you, I – '

His face changed, and he stopped in mid-flight, realizing how inappropriate such boastful exuberance was in her – in *their* – present predicament.

She was looking at him steadily, her fear sufficiently back in control to allow her the luxury of irony.

'What about *Whistling in the Dark*?' she asked him, with barely a hint of a smile. 'You got that?'

'What?' he blinked.

Come on, Arthur. Wake up.

'Dance tunes don't help, Arthur. What am I going to do?'

He had no idea what she should do. He couldn't take her home (Joan, I'd like you to meet a friend of mine –), and she couldn't live here in the store. Even now, however, even in the midst of his fear and her despair, he had to put down a momentarily tantalizing fantasy of him bringing her hot dogs and cups of coffee and them making love behind the counter before he locked up each night and went home.

What am I going to do?

The question was too important, and its implications too dire, for him not to concentrate. He *had* to help her.

But, no, he had no idea what she should do.

'Can't you go home?'

'No! I was already dead there!' she said passionately. 'This way feels like dying – but I can see everything, feel everything – do you understand?'

He thought he might. A new and strange concept was taking shape in his mind as he studied her. Perhaps it was simply the way she was now dressed, her make-up, her perfume: the signs and the symbols of her availability.

How could he ask?

'Did you – uh – ' he attempted. 'Did you *like* doing it? For money?'

Eileen hesitated. She knew that her reason and her sense of her own dignity wished, indignantly, to reject any such supposition.

'It wasn't as bad as I thought it was going to be,' she said. Tom's casual, insolent brutality came back to her, without revulsion.

Arthur found himself vaguely disturbed, and a little excited.

'My God,' he said, eyes brightening. 'You're something!'

But she did not like the male beast coiled behind his excitement, leering with lechery. She did not want to be dominated, nor abused.

'I'd rather pick and choose. I don't want to be a – I want to own myself, my own body. I know I'm wicked, but I'm still – proud.'

The tilt of her head as she said this was as vivacious an assertion as he had ever witnessed. He experienced again that puzzling awe, which, sooner or later, her presence and her movements evoked in him. She was finer than anything he knew how to measure.

'I think you are beautiful.'

'Do you?'

They stood in the griddle-shadowed, garish half-light looking at each other. Again, the sounds from the street, softened and made insinuating by the wet, entered their minds with the slow droop of a melancholy, or an unsatisfied yearning, too insubstantial for them to grasp.

It was either love or it was misery.

When Arthur was much younger he had heard a saxophone sending out its sobbing blue rhythms as he stood buying a ticket at the entrance to a small Chicago dance-hall. The music had been distanced by a wall and a pair of glass doors, and there were boys and girls milling about in the foyer. The boys hunted in packs, and the girls were in pairs. Jaws moved chewing-gum about drying mouths, and eyes whisked around the wall, too afraid to settle. The music from the makeshift band from within had the wistful suggestion of present and future loneliness. It seemed, to the young people who heard it, to be trying to say

145

something important. Find what you want or who you desire *now*, or be lost for ever. Crack your jokes, put on your style, curl your lip, but don't hang about on the edge of the floor . . . it will go, it will be gone, and the shine on the apple will dull and then rot, and your limbs will stiffen and decay, and the music will cease to play.

He could not tell her any of this.

But the sob of the saxophone was lingering even now in the ill-lit space between them.

Oh, she was so beautiful, and oh, time was so brief.

'Let's – uh – shall we – ?' he asked.

'If you've got five dollars,' she replied.

The calculated brutality of her answer rocked him back on his heels. Literally.

'Eileen!'

'I can't afford not to, can I? And the name is Lulu. Please.'

'That's disgusting!' he spluttered. 'Haven't you got any shame?'

She had not considered the question before. Few people ever do. Characteristically, she did not take it as an indignantly conventional scrap of rhetoric. It needed her attention.

'I don't think I have,' she said.

Arthur was totally unused to honesty of thought, let alone honesty of diction. Even when he felt otherwise, he tried to cast his words with more than due deference to the way those around him seemed to think was the appropriate means of valuing their lives. Salacious jokes with his fellow travelling salesmen gave place to sanctimony on other occasions.

When she *said* rather than confessed that she had no shame, he knew exactly what she meant. He recognized the part of himself he had never quite been able either to articulate or to act upon.

It thrilled him.

'We're the same sort, you and me,' he said, with obvious excitement. 'We ought to stick together.'

'But I can't rely on you, Arthur.'

'Listen to me!'

'I am. I am. Very carefully.'

So this was it. This was really it. His final chance, absolute and irrevocable. No time left for wheedling, for bluster, or rhetoric,

146

or dishonest exaggeration and easy emotional excess. No more 'final' chances after the final chance. He had called out 'Listen to me!' before he even knew what it was he truly wanted her to listen to. Vague yearnings and wistful desires were no longer worth a nickel.

And yet he did not know where to begin.

'I tell you –' he said, as earnest and without calculation as he could be. 'I'm choking to death. I should have hung on to you, no matter what. But I wanted my own record store!'

There was also the small matter of a gibbering apparition on a lonely road in the middle of a snowy night.

Eileen began to laugh.

'I know. I know,' he conceded, utterly helpless. 'It's enough to make a goddamn cat laugh.'

'You'll *never* be satisfied, Arthur. Not somebody like you.'

'Don't say that!'

'You're like the children in my class.'

She was hurting him. She was calling into question whatever it was that remained authentic in his dream. Was he, then, just a bag of bluster? Was he simply a child-like cheat and liar, with no strength, no resolve, no constancy?

You'll never be satisfied, not someone like you!

Arthur couldn't get out of it. His instinct came to his aid. When all was said and done, she still responded to him. Didn't she?

'But you're still sweet on me, aintcha?' he pleaded, his defences down. 'You still want me, huh? Eileen? Tell the truth.'

She examined him. He thought for a terrible instant, which came like he imagined the recognition of the moment of death must be like, that she was going to deny it, or sneer, or even laugh with that hard little tinkle of dismissal which belonged peculiarly to her directness.

Perhaps both of them held their breath.

'Yes. I do,' she said. 'And I'll go anywhere with you, or do anything with you. I've burnt all my bridges, Arthur. I'm not going home. I'm not going to walk the streets either. And I'm damned if I'm going to go hungry! Lulu I am, Lulu I stay. So what are we going to do?'

Right, it was up to him!

Now, not later, *now* he had to choose whether he really was that bag of bluster, that child-like cheat and liar. Whether he really was without strength, without resolve, and without constancy.

And most of all, whether or not he was a coward.

Her final question was almost bound to find him wanting. He could only approach decisiveness by havering his way towards it. It had to be that he must put up forms of objection which were only questions for her to answer or doubts for her to dispel.

She was the stronger one.

'Trouble is,' he havered, or quavered, 'I'm hard up.'

'I can always pick up some money. Now I know how.'

'I haven't even got my car any more.'

'We'll get another one. One day.'

''Course we will.'

And his mouth fell open. What had he said? He had moved from objection to acceptance in three easy moves!

'Course we will.

'So – what shall we do?' she asked him in a different voice. 'Where shall we hide?'

He swallowed. A path was opening up before him.

'I've got eleven dollars and five cents,' he told her.

'And I've got three dollars.'

Arthur put his foot on the path. He became excited.

'We can – we can live for a week – more! – on that,' he said.

'It's a start, anyway,' she agreed.

Perhaps there was still time to stop talking as though they meant it. He could not believe that he was committing himself with so little fuss. And neither could she wholly believe that he was. Her entire experience of him worked against it.

Arthur looked around his store. Without the overhead lighting, and despite its bizarre shadows, the place seemed, now, to be warm and safe. He had by now attuned himself to disappointment. It was almost his friend, his steady companion.

'What? Just go and – ' his eyes wandered over his stock, his fittings. 'Leave everything? Just like that?'

She nodded, expressionless.

'Just like that,' she said.

They looked at each other. They heard the swish of the traffic outside again.

And Arthur, he only heard the wolves howling.

'All right,' he said.

Relief and delight rushed at her. She could not wait another second, and grabbed at him to pull him out into the street. Somehow, it didn't seem to matter a damn what might be waiting out there. Nor even what disasters might be in store for the future.

'Then – let's get out of here. Shall we?' she gurgled, plucking at him.

'Yeah. But – hang on a minute . . .'

'What are you doing?'

Eileen imagined, at first, with a sickening plunge of dismay and contempt, that he was seeking a last-minute excuse. He had turned back. But then she was held by the expression on his face. It did not show what she had feared.

Arthur was picking up a pile of the phonograph records. He shuffled them through his hands, and began to read out their titles.

'*On a Little Bamboo Bridge,*' he intoned. '*Marie. You Sweet So-and-So. Dancing with my Shadow. September in the Rain.*'

He stopped. His insides were cracking open. He was staring a dream hard and straight into its face. She waited.

And he threw the records on to the floor. Then he jumped on them, again and again, frenzied. They smashed with the sound of breaking bones.

Eileen began to laugh.

He got hold of another handful. Nothing was going to keep him back. Nothing from his old life was going to stop him. He was so determined, he was panting. So serious, he was laughing . . .

'*You Couldn't Be Cuter,*' he gabbled out more titles. '*Isn't It Heavenly. Hand in Hand. Yes Yes My Baby Said Yes. Indian Love Call.*'

Again, the sacramental raising of the holy sacrifice, then – *smash! crash! splinter!* Shards of broken records went spinning across the floor, their magical black and shining grooves destroyed and made impotent.

Eileen joined in, her laughter edging into the relief of hysteria. She, too, plucked up a pile of the records, calling out their labels.

'*Seeing Is Believing,*' she laughed. '*Roll Along Prairie Moon.*'

'*Paper Moon*,' yelled Arthur, out-topping her. '*Whistling in the Dark. I Love You Truly.*'

Smash! Crash! Splinter! Two different piles were hurled down and crunched under feet.

'*Chasing Shadows*,' she screamed, and threw it to the floor in a frenzy. '*Pennies from Heaven*,' she yelled, lifting it above her head.

'No! Wait!' he grabbed at her. 'Not that one!'

But she wanted to break it, too. The frenzy had released both of them. It felt as though they were destroying everything that had misled, waylaid, hindered and cheated them. It felt marvellous!

Eileen tried to hurl the last record in her hands, but Arthur had got hold of her wrists. They were struggling, and they were laughing at the same time. Indeed, they were almost helpless with laughing, she to throw the record and he to stop her, so they cancelled each other out in a gurgling struggle.

They did not stop wrestling, not until, still laughing, they slid to the floor.

The struggle, the laughter, turned into kissing. They lay on the broken pieces of the shattered phonograph records, and with the same urgency, and an almost identical frenzy, began to make love.

Smash. Crash. Splinter.

24

The mystery of Arthur's disappearance, and the devastated state of the store he had left behind him, was at first a minor puzzle to the police and the subject of increasingly horrified speculation by Joan. The mess of broken records, the absence of any message, the lack of any warning, made her think that he had been kidnapped, or worse. She could not imagine what sort of ransom would be demanded, but knew that they would never be able to pay it.

Joan waited by the telephone, again, and watched the clock, again. If it were not for the broken phonograph records, she might have accepted that Arthur had run out on her again. But she believed that he would as soon smash up a record as tear a piece of sheet music to bits. A man like Arthur simply did not do that sort of thing.

And so she pestered the Chicago police. Every day she pestered them.

Their interest was low, and their irritation high. So, a small-time store keeper had disappeared for a while. Probably gone off with another woman. It happened all the time. And the broken records? Shrug. Shrug. Spread your hands and hide your yawn.

But they began to change their tune.

The car that Arthur, pressed for cash, had sold to a dealer off the Loop, was, in the slow and cumbersome way of the bureaucracies involved between two different police administrations, eventually matched to the number taken down by the gum-chewing cop on that snowy night of death and abasement.

BLIND GIRL RAPED AND STRANGLED.

Headlines had been as bold and as black as space and ink allowed. NO LEADS IN BLIND GIRL SLAYING duly followed. The beauty and vulnerability of the victim kept high the column inches, the speculation, the criticism – and the pressure on the police. It was not an election year, but there were still reputations to be won and lost.

The car number may or may not have been significant. The police never did rate the hoary supposition that a murderer always returned to the scene of the crime. But – well – it was a possibility, however remote.

Much more important – and many heads and hands had pondered and mauled over their meanings – were the plaster cast of the footprint and the tossed-away, empty pack of Lucky Strike cigarettes.

Gradually, Joan found that the police were, after all, as interested in what had happened to Arthur as she was. She had already had two visits from them, the second by a lieutenant of

151

detectives who looked at her 'in that way', as Joan preferred to put it – if she ever put it at all.

She had just baked a cake and was cleaning the house when he called again.

The set of his face, and something sombre and restless in his eyes, made her fear the worst.

'He's dead! Isn't he? Murdered!'

The lieutenant found her attractive, especially when crying out like this, eyes wide, body tensing.

Wonder what she'd be like in the sack. Pretty hot, he guessed. As Arthur, too, had once guessed, seeing her on her father's veranda.

'No, no, no,' the lieutenant said, with a confident assurance which went a long way to quieten her. 'Now – this is what the police know so far – '

'Is he in trouble?' she asked, in a different voice. 'Or – *kidnapped*?'

He spoke in a gentle voice, partly to gain her full co-operation, but mostly because he wanted to cup her elbow in the palm of his hand. The lieutenant was very fond of a pretty woman's elbow. Touch it nicely, and the way was nearly always open to even nicer parts, like the knee, and eventually the hip bone.

'Nothing like that – Mrs Parker – listen to me.'

She listened, pleased by his tone.

'Your husband left his store at close of business and went to a bar in the neighbourhood. He was later seen by a reliable witness to return to his store.'

He looked hard at her, delivering up implications in his voice and his eyes. It was the sort of manner that he had used to let the person he was visiting officially know that someone was dead, without actually saying so. The lieutenant was an expert at letting meanings hang out just beyond his words.

She picked it up, and her face was already beginning to harden.

'Who – who was he with?'

The lieutenant needed her active co-operation. There was always a very strong possibility that Parker would try to contact her. He might even call at the house. She had to be on the right side. She had to want him caught.

So when he told her, he spoke in such a way that her potential sense of humiliation would be instantly engaged. The lieutenant wanted her to think that what he himself considered to be quite normal behaviour – a lay, what the hell – was peculiarly abominable.

'He was with a young lady,' he said, heavily. 'Well – when I say *lady* . . .'

He waited.

Joan stared at him, and bitterness overwhelmed her. So it was *that* was it? It was all that stuff. He never could get enough of it, and so he had gone looking for it elsewhere. Among the dregs. In the gutter.

'Go on,' she said, in flint.

The lieutenant was pleased, but hid the pleasure. He wanted to make a meal of it. His sympathy, of course, would make her feel worse. No woman wants to hear condolences about the sexual misbehaviour of her husband.

'We've been piecing things together,' he said, in an air of sad resignation, 'and – I'm sorry – but this woman was a prostitute.'

The bald word sickened her. She saw soiled limbs, soiled bedsheets, smelly genitals, illicit thrashing and gasping, discarded condoms, filthy words, and –

Her face was twisting in disgust.

Oh, boy, oh, boy, oh, boy, I've got her. I've got her.

He nodded in answer to her expression.

'You mean – she went there to – to – '

Her hands went up to her face. The lieutenant came as near to her as he dared, wanting to touch her.

'He was – like that?' he asked, instantly.

'He – '

But she stopped. About to launch into a passionate denunciation, she stopped. She had picked up something in his tone, or in his manner, which put her on her guard. Perhaps, she thought, he is trying to trap Arthur. Maybe they already have him for something he didn't do, or –

'How do you mean?' she said, warily.

'Was he disturbed in any way? About anything? Odd. Restless,' he paused. '*Nuts.*'

Joan's eyes narrowed. It was sex. It surely was sex. Arthur had done something disgusting.

'Has Arthur done something else? Is that why you took his shoes?'

They said that it would help them locate him. But now she could see by the firmness, and the care, in this nice policeman's attitude that there was more to it than she had bargained for.

Joan, dreading yet more humiliation, desperately wanted to trust the lieutenant.

'Please think,' he said, as though appealing to everything decent in her. 'Was he acting strange in any way?'

Strange! My God, she had often thought so! He wanted to make love on the kitchen floor. Love before breakfast.

And that wasn't the half of it.

She looked at the lieutenant. Yes, it was time she told somebody.

It was not an easy thing to talk about, and never could be. But if Arthur was – well – *nuts*, then –

'He made me wear – ' she hesitated, excruciatingly embarrassed. 'Lipstick.'

There! She had almost said it! Her own now less than vivid nipples went stiff and tight with sexual anxiety.

'Oh,' said the lieutenant, incredibly disappointed.

No, more than that. Her reply made him feel that *she* was the nut. My God, he thought, if wearing lipstick was such a big deal, the supposed proof that her husband was 'acting strange' in asking her to use it, well, no wonder the poor slob went bananas and tore the pants off some girl in a field.

Joan reacted to his flat 'Oh.' She felt a fool.

'No – on the – on the – ' she struggled, 'on the points of my bosom.'

He wanted to explode with laughter. He would have liked to shout out and throw himself on the carpet and roll round and round, over and over, howling in hilarity.

Instead, his face twitched.

'That's – well – that's –,' he began, but the laughter was hurtling up into his chest and throat. 'Excuse me,' he said, and, just in time, blew his nose into his handkerchief.

Joan could see that he was deeply shocked and moved by the barbarism that had been so wantonly inflicted on her. Even now, it was evident that he was trying to stop her seeing his pain and his compassion. His face had gone tight and red with the effort of bottling up his feelings.

Hoo! Hoo! Hoo! Hoooo!

But he didn't let it out. He deserved the Police Medal. Christ, he deserved a presidential citation.

Joan, encouraged by his demonstrable sensitivity, was encouraged enough to venture further with her tale of woe.

'And he asked me if I – if I would stop – '

She could not make the words come. It was too embarrassing. Her eyes swivelled away from him.

'No. Go on,' he said, strained. He coughed. 'Please.'

Joan's voice dropped to a near whisper, and the effect of this on him was to make his gut ache. What was she, a cabaret performer?

'If I – if I would stop wearing – a certain garment,' she continued, oblivious of the comedy. 'A certain item of – underwear.'

He again just managed to turn what he wanted to do into the merest twitch of his cheek.

'An upper or lower garment?' he asked her, with difficulty.

She said something, but he found he couldn't hear it.

'What?'

Joan twisted her hands. 'Lower,' she said.

The inner scream of laughter went out of him. Right out. A new thought clicked home as clean as a pool ball into the pocket. A detail matched. One more detail matched.

He leaned into her, suddenly sharp and crisply urgent. It was a police voice and he wanted answers. Even if he did not get to touch her elbow.

'About six weeks ago – can you think back? – your husband travelled back late one night to Chicago along Illinois Route One.'

'He – ' she stopped, and looked at him, wanting to help and, in any event, intrigued. 'That must have been the night he said – he said – he'd seen a *message*.'

The lieutenant stiffened. That was *real* nut talk.

'He was very upset. He said – "I've got to change. I've got to be good."'

Joan repeated the words in great bitterness, and the irony of them made her put her hands to her face again. She had been

155

appallingly betrayed, and her suffering was now extreme.

'Got to be good?' hissed the lieutenant. 'The hell.'

'Oh, he's bad. He's bad all right!' she cried out in her pain.

The lieutenant stared at her, but he was not seeing her. In his mind was the car number, the cast of the footprint, the pack of the brand this guy smoked, the pants – or the lack of them. All shaking together into such a neat pattern.

'I get the picture,' he said, almost to himself. 'Things are beginning to fit together.'

Joan knew now, for sure, that Arthur had done something terrible, and that there was no hope left for their marriage. He had copulated with a whore in the store her father's money – *her* money – had provided. Money handed over because of emotional blackmail, because of her fear of being abandoned. The fear that made her put that lipstick on her nipples, and submit – oh God, *submit* – to his appetites.

To his *thing*!

How many whores had he had before he came back to her? How often had she been betrayed?

Joan felt the need for vengeance. Her humiliation, and her terrible, desolating hurt, spewed away from her in a shriek of rage and torment. She concentrated her venom on the offending object.

'Cut his thing off!' she cried. 'I want them to cut his thing off and – and – bury it!'

The lieutenant remained calm in the face of her assault upon the male member.

'That's the one and only cure, ma'am,' he said.

25

The shine had gone off the apple, and the glow had left the cherry. Arthur and Eileen had enjoyed some laughter, much passion and many other moments of mutual exploration. They had talked about their own childhoods, their memories and their expectations. But now they were not at all sure whether they were hiding out or running away. It was no longer clear to them whether they were going towards a new life together, or retreating from it. Once more, the brighter colours had begun to fade, much in the fashion of the ancient and flaking paint on the walls too close around them.

There were even a few nights now when Arthur and Eileen, upon going to bed, went straight to sleep.

The bed was hard up against a cracked wall. There were also a table and two chairs. A wardrobe, a sink and a stove. All pressed together in a tawdry hotel room, made intermittently noisy by the racket from the Elevated below their grubby window.

His eleven dollars and five cents, and her three dollars, had gone less far than a seven-stone weakling could throw a handful of sand. And there was none of it left.

One of the riches left behind by the previous occupant of the hotel room, and miraculously not claimed by the grasping proprietor, was a jigsaw puzzle. So at least there was something to fit together properly.

Arthur could not get even this small diversion to come right, however. He was tut-tutting and sighing over it, just as though it were important.

Sallow and unshaven, and less like the handsome Prince in Eileen's all but forgotten fairy tales than he had ever been, Arthur was at the table trying to get an oddly shaped segment of the puzzle to go where it palpably did not belong. He bent the edges in frustration.

Eileen could care less. She was at the only mirror, carefully over-making-up her lovely face, and not listening to his repeated sighs.

Mirror, Mirror, on the wall
Who is the fairest of them all?

She pursed and pouted her lips to apply the lipstick. Even that was low down in its tube, a stump rather than a slenderly shaped finger of crimson.

Down below them, a train on the El clanked and groaned like an enslaved giant forced to drag endless chains behind himself. She paused in her excessive beautification, and made a face at herself in the mirror. Not a pretty one, either. There looked to be some kind of contentious decision – or outright rebellion, even – brewing up in her eyes.

'This goddamn sky,' complained Arthur, at last. 'It's very hard. It's all blue except a bit of white cloud here and there.'

'Blue skies,' she said, in her special flat voice. 'Nothing but blue skies.'

He tried to make another curved piece go where it did not want to go. An isthmus that failed to lock into the surrounding ocean of insipid blue. Arthur could so far make only the wisps of white cloud fit into place, and they were all in one corner of the sky.

'What?' he asked, in mere irritation rather than because he had not heard.

'Wish it was,' she said, just as flat as before.

A train clacked and thundered by, hard on the tail of the previous one. Its brakes squealed on the curve.

'God! What a rat hole!' she exclaimed, and this time the animation made him look up from his bewildering puzzle.

'What are you doing that for?'

There was perhaps a touch more hostility than anxiety in his voice, but that would change. She did not turn round, but stayed looking almost quizzically at her own painted and powdered reflection. There was a small dab of lipstick on the edge of one of her teeth. She wiped it off. It was too much like blood.

'*What are you doing that for?*'

'To go out.'

'Where to?'

'Anywhere,' she said. 'Just *anywhere* out of this place.'

He put the piece of jigsaw in his hand down on the table, disgruntlement all over him.

'What about me?' he asked in his most peevish voice.

'Look in the mirror, Arthur.'

Arthur rubbed his hand across the bristles on his chin. It sounded like a hedgehog rubbing its back on a rough old garden wall.

'I know. I know,' he snarled, half ashamed and yet also resentful of the implied accusation. 'I'm a slob.'

Eileen did not answer. The resentment did not leave his voice, but it was joined by boredom – always a fine pair.

'But we got no dough anyway. Where's to go?'

Eileen turned away from the mirror, abruptly. She no longer wished to see the face that was in it. Besides, she was ready. That part of her was ready. As pretty and as dead as a pinky-white china doll.

'I'm sick of being poor,' she said.

It was time for him to start getting worried by her tone, and her manner. He was already a little frightened of her, though not in anything like the same way he had been of Joan. He even rather liked his fear of Eileen, if that, indeed, is what it really was. *Awe* might be a better word.

'I'll find something soon', he promised, but without much conviction. 'Maybe *tomorrow*, huh?'

'Yeah. Maybe.'

The disbelief, and the edge of potential sarcasm, stung him. It wasn't *his* fault, was it? She hadn't been too hot at getting a job, had she? There was no call to blame him and make him feel small.

'Now look, Eileen – you're beginning to sound like my wife!'

'I'm not surprised. Poor woman.'

Good God. Oh, good God. Jesus Jiminy Cricket Christ almighty. Don't say all *that* is going to start over again!

Arthur knew again the pains of the martyrs, and the burdens of the saints.

'What is it about women?' he asked indignantly. 'Do your mothers teach it to you, or what?'

'I hardly ever knew my mother, poor soul.'

'I didn't mean – ' He didn't either. Never bring family into it.

'She worked her fingers to the bone – and for what? For a life at the stove and the wash-tub and – oh, what's the use. She was

159

dead at forty-five. We've only got one life, Arthur.'

'That's no news,' he said, morose, sorry to have opened this particular can of worms. It looked as though they were going to have a fight.

'And I was content with mine,' she swept on. 'I didn't *think* about it, just accepted it. But you changed all that. You killed off my old life.'

'Blame, blame,' said poor Arthur, trying to roll his eyes.

She looked at him, and saw his dejection. No, this wasn't right. This wasn't what she meant. What they had, they had made together. And what they would have, they would make together. Even in argument, her heart never stayed long away from him. She knew she was the stronger, and knew that it was fear – and especially his fear of failure, of disappointment – which was keeping him down.

'No – I'm *glad* you did,' she told him. 'When you made love to me and – I don't know. I became very – I saw things differently. I just had to get away. I had to see something else – '

But she was looking around the tawdry little room again.

'Something more,' she said.

And then she stared at him, implacable and not imploring.

'I want nice things, Arthur.'

'And you'll have them, honey,' he said, worried.

What was she doing? Where was she going? Suppose she didn't come back? Sooner or later, he thought, she is not going to return.

What would he do without her? What could he do for her?

I want nice things, Arthur.

And you'll have them, honey.

She was looking at him too steadily. That old trick of hers.

'But I don't want to wait. There isn't time.'

'Don't say that!' he begged.

A premonition had entered the room, and she had let it in. He went cold inside. It was tapping him on the shoulder with a bony hand.

'No. There isn't,' she said. 'I *know* there isn't. Don't ask me how. I just *know*.'

Her saying this, and saying it with such conviction, was not the same to him as the ghoul or apparition or whatever it was that

160

had jumped out at him in the middle of the night. It was not so dramatically scaring. But he was deeper down troubled by her words. They did not gibber and gesticulate, but they did come out of some kind of darkness. There was a chill on them which he felt reaching into his bones. Tap-tap, on the shoulder. Tap-tap.

For he, too, sallow and unshaven, felt that time was running out. All he could do was sit there and watch it dwindle. *Tick-tock.*

But she wasn't. She was going out. Where? Why?

'What's happening?' he asked her in alarm. 'Where are you going?'

Eileen turned brightly about, her head over her shoulder.

'Are the seams of my stockings straight?'

She was showing him her legs. The sight of them cheered him up.

'You got terrific legs, baby!'

'Let's hope so!' she said, in a brittle throw-away.

She looked sexier, harder and falsely brighter. But she was also exuding danger. It hung in the stale air of this miserable little room with the weight and the pungency of the remains of the perfume she had drenched over herself. A smell which went into the back of his nose and throat. Like all excessive sweetness, it had a little of the stench of death about it.

I want nice things, Arthur.

And you'll have them, honey.

But I don't want to wait. There isn't time.

She had turned away again, satisfied that her seams were straight. Her face was set. Her lips as tight and as red as a slow wound.

'Hey – what are you going to do – Eileen!'

'Get some dough.'

Arthur had no doubt about how she was going to get it. The certainty hit him hard and fast, broadside on. She was going to sell her body.

She saw the effect of the blow, and hesitated.

'It doesn't *mean* anything, lovey-dovey,' she said, as soft as a purr, her language already preparing for trade.

She blew him a little kiss from a pursed red mouth and long red fingernails, as sweet and tart as her mother's apple pie.

161

Arthur was too slow to catch up with her as she closed the door. His remonstrances, in any case, would not make the slightest difference. The door would shut in his face.

He was alone, with his anxiety, his anger, and the bits and pieces of a jigsaw puzzle that, try as he might, he was still not able to fit together. A few important shapes must be missing. Either that, or Arthur was too confused by such a large and unbroken expanse of a sky which was not always blue.

26

This is not so much a chapter, as a hole in the narrative while Eileen Everson sells her body on the streets of Chicago.

'Who would read a novel if we were permitted to write biography all out?' asked a famous English writer in 1934, in the same year that these events were happening. He knew, and you know, that novels and similar entertainments and diversions, to claim no more for them than that which is probably the most valuable element they possess, are produced in an atmosphere of security (or calm manipulation) to enable the equally secure to pass the time in a reasonably refreshing or stimulating manner.

Eileen is standing on the sidewalk in the red-light district. She hesitates and then smiles as men pass and linger, their footsteps ringing on the stone, before scuffing in an apparently similar hesitation.

What if one could indeed write her biography – all out?

Well, then, we would have no more need to speculate about her character in this story. You and I could sit, so to speak, in her mind as she sees first this man and then that man approach, hesitate, speed up his walk or hang back with dark eyes brimming with the thought of sex.

Eileen needs the money. She can be bought for brief periods. We can see now, in our privileged position as we sit in her own personal theatre, that she also needs – just as urgently – to break with every scrap of the security, the established standards, the assumption, the *everything* which marked her old life on the farm and in the little school in Galena.

She has been too shaken up, and too much has happened to her, for her not to hunger for a new identity.

Every memory of her old life has become altered and contaminated. The past of each one of us is continually being adjusted and shifted around by what is now shaping us. We needs must keep altering, trimming, extending, freshly colouring, our own recollection of the past in order to keep up with ourselves in the present. Violent change violently alters everything prior to it.

Eileen needs more than the money. She wants the space.

'But I don't want to wait. There isn't time.'

The premonition that she had allowed to enter into the cheap room she shared with unshaven Arthur had not stayed behind when she left. It was following close behind her, and sometimes it jumped ahead of her, just like the way her shadow did when she neared and then passed the street lights. It had become her constant companion, though not her friend.

Listen, it was saying, if it ever spoke at all, *listen*. You have been changed beyond your own recognition of yourself. But it won't be for long. Look hard at everything around you, while you can. *It won't be for long.* See the glisten on the sugar crystals, feel the texture on the crust of your bread, taste the water on the back of your tongue, hear the sound of your shoes on the stone stair, catch the movement of people who scarcely know that they are mortal beings, too.

And accept what is unacceptable.

She was no longer afraid of Tom, the pimp, even though she did keep a wary eye and used a different district from the one small section he tried to control. She was no longer afraid of going to another cheap room in yet another cheap hotel with men she had never seen before. She never lowered her gaze in shame.

While they panted and laboured upon her naked body, she let her eyes roam around the walls and ceilings, tabulating the peeling paint, counting the patches of damp, and listening to the changes in the creaking rhythms of the bed springs.

While they talked filth at her, or sometimes stumbled out, in

163

surprise, their own ache, their own yearning, she simply set her face in the appropriate, paid-for response and continued to think her own thoughts.

She did not care a damn for anyone or anything else. Not any more. No one and nothing.

Except Arthur.

Sallow and unshaven and weak and disappointed Arthur. Brooding alone in the nasty little room above the noisy Elevated rail, a room which still had a bed hard up against a cracked wall, a table, two chairs, a wardrobe, a sink and a stove, but no Eileen in it breathing the emancipating fatalism which he mistook for a more highly developed brand of the confidence and optimism he recognized in the songs he loved.

It was this silly, soft dream of his which had brought them together, and that still drew her so strongly to him. The betrayals were now of little consequence. His disappointment did not matter too much. She was going to change all that.

'Would you like a nice time, honey?' Every time she said it, invitingly, to a stranger she was saying it to Arthur.

There is no need – and, in any case, no possibility – of describing 'all out' this section of Eileen's biography. It was a series of sordid encounters and degraded copulations, where she counted the money first, a dollar at a time. It was a descent into the nether land of the flesh, where all that is not tinted is irredeemably tainted.

And yet it did not seem to touch her.

This is why there is a hole in the narrative, and why the chapter is not a chapter. There is no possibility of representing the manner in which it is true to assert that what she did, day upon day or night upon night, had no effect upon her. She was changing herself, certainly, but by other means.

She would do anything to be what she now saw she *had* to be. The means did not matter by one grunt, gasp, or ejaculation – or many of them.

Anything goes! Music, maestro, please!

Here among the hookers clack-clacking their high-heeled patrol, a hard, fast, smack-eyed street dance would do better than words to get closer to Eileen. A clicking, precise, neon-lit beat to the insolently accurate words of the song.

164

ANYTHING GOES!

For Eileen had reversed the poles in her own mind, and stood everything from her past upon its head.

Except, perhaps, the odd line in the occasional fairy tale.

27

The evidence against Arthur was flimsily circumstantial. It had to be. He was not, after all, the man who had raped and murdered the blind girl in a field beyond the billboard advertising *Love Before Breakfast*. The fragments of human flesh and blood taken from the dead girl's fingernails would never match up with Arthur's. The semen taken from her ruptured vagina was not his – even if, at the time he first saw her walking so slowly towards him, he had at least considered the possibility of putting some of his own joy-juice (as Al called it) in precisely the same place.

The murderer was now at rest in a pauper's grave, partly paid for by the sale of the battered piano accordion he had left under the bed in the flop -house. Enough to pay for the mumbling priest but not the pine coffin.

And so, in reality, the police had nowhere to go in their hunt for the killer.

Popular imagination, however, had taken hold of things. The dead girl was both astonishingly beautiful and grievously afflicted. If she had been ugly, the matter would have been dropped much more quickly by all but the most local of news-papers. If she had been stone deaf, or if she had worn an iron leg-brace, her beauty would have had less significance. The column inches in the papers were measured in terms of human sentiment and not in obedience to cosmic injustices.

The result was that the public – or so the papers said – wanted the monster who had killed her to be caught and executed, with an intervening trial if possible, and a shoot-out if not.

The police had not delivered the goods. There was a lot of carping about their inadequacies in the public prints. The pressure was on them to make an arrest.

In these circumstances, flimsy evidence tends to harden very fast.

The lieutenant who had called upon Joan was one of those policemen, sometimes a danger to the public at large, who congratulate themselves on the nature and veracity of their intuitions. *Hunch* is the word they use to justify short cuts, planted evidence, perjury and every other undue process. And the lieutenant had persuaded himself that Arthur Parker was his man. I mean, as he said with a wink to his colleagues, a man who makes his wife put lipstick on her tits is capable of *anything*.

He was arguing the same kind of thing in a far more restrained tongue on the telephone as he called from Arthur's former home.

Joan had been as co-operative as he could have wished. She could see and feel little but her own humiliation and abandonment, and the reasons she gave the pleasant, sympathetic lieutenant were precisely the ones he wanted to coax out of her. That is, they were highly coloured and extremely tendentious accounts of his villainy, and, notably, his sexual excess. By the time she had finished, Arthur was indeed a lustful psychotic, ever touched in the head and perpetually hard in the loins.

'Look – ' he was saying on her telephone, 'there's enough to get an indictment. His shoe fits the print made at the scene. His fingerprints are on the cigarette pack found at the scene. He said he'd seen a message that night. He is on the run with a tramp . . .'

Joan was watching and listening with a martyred satisfaction which could not be wholly free of remorse and regret. She felt as though it had somehow gone way beyond any control or influence she might have had. True, she dearly wanted her treacherous husband to be caught and punished, but she was no longer sure for precisely what. Except, of course, the crime against her.

The lieutenant had touched her elbow in order to comfort her. She smiled back, a little anxiously.

But, listening to him now, on the telephone, and watching his face darken, she had the unsettling feeling that she was falling away from the endless drama that was Arthur like a minor character in a black-and-white movie.

The kind of film which Joan liked allowed you to cry and yet also be pleased. In the same way, she wanted Arthur to be caught and punished, but at the back of her mind there were still remnants or glimmers of the assumption that he would then, somehow, be returned to her, as good as new, and better than of old.

That sort of movie let you have your cake and eat it.

It was exactly such entertainment that Eileen and Arthur were now watching in a movie theatre a few miles away in the heart of the city.

The second feature was rolling towards its end with an old Hollywood confidence about engaging the interest and emotions of audiences for precisely as long as the reels of film in the projection room at the back.

Arthur and Eileen, so much sprucer, sleeker, better dressed, were raptly absorbed in the tale set out before them. They were holding hands.

Lovers had good reason to like the magical caves of the Biograph, the Roxy, or whatever. There was a soft darkness immediately around them, and everyone's attention directed elsewhere. Blue cigarette smoke coils in lazy, drifting layers into the multi-stranded and ever-flickering projection beam. And, above all, there is the story up on the big white screen, where a kiss comes after a tear, and the good (but not too good) get away with everything.

The movie they were watching had been specifically made to dampen cheeks with easy tears. The makers had not gone so far as to let a pet horse drop dead with exhaustion on the lawn of a house being repossessed by the broker's men, right in the middle of a birthday party for a sweet little girl who had just begun to speak again after the trauma of saving the wicked landlord's sister from drowning. They had not gone quite as far as this, no, but what they *had* done was even better.

The tired usherette in the aisle was about the only one not

moved. Her feet ached. Not quite enough compensation for being in the movie business.

When the final credits began to roll, showing that guilty men were not afraid to accept attribution for their share in the story, Eileen was as close to tears as she now allowed herself.

'That was good!' she said, nestling up to Arthur. 'It made me want to cry.'

It was the duty of men in these situations to pretend that they, of course, had no lump in the throat because of such nonsense.

'How can it be good if it makes you cry?' Arthur duly laughed, squeezing her hand, and wanting to kiss her eyelids.

Eileen dabbed at her eyes. It had been good to submit to the celluloid characters on the screen. The catharsis was a minor one, but it had its uses.

'Oh, I like a weepie,' she affirmed.

'Naw!' said Arthur with conviction. 'Can't beat a good musical!'

Fred Astaire and Ginger Rogers. That's what they had come to see in their new car. The main feature.

In their new car. In their new clothes. To see a musical.

Me? No chance! I'll tell you guys something! Everybody who has ever lived in the entire history of these here United States would wanna be me if'n they only knew what I felt like inside.

What's wrong, Arthur?

You just can't begin to see what a fantastic world it is we live in. No – c'mon! Get your goddamn chins up off the floor! Beautiful! It is! Shining, the whole darn place, shining! Can't you see it? Don't you feel it?

What's wrong, Arthur?

In your new car. In your new clothes. To see a musical.

What's wrong, Arthur?

Everything I've ever – everything I've ever dreamed, hoped for, longed for, deep inside me, here in my heart, everything! Years and years I didn't really know what I was selling. The songs! What they are all about! The way they do – really do – tell the truth, the honest to God truth. And they do! They do! Goddamn it, they do!

WHAT'S WRONG, ARTHUR?

Somewhere the sun is shining. And do you know where? Inside! Inside yourself. Inside your own head – in the spaces in between!

168

That's where the blue and gold is. On the other side of the black!

But what's wrong, Arthur?

'Naw!' he said, vaguely wistful. 'Can't beat a good musical!'

Eileen looked sideways at him, smiling with a tender affection, and squeezing his hand.

'You want to be a song-and-dance man, Arthur?'

'Oh, but I am,' he said at once, with a rueful grin. 'Inside, I am!'

And that was the truth of it. Inside, he was. His faith had been preserved, more or less intact. Whenever the song ended, the melody lingered on.

'No regrets, darling?' Eileen asked him.

'What do *you* think?' he answered, moved.

'We can start to live a little,' she whispered. 'I'll take care of you, my love.'

Arthur looked, then, at Eileen with his old sense of wonder. She was so beautiful, especially in the cinema light. Her eyes were glistening, and her lips were slightly parted. He did not know how it was that he had ever managed to get her, and, more, to keep hold of her. In the night, when she turned sleepily into him, he was entranced. In the morning, as she laughingly pinched and punched him, he was still entranced.

How warm, how marvellous a thing it was, he felt, when she bit the lobe of his ear and whispered that she would take care of him!

'Yeah – that's what I don't understand,' he admitted. 'You could have *anybody*.'

She laughed, in a brazen gurgle.

'I do have anybody!'

And although he thought that she had said it too loudly, so that people turned their heads, he laughed too. Perhaps a little uneasily.

The big picture was about to begin, and the lights dipped. If he looked up, he would be able to see where the blue and the gold was. On the other side of the black. Or this side of the titles.

Meanwhile, almost exactly as in the plot of the good bad movie they had just seen, with an aptness that could be said to owe more to economy than to confidence, the miniature idyll in the movie theatre was being interrupted by the rolling presses of the newspaper business.

Big black headlines were falling in their thousands on top of each other as the presses spat out the news.

CHICAGO SONG SALESMAN HUNTED IN BLIND GIRL MURDER

Arthur had insisted – without much resistance – on sitting through it all again. Newsreel. Weepy. Fred and Ginger. Why not? There wasn't enough magic around to turn up the chance of spreading it on another slice.

In the gleaming dark, Eileen watched him without him knowing it. A musical number was just concluding, leaping out of the narrative with an astonishing exuberance. Arthur's face was alive with the sheer joy of it all. His eyes were fixed with the utmost attention on the screen. She was pleased, and a little amused, by the extent of his rapture, and leaned in to kiss him.

For once, he scarcely noticed. His eyes never left the screen.

She, too, looked at the picture and enjoyed herself in her own cooler fashion. But she kept darting glances at him, to share his pleasure, and also to monitor it. He was like a kid with a candy bar.

Gradually, though, the very intensity of his attention, the joy on his face, moved something very deep down inside her. She hesitated to interrupt, but then leaned in to him in order to whisper.

'I'd like that baby one day!' she said. 'I'd like to have that baby. And then . . .

She stopped, thinking that he was too absorbed to pay attention to what she had surprised herself in saying. She stopped, also, because her throat had tightened, and it was not possible to finish the sentence. Eileen did not know where it would lead.

Up there on the screen, they were easing themselves towards yet another song and dance. She needed the same uncomplicated transition if she were to get the words out. The trouble is, she did not know what the words were going to be.

Arthur *had* heard. He was only momentarily distracted by the dialogue cues for the obviously forthcoming number.

'And then what?' he turned to her.

'I don't know.'

He wanted to look at the screen again, but then was surprised to see the strain on her face. He made himself pay attention.

'Come on,' he said. 'What were you going to say?'

She did not know why the idea of the baby, and the fate of the child she had so briefly carried, had come back at her in such a swift and poignant manner. Eileen had thought herself especially skilled in destroying inside herself (in this case quite literally) the fruits of her former life. She had resolutely turned her back on the days before yesterday.

Arthur was dismayed to see the threat of tears.

'Hey!' he protested, a little frightened. 'You're not going to cry. Are you?'

Unable to speak for a moment, she was nevertheless able to smile a 'No', but her eyes were dangerously moist. She knew now, if she didn't know before, that you could not kill off the yearning inside yourself. There was still a high tower without a door from which she had to escape. And even while remaining locked away inside it, there were still consequences to face . . .

Fred Astaire was at the introduction to *Let's Face the Music and Dance*.

The music swirled around them, but they were looking at each other, troubled, and not at the screen.

'Listen,' said Arthur, sensing the surge of pain in her. 'There's gotta be *something* on the other side of the rainbow.'

'There always is,' she whispered, as her eyes at last brimmed over with tears.

Arthur groped for her hand as the song burst over them. He could not bear to see her so upset. They clutched at each other in the cinema darkness, and, as if by consent, for confirmation rather than comfort, let the cruelly appropriate song speak for them. The first time round, Arthur had heard it without turning a hair. He had enjoyed its accomplished theatricality.

Looking for relief, and trying to shut out the renewed sense of menace and doom which the real world had once more revealed to him, he tried to enter again into his former enjoyment of Fred Astaire and Ginger Rogers in the number on the screen.

Let's Face the Music and Dance.

In his imagination, now, seeking to be assuaged, Arthur was up there on the flickering and shimmering screen. A great song-and-dance man. He was Fred Astaire. And, yes, Ginger had turned into Eileen. They swirled together about the shining set, without a care in the world; or rather, determined to ignore the cares of the world now that they were in their dancing shoes.

Was it possible to escape this fantasy? Could they not thus hold back his fear and her tears?

Let's Face the Music and Dance?

In the set which was not a set, on the screen which was not a screen, the anxious mind had its own way of subverting the dance. Chorus lines of male dancers in top hats, white ties and tails were tapping their sticks in ominous precision on the shiny floor, the dreaming mind. Arthur shifted in his seat, seeing 'Arthur' threatened.

In their dance which was not a dance, the choreography of their thoughts, Arthur and Eileen were being surrounded by the male dancers and their sticks. They were both puzzled, and their movements slowed as they clung together. And when the top-hatted dancers disappeared, the sticks stayed where they had been left, upright on the gleamingly polished floor.

Sticks which became like huge prison bars tightly surrounding a miniature Arthur and Eileen. He looked across at her in the strange light of the movie theatre, the projection beam switching and thickening in its smoke-laden shaft above them.

They watched the remainder of the film in silence, holding hands very tightly.

28

People coming out of the movies often blink with a small variant of astonishment at what they take to be the change of light in the street outside. It is just as likely that the real reason lies in the transition of their mood from the neat, topped-and-tailed make-believe they have just enjoyed into the less satisfactorily shaped, far more complex and intransigent realities of the world beyond the screen, and their lives in it.

Thus, it takes a few blocks of walking for the dangle-fingered, loosely alert expression, and gun-fighter lope to disappear completely from the stride of many a young man who has just seen a Western. Coming out of the movies, a man can jut his jaw or square his shoulders, and a woman can turn her head with a celluloid delicacy, stars spangled upon her.

Sometimes.

Just as often, alas, the smack of the outside is delivered so swiftly that all but a trace of what has just been seen in the movie house is instantly swamped. The pimpled youth knows too quickly that he would run from an ambling cow if it had an even passably curled horn. And a man cannot easily square his shoulders if they are already sloping with the worries he took in with him.

As Arthur and Eileen came out in the jostling throng, they could see that it was drizzling with rain. They had gone into the theatre in bright daylight, but now it was dark and miserably overcast, in that urban depression where the sky sits on top of gloomy buildings and weeps in wretchedness.

The short horizon had smudged into itself.

Arthur looked at the lowering sky, and screwed up his face in rueful dismay.

' 'S always the same!'

'What is?'

Eileen was subdued, and not looking around. Her eyes were cast downwards, but she was not searching for lost coins or old tickets.

'When you come out of the movies,' he complained, 'the world has changed! Goddamn rain.'

When you come out of the movies, that is, the world has *not* changed.

But she would have known exactly what he meant – if she had listened with a full attention. An odd warning was swelling up inside her abstractedness. Eileen was watching a truck driving past, tossing out bales of newspapers. It was as though the act had enormous significance for her.

She felt that it was the opening fusillade in a barrage of events she had already lived through. Premonition, or precognition, was galloping fast towards her. She touched Arthur's arm, and indicated, without words, that he should buy a newspaper.

Puzzled by her manner, by the tenseness around her, Arthur did as he was commanded. He glanced quickly at the folded front page, and the screaming jumble of black print settled with an abrupt jolt. The colour drained from his face and the air was knocked out of his chest.

'Jesus Jiminy Cricket Christ almighty!' he gasped.

And then, as she closed on him, eyes widening –

'I'm going to be sick – Oh, God! Eileen!'

The deadly combination of fear and shock and total incredulity did not so paralyse him that he was unable to reach their brand-new car, parked along the street. Arthur could not see anything as the electricity of horrified astonishment burned into him, but some still active sense made him act to get away. His mind could only register the urgent, the paramount need to escape. To run! To *run*!

He started the car as though it were the classic get-away vehicle in a bank heist. It bombed away in an aggressive stop-me-if-you-dare snarl through the congested streets of the city, his hands gripping the steering wheel so tightly that his knuckles whitened.

Eileen, badly shaken, had taken the newspaper and stared at the front page as the automobile swerved, jerked, rushed and tooted a dangerous path through the traffic.

CHICAGO SONG SALESMAN HUNTED IN BLIND GIRL MURDER.

Black scream above a photograph.

A photograph of Arthur! A grinning Arthur!

They were clear of the wider streets and the brighter lights, and already the outer limbs of industrial Chicago had tightened in around them. Only now could Arthur pay any kind of attention to anything other than the imperative shriek in his head to get away from the city centre. The place of maximum danger. One big identity parade.

174

He became aware of Eileen in the car beside him. She was staring at him, holding the newspaper, an odd light in her eyes.

CHICAGO SONG SALESMAN HUNTED IN BLIND GIRL MURDER.

'You don't think I did it!'

Eileen studied him a long moment. Was there doubt in her eyes? Could she possibly imagine even for a fraction of a second that he went around killing blind girls? He was aghast.

'No,' she said, at last, and with blessed conviction. 'You couldn't.'

Her very avowal of his innocence had the opposite effect upon him to the relief he should have felt. Paradoxically, it threw into even more ominous detail the question of his presumed guilt. The panic which had provided him with the blind impulse to get away, and thus to do something urgent and mechanical, now tore at him with worse claws. And there was nothing he could do.

'What'll I do?' he croaked.

Eileen did not answer, because she had no idea what she should say. Instead, she bit her lower lip, pensive. The run-down decaying landscape scudding at her through the car windows gave her no clues. It had no human dimensions.

'Eileen!' he exclaimed, demanding her attention, begging for an answer. He could not think. He wanted to be told what to do. The black headline had reduced him to a helpless quiver in which the dread was so overwhelming that it made him think he really was guilty. Maybe it was all his fault.

Do you need somebody to walk with you, miss? It'd be a great honour.

That's very kind. But – no. Thank you!

But you ain't got a stick! The ground is very rough, miss. It's not safe!

It's not safe! My God, how right he had been.

Not safe – not safe – not – safe – not safe hammered out in his brain. He was in appalling danger. They would snap his neck at the bone.

'Go to the police . . .' Eileen said, but too tentatively.

'Are you crazy!' he yelled.

'But you're innocent, and – '

'They'll hang me!' he half sobbed back at her, already imagining the hood and the noose and the swing of his choked carcass below the trap door. 'I gotta get away!'

He hadn't got a stick, and the ground was very rough. He couldn't see, and he did not know where to go.

I gotta get away!

'Where to?' she asked him, her reason asserting itself, the steady calm characteristic of her back in her eyes and her voice.

'What?' he asked, too confused, too frightened, to register any sort of question which demanded thought and motive from him. He had no idea at all where the car was going, except that it had to keep going. At all costs, he had to keep running.

The hood. The noose. The slow swing of his dead body at the end of the rope.

The steps up to the gallows.

And what about his Adam's apple? Suppose it got sort of caught in the knot of the rope, or – after all, when he swallowed, when he gulped with fear, as he surely would, his Adam's apple went up and down. Like an elevator.

'Where to?' said Eileen.

So what if it went up and down as they put the rope around his neck? Suppose, oh dear Christ, it somehow slipped under the knot at the very moment they pulled the lever and the trap door lurched open at his feet? Then he wouldn't hang properly, would he? He would be slowly strangled, and his feet would be dancing the wrong kind of dance. A quickstep in mid-air.

Suppose they – suppose . . .

'Arthur,' she was saying, firmly. 'Where are we going?'

He heard, but he did not answer. The panic was growing all the time, worse and worse. His head and his eyes and his hands were hot. His limbs were clammy. He did not know whether to sweat or shiver. In fact, he was doing both.

The gallows loomed in black silhouette.

Arthur slammed on the brakes, as though trying to put his foot through the floor.

Eileen jolted forward as the car skidded to a violent stop on a beat-up stretch of road in the middle of weird industrial desolation. She thought they had hit something, or been hit.

'A cat,' he mumbled shakily, the dank inner fear coming up into his dried mouth.

Better than the gallows. Better a cat that wasn't there than gallows which were.

'A cat . . .'

'What – ?' she gasped, shaken. 'Arthur – ?'

'There was a cat. Ran across in front of – ' his voice fell away into a sick mumble again. 'A cat. Black cat.'

'I didn't see it,' she said, looking at him, and beginning to hate his fear.

He took no notice. He was staring ahead with horror, seeing the steps of the gallows, and himself climbing them.

'Maybe it was a rat,' she added, sardonic. What could she do to jolt him out of it, to make him think straight, to act like a man?

Arthur put his hands to his face. It was wet with sweat. The terror was so bad now that it threatened to make him incontinent. It was like the last few minutes before the execution. He could sense with an awful certainty what was going to happen to him. Everything in his life, he could see now, everything had all the time been pointing forward to this inevitable end, this dark injustice and cruel terror. There was nowhere to go to escape it. There was no hiding place.

The ghastly apparition with the gesticulating arms and humped back which had jumped out of the night at him had carried a message, after all.

'I gotta be good!' he had sobbed out to Joan on his return. But it was too late. He had been bad too long. It was already too late. His goose was cooked, and basted with sizzling hot fat.

I'd cut off my right arm if I could make you see again. I'd – I don't know what I'd do if I could – if I could . . . If I could get into your pants.

His hands were at his face. And his face was wet with his own clammy fear.

'I'm scared, Eileen,' he said, in a helpless appeal.

She did not answer. She was looking at him, and her expression was hardening.

Arthur dragged his hands away from his face and held them in front of him as objects of terror in themselves. He stared at his hands like a crazed man. They were shaking badly.

'Can you drive?' Eileen demanded, in a brisk, no-nonsense voice.

What the hell were they doing, sitting here in the car in the middle of an industrial nowhere, polluted with grey decay?

'They'll hang me,' was all he would say, his words hollowed out. 'They're gonna hang me. They're gonna hang me. I know it.'

'Stop that!' she said severely. 'Stop it, you hear!'

'They'll string me up!' he screamed in hysteria. 'Don't you understand!'

Eileen examined him, as calmly and as objectively as she could. His breath was coming in shuddering gasps like a drowning man. His eyes were points of cold fear, obviously seeing nothing except the shapes of dread. It was clear to her that nothing she could say, no words, would cut through such an animal terror. Might as well reason with a rolling-eyed horse when the stable is on fire, or seek to reassure a hog at the slaughterhouse when it has smelt the butcher and seen the knife.

She had to do something much more dramatic than just speak to him. He had to be jolted back into self-control.

Eileen got out of the car.

She said nothing to him, but with abrupt deliberation opened the door and got out into the night.

As she closed the door she looked at him with what seemed to be a cruel contempt. 'See you, big boy,' she said, harshly. She could not quite manage the final gesture of brutal dismissal, however, and hesitated slightly before she closed the door.

Arthur did not even seem to notice, neither her leaving, her harsh valedictory dismissal, nor her minuscule hesitation. The fear had exploded inside him. She shrugged, and closed the car door.

'I always knew something terrible was coming to me,' he mumbled, as though she were still sitting beside him. 'All my life I've been waiting for – '

His words sank back down into his fear. He was astonished to see Eileen in front of the car. She was walking slowly ahead of it, her shadow elongated and thrown forward in black aggrandizement by the headlights he had left burning.

'Eileen,' he said to himself, bewildered. For a moment, he thought he was hallucinating. He could not work out what she was doing, walking ahead of the car when he had assumed she was sitting with him inside it.

He did not even know why the car was not moving.

'Eileen?'

And then anger flooded over him, as she had hoped it would. She was out of the car and walking away from it because she was abandoning him! She was leaving him to stew in his own rancid juices! The bitch!

Enraged, Arthur pressed the hooter.

Parp! Pa-aa-aarp!

Eileen, her back to the car, stopped walking. She and her shadow waited.

She and not her shadow smiled faintly, with relief.

She could hear Arthur running up behind her, the headlights lurching and bumping his shadow towards her. Eileen did not turn. And when he caught up with her, the two of them were thrown by the car light and the dark into a vivid, dramatic chiaroscuro, especially when the shadowed man grabbed the shadowed woman by the shoulders and whirled her round into the pool of light to face him.

'Are you running out on me, you bitch!' he spouted out at her.

Eileen did not move a muscle. She stared back evenly at him, expressionless, facing down his rage.

'Well – it's no fun, is it?' she said in her special flat voice. 'No laughs.'

Arthur was completely thrown. No fun? No laughs? Was that what it was supposed to be about?

He gaped at her, so nonplussed that he could not keep his lips together.

'But – but – don't you love me?' he spluttered.

In return, and not as he expected, Eileen gave him a brittle little laugh. A sound that seemed to occupy that miserably confined space between boredom and sarcasm.

'That question – ' she said.

'Wh – what about it?'

'What do you want me to say?' she asked in the equivalent of a shrug, being as callous, or as coldly indifferent, as she knew how.

'But – *do* you? Eileen?' he pleaded. Oh, God, this was terrible. Please God, this couldn't be happening.

She was giving him that steady, cold fish-eyed look again, and it made him quake in his shoes.

'*Not when you are so scared.*'

The crisp emphasis of it shook him even more. His mouth sagged again as the implications rammed home.

'But – listen – you mean – you'll only stick by me if I keep smiling?' he gulped out his incredulity. 'Even with the rope around my neck?'

Let's Face the Music and Dance? But what sort of music, what sort of dance? A prison dirge and a mid-air tap-dance?

Eileen wanted him to understand something. It was not an easy thing to understand, because she did not wholly comprehend it herself. But that had not prevented her from accepting it. Everything that had happened to her since she had innocently wandered into Barret's music store in Galena to ask for part-songs for the children's choir, the whole process of action and reaction, desire and betrayal, joy and punishment, had led her into this acceptance. She had made herself strong because of it, and she knew she could endure anything since it had come upon her. And now she wanted Arthur, whom she loved, passionately loved, to see it too.

She put it in the simplest terms possible.

'We've only got one life, Arthur,' she said, matter-of-fact. 'We both know we've made a mess of ours. It doesn't seem to matter much how it ends. Does it?'

Arthur was puzzled, and he was scared. The bleak implacability of the proposition was against his nature. He was a child in this, forever wanting to be assured that there was always icing on the cake, and cherries on the bough.

'Doesn't it?' he asked, numbly.

Eileen waited. She let him stare at her.

'No,' she said.

Arthur took it all in, her word, her expression. He saw with relief how hard and strong she was.

'You're a – what they call it – ? A *fatalist*, right?' he said, touched by awe.

'That's the only word that's left, lover,' she smiled, sardonic now that he nearly understood.

Arthur took hold of her hand. He lifted it in a truly humble caress to his lips. She was a princess, and he was the croaking frog by the sedge-layered pond who had been turned back into the

180

prince of his own different dream. He wanted to acknowledge her strength, and take some of it for himself.

Eileen had won. He had lost his hysteria. He was calm, now.

'I love you,' he whispered. The awe had not disappeared.

'Yes.'

'I want you,' he then said, with a quiet intensity.

She looked at him, eyes softening.

'I want you now,' he said.

'What?' she whispered. 'Here?'

And so the handsome Prince stepped out from the trees and looked up at the tiny window at the top of the tall, tall tower that had no door. 'Rapunzel! Rapunzel!' he called. 'Let down your hair!' And thinking it was the old witch, Rapunzel let down her hair. Long, shining, golden hair all the way down, down, down to the ground. And. And then –

The Prince climbed up!

Just as he had seen the old witch do! But when he came to the window, Rapunzel stepped back in fear. Oh, my, she was scared! She had never seen a man before!

There was tittering at the back of the class.

Yes – some of you boys can laugh! But, his face was so nice, his eyes were so kind, his voice was so gentle, that she . . .

'What?' she whispered. 'Here?'

Arthur laughed a hard little laugh, but he did not break the spell, nor want to.

'It's the only way I can keep going,' he said. 'Besides – we ain't never done it in a car. Have we?'

Eileen found the resurgence of the old Arthur, and his rapid shift from tender humility to raunchy adventurism, intolerably moving. It was part of what made her love him, and yearn for him. She had always, with him, seen her body as her gift to him, and the pleasure he got from it, and in it, was at least as great a pleasure to her. And then her body became her own gift to herself, just as his did to himself.

'We must be crazy,' she said, her voice breaking.

They stared into each other, grappling for the centre of each other with their eyes, only their eyes. Hers began to sheen with tears. A slow freight train clack-clacked beyond them, threading its burdened way through a sleazy urban nowhere, as desolate as an abandoned planet on the cold side of the sun.

Suddenly, and violently, mutually locked in their own emotion, their own urgent need, they plunged into each other's arms, and clung together for dear life. The car headlights made them seem one person, not two. One human being swathed in a small beam and a long shadow.

The cumbersome, slowly clanking freight train let out a sharp and plangent whistle, like a cry in the night.

Arthur and Eileen spent the rest of the night in the car at the place where they had left it. This was partly because they did not know anywhere else to go, and his feverish desire to escape, blindly, had subsided. But it was mostly because they could not wait to make love to each other.

'Besides – we ain't never done it in a car. Have we?'

They had now. They had loved each other with a passion so urgent, so generous and yet so tenderly laced with a soft and subdued grief that it was as though they knew they would never be allowed to touch each other ever again. They were cramped for space, sometimes in a way that made them laugh, and they were cramped for time: future time.

Eileen, especially, and in a sadness that wrenched her soul even as she cried out in physical abandonment, sensed beyond sense that this was the last time Arthur would ever enter her.

He had not put it that way to himself, but the urgency, and the alternating tenderness, the almost angry thrusting so that her head all but banged against the car door, and then the slow, stroking, murmuring wonder, seemed to convey the same order of knowledge.

Nobody disturbed them. No other vehicle passed them in the night. Only an occasional freight train clacked along on the rusted iron bridge beyond and above them. They had stopped, by accident and not design, in the midst of an empty, blighted and redundant sprawl.

Theirs was the only human passion in half a dozen poisoned acres of human waste.

29

Morning came in a clear sallow light which scarcely bothered to burnish a landscape that was far too run down to be ever again gilded. Arthur and Eileen, uncoiling themselves from each other's cramped and awkward sleep, discovered that their limbs ached, their problems had not disappeared, and that they were hungry.

Arthur was also in the middle of finding out that he could not start their splendid new car. It was coughing and spluttering like an asthmatic old man on a cold and foggy morning. Too geriatric a distress for such a smart new auto.

'Come on – come on!' Arthur angrily urged the stubborn vehicle, but the car refused to turn over.

He glared at it as though it were a living creature, and the pointless ferocity of his expression made a rumpled Eileen start to laugh.

'A bargain, he said. Best car on the lot, he said. I tell you, Eileen, salesmen got no goddamn morals!'

Her laughter was making him act up for her benefit. Oh, wouldn't it be lovely if there were nothing dreadful hanging over them! They were surely born to laugh and act the fool like this on a clear morning with nowhere special to go. Arthur consciously pushed away the first cold fingers of a renewed terror – CHICAGO SONG SALESMAN HUNTED IN BLIND GIRL MURDER – and addressed himself to the intransigent automobile. Perhaps the battery was flat.

'Any idea where we are?' Eileen asked, as though it were a matter of absolutely no consequence.

'In the middle of nothing,' he snorted. 'Just where I always wanted to be.'

She laughed, and looked about. It certainly *did* look to be in the middle of nothing. The very epitome of an urban nowhere, of the kind to be seen on the fringes of many a large industrial city.

'Well, we'll just have to stay here,' she said cheerfully. 'We'll stay here until they find us.'

Arthur didn't like that so much. It was not the kind of remark which he considered to be at all goddamn cheerful. Why'd she say *that*!

He violently kicked the car's front tyre and the effect was comic. He hurt his toe in doing so, and, as her laughter pealed out, he hopped on one leg, holding his injured foot.

'Goddamn car!' he shouted at it, jigging up and down with an exaggerated pain.

'Kick it again, Arthur. It didn't hear you!'

Everything was so ridiculous that the clown in Arthur rose to the occasion – or, rather, hopped to it. Holding his foot, he bounced up and down on the spot, warbling with an almost manic glee which (she knew) hid the hysteria that was again threatening to rise and grab hold of him.

'Champagne doesn't thrill me at all,' he yelled, well over the top, 'but I get a kick out of you!'

Holding his foot in his hand, he suddenly froze.

'Arthur – ?' she asked, fear flying up.

A pair of police motorcycles had come into view. They stopped. Perhaps the riders simply wanted to help out, probably they were just curious, as is their way. But whatever the reason – and they naturally claimed later, that it was because they were good and alert cops – one of them got off his motorcycle and began to amble in a Chicago police slouch towards the still ridiculously one-legged Arthur.

And as he approached, Arthur's nerve cracked. He could see the cop staring at him with a puzzled first glimmer of recognition.

Arthur turned, and fled. Arms and legs going like pistons.

The policeman was very startled. But if there is one thing a cop knows absolutely for damned sure (and he will, of course, insist that there are many things) it is that a man who runs when you approach him has been up to no damned good. The wad of gum stopped shifting about in his mouth, and his hand went down automatically to his holster.

'Wait!' he yelled.

Eileen could see that he was going to pull his gun.

'Arthur!' she yelled, fearing for his life.

But Arthur was going hell for leather towards the nearest cover. He was running as though all the hounds in the world were

184

snarling at his feet, and the breath was pumping out of him in sobbing gasps of panic and desperation. The cop took after him, followed by his companion. The chase was on.

It did not last very long. Arthur was far too frightened to demonstrate any skill in evasion. He had hurtled into some kind of factory yard, full of rusted and discarded junk, and found himself at a dead end. There was a high wall in front of him, and the cops behind him. They had drawn their guns, and, scrabble as he might at the elderly brickwork, there was no place for him to go.

Arthur turned to face his pursuers. He raised his hands. He knew his song was winding down now towards its end.

'I'm innocent! I'm innocent!' he cried. 'I wouldn't hurt a fly!'

But when they snapped the metal cuffs on his wrists, Arthur fell silent. All at once, and with a determination rare to him, he decided that he was not going to say another word. They were taking him away from Eileen, and he was not going to speak until they could be joined again.

30

Bad news sells papers. And so do accounts of murder trials, especially when the defendant is likely to be executed. The verdict is awaited with a degree of interest almost exactly proportionate to the horror and degradation of the crime it allegedly wipes from the books of justice.

The blind girl had come alive again in the courtroom.

She was, apparently, a paragon of all the virtues. One witness went so far as to call her a saint, and was not rebuked. She had possessed a remarkable beauty, and had been greatly beloved by her elderly parents and all who knew her. Her courage in overcoming her sightlessness was a beacon to set before others. She had learned to do most things tolerably well, and some things exceptionally well. Amy Farr – as she was called – had even learnt how to walk across the fields of her father's farm, alone and unaided.

Who had stumbled upon her on one of her walks?

Arthur said little, attempting to keep his vow, but he did, in the unwisdom of his fear, deny that he had ever been in that field, or ever seen her. And he did deny that he had been anywhere *near* the field on that fatal day. No, no, he was someplace else altogether. Never went near the place!

Exhibit A was the perfect cast of his footprint. Exhibit B was the pack of Lucky Strike, covered with his fingerprints. Exhibit C the gum-chewing cop's notebook, complete with the number of Arthur's old car.

It was after this that Arthur finally clamped shut his jaws. He waited for the inevitable.

Contradictions and holes in the evidence were not met by competent counter-argument. A lattice of circumstance was bent and shaped to fit the lethally compelling case for the prosecution. All the lies, adulteries, casual fornications and crude little dishonesties which had littered and splattered the accused's previous life were diligently excavated and brilliantly presented.

Arthur remained silent. He just pursed his lips and shook his head. What could they know of him, these people?

He had always told what he considered to be little white lies. He had always exaggerated a little bit here, and a little bit there, putting himself up in order to get by. Life was tough enough as it was, and there was no point making it even harder for yourself by always telling the truth, always sticking to the rules.

It wasn't him who had made these so-called rules. Somebody had built the maze – and built it with great cunning, devilishly so – and people like Arthur were the poor blind rats made to scurry and claw up and down an apparently endless series of dead-ends and blocked-off alleys. Were you supposed to be a good little rat and accept your plight, squeaking a rodentine thank you at each false opening in the maze? Well, he wasn't going to make these pathetic little squeals of gratitude. Drop dead! Take a powder! Leave me alone!

And as for all these so-called fornications – the hell.

186

Here you are, trapped in the maze, thrown little rewards to nibble on now and then, and all the time you have this – um – this equipment, right? You have these *urges*. You accept that? Look at those sawdust faces on the jury: don't they ever screw, or leer, or crack a dirty joke, or surreptitiously rub their knee up against a lady's leg?

O.K. So they say it's dirty. Filthy. Who's *they*, for God's sakes!

Sometimes when out on the road, in the years of selling song sheets in East goddamn Central goddamn Illinois to dumb goddamn storekeepers with corn syrup coming out of their goddamn ears, he had bought a woman a few drinks in a no-good bar or worse roadhouse and then made his car's springs rock and creak with a little back-seat activity.

It had not been very good, but it hadn't always been all that bad either.

There was powder on your vest, and cheap perfume bought by the gallon lingering on your clothes, so that you were almost too scared to go home. And when you came, it was no big deal. You weren't shooting out paradise, or anything like. It helped you keep in touch with something you wanted . . .

What did they know of him, what did they care about his needs and his yearnings?

Sex was just 'all that stuff' to Joan. A furtive wrestle over and done with in a couple of minutes to a few of the others he had had. He, too, had felt repelled and attracted by his physical desires – or, rather, their consequences. But beer and baseball and the roadhouse pin-tables were not adequate substitutes.

A hurried grope with a powdered whore was not what he was about, either – but if you closed your eyes, if you seized the moment, even this would do on a lonely wet night in a little town in the middle of the flat lands.

It was the same with the lipstick on the nipples.

He didn't want to humiliate his wife. It was she who chose to humiliate herself. He wanted to turn sex into a thing of wit and fun, rather than the standard humping and heaving, bumping and grinding, with the light out. Vivid red nipples. Black underwear. Silky things. He couldn't for the life of him see what was so very wrong in all that. Didn't you put salt on your food, and cherries on your cake? To aid the appetite, right?

He had never been able to explain it to anyone. His buddies turned it into a dirty joke, and cracked walnuts with their eyelids. His wife had thought him some sort of depraved monster. But he didn't feel it was a snickering, sniggering thing at all. He was awed by the power of it, and knew, dimly, that people had blocked it off, subdued and subverted it, and used it to sell anything and everything except the human spirit and the human imagination. *His* spirit. *His* imagination.

No, he had never been able to explain it to anyone.

Until he had met Eileen Everson. And then – glory be! – he had not found it *necessary* to explain it.

Whether it was the way she understood his story about the couple in the hotel elevator, or the manner in which she slightly opened her mouth when he kissed her, or the clench of her legs when under him, she was the woman who made *him* understand what it was he had never been able to explain to anybody.

He had come up behind her under the trees, and when she had turned in alarm he had said, without design, that it was like the song, and songs told the truth, songs did.

CHICAGO SONG SALESMAN GOES BANANAS.

Arthur was now prepared to concede that to more sophisticated eyes he was, not to put too fine a point on it, *nuts*.

He had not heard the exchange between sad Mr Warner and Eileen in her classroom at one of the low points of her life. She did not discuss such things. He never had access to her thoughts about the past.

'These children. Look – here is a tree one of them has drawn. And it's like a diamond. With different kinds of fruit on the same branch. A tree out of the Garden of Eden. That's how they see things, you know. I think they really do see things in a way that – in a way that they eventually lose. Not only lose, but forget they ever had.'

'Yes. So why do you – ?'

'You were going to ask – why, if I understand *that*, why do I *hit* them so often?'

'Yes.'

'So that they can learn enough to bend their backs in the fields, Miss Everson, or endure the wearing out of their bodies and their spirits on the assembly line. What do they want with visions, or trees shaped like diamonds? Or any memory at all of the Garden of Eden? Cheap music will do. Cheap music. And beer. And baseball.'

He had not heard it then, but variants of it had been in the very air he breathed. Eileen understood that Arthur, after his fashion, and deeply flawed as he was by his own compromises and evasions, nevertheless retained what Warner called 'some memory of the Garden of Eden'. His trees, too, were sometimes shaped like diamonds.

CHICAGO SONG SALESMAN FINDS GOD.

No, it wasn't quite as bad as that. Jeez-us Jiminy Cricket Christ almighty! Arthur would have considered himself very insulted if such a thing had even been *whispered* in his ear.

> *Rejoice in the Lord, O ye righteous: for praise is comely for the upright.*
> *Praise the Lord with harp: sing unto him with the psaltery and an instrument of ten strings.*
> *Sing unto him a new song; play skilfully with a loud noise.*

The Psalms were not for Arthur. As he said to the accordion man when giving him a lift into Galena along the murderous stretch of the highway that contained the LOVE BEFORE BREAKFAST billboard, 'This is not for the likes of you.' No, sir. They got no real rhythm, no swing.

And yet – even as the members of the jury file back into the courtroom, refusing to look at Arthur, all twelve of them – the surge of joyous exhortation manifest in the psalmist has not totally dwindled to zero in a secular Arthur making his sorry way in a secular world.

'Members of the jury. Have you reached your verdict?'

'We have.'

'And is it the verdict of you all?'

'It is.'

He does not sing with the psaltery and an instrument of ten strings. He does not even celebrate life with a new song, though he thinks it is one.

Arthur's new songs are half as old as the hills.

Neither the circumstances in which they were composed, nor

the motives of those who wrote them, can altogether change his eager understanding of the wisps and remnants of the ancient dream that still lies embodied within them.

He could not have stood up in this court, or in any other assembly, whether friendly or hostile, and delivered up his comical little faith to the spectators, to any sort of judge, or any kind of jury. Arthur had never been good with words.

But – but – I wanna live in a world where the, where the songs come true!

I – Why not? Why not? There must be someplace where the songs is for real!

It was there, in a darkened store full of phonograph records, and griddled by ominous shadows, that, in a cry of anguish, he had come nearest to rising up and shaking his fist at a universe in which God had, allegedly, died.

'*Happy Days Are Here Again!* Is that it, Arthur?' Eileen had responded, with a bitter irony, and eyes full of tears.

Her own pain, and her own intelligence, had not stopped her from seeing what he meant. Her response to him was partly mediated through this impossible dream of his. And even though he had seduced her, and twice betrayed her, she could still see its crumpled, crumbled, peg-legged, one-eyed authenticity.

'Arthur Parker, please rise and face the court.'

The moon is high and silver. The roses are around the door. Every lonely road I walk along, you are there. Across the crowded bar. Love is true. Heaven is in your smile. I stroll down the lane with this, the happiest refrain. Somewhere the sun is always shining, bird with the yellow bill sings out its heart. The stars are spangled in dark blue velvet. Paradise. In all its twinkling varieties.

The covers on the song sheets he used to try to sell are not unlike the crude emblems of a debased civilization that has forgotten the origins of its yearning for perfection – or for life to be, at the least, better and sweeter than these our mortal pains and casual cruelties have so far allowed – but still partly remembers, in occasional glimmerings, as in a mental fog, the traces of those long-abandoned origins.

These emblems and what was sugared and syncopated with a one, a two, a three, within them were the staff of life to Arthur.

No good now, though, Too late, old pal, old buddy.

'Arthur Parker. You have been found guilty of the murder of one Amy Farr. Have you anything to say before sentence is passed?'

No, he didn't. Goddamn it, no. What the hell. No!

How come the sweaty, dank terror has almost disappeared? Is that a tiny smile threatening to twitch at the corners of his mouth? He is led away to the death cell, and he all but shrugs.

Bad news sells papers. And so do verdicts in murder trials. The news stands were soon shouting their wares. The black print above Arthur's picture on the placards had one pithy word to sum up what might be said by the uncharitable to be his entire life, his whole squalid existence: GUILTY!

A newsboy on the Loop was crying it out with a high-pitched brutal satisfaction, letting the words run into each other in a refrain that would have been as mechanical as the accordion man's chant of thanks had it not contained one vital human element: sheer relish.

'Song Man to Hang! Song Man to Hang! Song Man to Hang! Song Man – '

A cry eventually lost in the hoot and roar of the traffic, and the intermittent clack of the trains on the Elevated rail. People were still going about their business. They could not be diverted long by another's misfortune.

He was only getting what was coming to him.

Joan, at home, and wearing a pretty new dress, picked up the evening paper with a frown and a hollow space in what she would always call her bosom. GUILTY! came out at her like a finger of accusation. Her expression remained tensely ambivalent as she read down the column.

. . . *overwhelmed by the enormity of his crimes, Arthur Parker said not a single word in his own defence. There were no tunes left for him to whistle in the darkness of his mind.*

She put the paper down. Whistle in the darkness of his mind?

'Arthur?' she said to herself. She was not sure of the provenance of the question, nor to whom it was really directed.

It was dusk, and the light in the room where they had spent so much time together was fading fast.

Joan got up to close the drapes. For a moment, it looked as though she was going to cry. At the window, she stared out for a few seconds, not seeing what was to her a familiar scene.

'Guilty?' she whispered to herself, so softly that no one in the room with her would have been able to hear it. The question mark was important. Anyone in the room with her would have been able to see it.

GUILTY.

It was the title of one of the songs that Arthur liked – though he presumably cared a great deal less for it now.

The right thing, the nice thing, the impossible thing is for Joan, in her pretty dress and her tight, pretty face, to sing such a song. Almost any song. The thought might not have been too far from her mind.

As she turns back into the darkened room from the window, she goes to the table which is laid for dinner for two. Dinner for two. Dinner for *two*? She lights the candles neatly placed at the centre of the table. The cutlery gleams. Her eyes gleam. There is a single rose in a slender crystal vase to heighten the effect, and its petals look to be made of velvet in the soft glow of the candlelight. Everything is set for music.

Dinner for two.

It surely cannot be for Arthur, this elaborate preparation. He is sitting brooding, silent and melancholy in his cell on Death Row. Attempting to summon up the harder parts of what is almost too tattered a thing to call his Philosophy . . .

He is still worrying about whether his Adam's apple will slide over or under the knot in the rope as the noose goes around his neck.

The doorbell rings at the house on South Campbell he will never see again. She has a visitor.

Joan stops her activity in mid-note, so to speak, or, rather, so not to sing. As she goes into the hall in order to open the front door, she hesitates at the mirror. She smoothes down her dress, and pulls it up a little at the neckline to make sure that no eyes will find it too easy to peep down at her, ahem, *bosom*.

All in order now, she opens the front door.

The lieutenant of detectives is standing there, very smart and grinning hugely. He is her guest for dinner. The burning candles and the single velvet rose in the slender crystal vase, the pretty dress and the pretty smile, are for *his* benefit.

He is carrying a bouquet of flowers, as fresh as her perfume.

The welcoming smile wavers on Joan's face. She is looking at the beautiful flowers, a gift in living polychrome, the severed stems dressed and bandaged by cellophane and ribbon.

'I don't really like to see a man with flowers,' she said, primly. 'Do you?'

His face fell.

It would take him a lot longer than he was yet to realize to touch any joint in her neat body besides her elbow.

But at least the two of them had done for Arthur.

31

The ghastly ritual of legal execution was unfolding itself with due solemnity and appropriate genuflections towards the religion which values above all earthly things the sanctity of human life.

Arthur Parker, wrongly condemned, walked with two taciturn guards, a mumbling priest and the morose warden down a long corridor between two high buildings. There was a grille at the end of the walkway.

The steps and the noose were waiting, as in a bad dream.

Arthur was trying hard to think of something else.

The image of Eileen calling out his name had not left him. She had appeared to him in a thousand different guises, and he still felt himself to be a part of her, as she was of him.

But there was something else . . . definitely something else . . .

O Come, let us sing unto the Lord: let us make a joyful noise to the rock of our salvation.
Let us come before his presence with thanksgiving and make a joyful noise unto him with psalms –

No, no. *Something else* . . .

He was mounting the steps of the gallows, and, to his surprise, his knees did not buckle, though his mouth felt full of hot, dry sand.

There was something in the corner of his mind, not unlike a remembered taste. He could not quite get his thought around it. And yet his head felt so clear now, so light.

Whatever the priest was saying didn't bear thinking about.

'Do you have anything to say?' the warden asked him, properly solicitous.

There was something, if only he could get it up into his head.

'It's impossible to explain. It's not the sort of thing you can put into words,' he was saying again to good old Ed and good old Al.

'Oh, yes it is!' they had exclaimed in gleeful unison.

Years and years I didn't really know what I was selling. The songs! What they are all about! The way they do – really do, tell the truth, the honest to God truth. And they do! They do! Goddamn it, they do!

'What? Them songs?' said Ed, incredulous.

'Do you have anything to say?' said the warden, solicitous.

And the Something he had been searching for inside himself came all at once, as clear as a bell, into his head.

Of course! It was the song. It was 'Pennies from Heaven', and the lyric jingled like small silver coins in the pockets of his mind. Small change that was the only assertion he could now make – and he knew the words by heart.

Arthur spoke aloud the words of the song. Bless his heart, he said all of them, line by line, as though the cheap little lyric were a sonorous passage from the Holy Bible or the finest Shakespeare sonnet.

But they hanged him all the same.

And at the same time as Arthur prepared to hurtle down into eternity, where he would presumably arrive with a broken neck and a poor taste in literature, Eileen his beloved was standing bereft at a city window staring down at the empty street.

She was counting the seconds as the Wrigley Clock counted a slow minute. Time was too slow for her head and its hand.

There was nothing left for her. She could live by selling her body, but she had no one left to live for, and nothing else that she sufficiently desired. Life had no remaining value if he were not to be a part of it.

She was, as usual, utterly matter-of-fact about it. She had looked inside herself with the same cool, steady gaze that she so often turned upon the world outside her. And she did not like what she saw.

Perhaps the only image that still puzzled her was the unbidden one of her father's hogs squealing and grunting and slurping at the trough. Their greedy pleasure gave her momentary pause.

'I don't want to talk about hogs,' Arthur had said, surreptitiously reaching for her hand. It helped her to block out the eager grunts.

Otherwise, everything else was in order. She looked at the street. She prepared herself for the jump, and winged a deep pity towards Arthur and his unspeakable ordeal. Eileen well knew that he was not the bravest of men, and she hardly dared to imagine the weeping and moaning and pleading as they dragged her poor darling to the gallows. The ache of her love, the pain of his pain, was in her bones.

Eileen began to count.

'*One*,' she said to herself. Arthur's hands were being tied behind his back.

'*Two*,' she said. '*Three*,' she said. The bag was being put over Arthur's head, and his childhood somehow pressed close around him.

Four. Five. Six. The rope was now around his neck.

'*Seven*,' she said, and a cry rose silently in the black grief. Oh, Arthur. Poor Arthur. I love you. I love you!

'*Eight*,' she said. '*Nine*.' The hangman's hand was on the trap.

'*Ten*,' she said.

The trap opened.

'*Eleven*,' she trembled.

Arthur's body swung, and kicked briefly, and then was still.

'*Twelve*,' she said, before everything went black for both of them.

They hanged him all the same. And she was out of it, too.

Epilogue

'Arthur!' she says, her eyes wide and clear. 'What are you doing here?' Her words are spoken as in the moment of waking.

He laughs, full of glee. As full of himself as he ever had been.

'Who ever said you could stop a dream?' he says, triumphant.

Arthur and Eileen are embracing. So tenderly. So lovingly.

'We couldn't go through all that without a happy ending,' he is saying. 'Songs ain't like that! Are they?' Well, they are not, are they?

They both turn, and they are looking at you. If you want them to.

'The song is ended,' they say. 'But the melody lingers on.'

And from all around, the music is playing. Arthur and Eileen are singing.

The Glory of Love.

The world was through with them, but they still, it seems, had each other's arms. In a brilliant sky, cavernous, clear and endless. A space in the head.

Where is this place? Where can it be?

Why, Chicago, of course. And you'd better believe it.

The same sky joins up all the places you have ever known, some you do not know, and at least one you do not yet know. Look for the patch of blue. Arthur maintains it is inside yourself, and, for once, he might just be right. Half-way right.

Don't switch off the music! The world would go even crazier than it already is if we stopped the music altogether.

'There must be someplace where the songs is for real.'